CH00428574

# When Stars Will Shine

Helping our heroes, one page at a time

This is a work of fiction. Names, characters, places, and incidents either are the product of the author's imagination or are used fictitiously. Any resemblance to actual persons, living or dead, events, or locales is entirely coincidental.

Copyright © 2019 by Emma Mitchell, Creating Perfection

All rights reserved. No part of this book may be reproduced or used in any manner without written permission of the copyright owner except for the use of quotations in a book review. For more information, address: emmamitchellfpr@gmail.com

First Edition December 2019
ISBN:9781713181781

Cover design by Amanda Ni Odharáin of Let's Get Booked
Edited by Emma Mitchell of Creating Perfection
Proofread by Kate Noble of Noble Owl Proofreading

Published by Creating Perfection

www.edmcreatingperfection.com

# A note from the Editor

One of my earliest memories of home is picture of my dad with his army regiment. He was only a teenager. He was medically discharged after breaking his leg playing football one day after training and I know that devastated him at the time. His sister and her husband were in the RAF and I remember how they travelled the world and were always away in some far-off country.

A friend of mine from school was in the navy and we kept in touch for years while he was away. I'd get letters on blue paper from all the exotic places he visited and so, when I was nineteen, I decided to sign up. I was so excited to be a part of something so special but due to medical reasons, I couldn't join.

Over the years, I've seen friends go off to war zones, and have seen the devastation our service personnel face first-hand but I've never found myself in a position to be able to do anything to help.

Until now.

For the last three years I've held online book auctions to raise money for a cancer charity which was part of the fundraising efforts with my local pub. I'm not involved with that anymore and so this year, I decided to do something different.

Instead of putting a call out for signed books I could auction, I asked if anyone would be interested in writing a short story for an anthology, the profits from which would be donated to the charity. To say I was blown away by the response is an understatement. Within two hours I had over forty offers, and because I didn't restrict the submissions to published authors, aspiring authors were able to submit too. The quality of the submissions was phenomenal – as you will see when you read on – and it was so hard deciding which to use but I think you'll agree, I chose wisely!

It devastates me that there are ex-forces members living on the streets. Service personnel with injuries, both physical and mental, struggling through life after service and Help for Heroes does so much to help them. There isn't anyone in the country who hasn't benefitted from our armed forces, whether they realise it or not, and we owe these people so much… this anthology is our way of saying thank you, and the proceeds will hopefully provide some help to those who need it.

It has been my absolute pleasure working with these wonderful authors to deliver you this book, and I hope you love reading the stories as much as I did.

*Emma Mitchell*, 2019

# Megan's Poem

The events from a hundred years ago still seem unreal,

For the world today is all so still.

Although the guns fell silent at 11 a.m. today,

Fathers, husbands, and sons have still passed away.

They gave their lives because they cared about us,

And now we don't have to worry or fuss.

In No Man's Land there was a night of peace,

A single night,

When guns would cease.

In Flanders Field the poppies grow,

With our pride and gratitude in which we show.

Eleven o'clock of the eleventh day of the eleventh month,

The fighting ended on the battlefront.

*Megan Steer, aged 11*
*7 November 2018*

# Fredrick Snellgrove, Private 23208 by Rob Ashman

The white feather fluttered in the breeze. I stared into the eyes of the woman blocking my path, her young face framed with ringlet curls. She held it between her fingers and extended her hand towards me. I tried to speak but nothing came out.

I knew her, in fact I knew her entire family – Welsh Valley towns are like that – everyone knows everyone. I thought they were my friends… but not today.

I reached out and plucked the feather from her grasp. My chin sank into my chest as she gathered her skirts and scurried past. The message had been delivered.

I'm the second eldest of four brothers, all of us sons of John Snellgrove. My dad is a pillar of the community; a lay preacher, a local councillor, a Labour Party activist, but he has a weakness – his sons are at home.

My elder brother, Will, works in a reserved occupation, and my two other brothers, George and Bert, are too young to enlist – which just leaves me.

I've been stepping out with Annie Maude for some time and it's the real thing. I live on Cwm Cottage Road in Abertillery and she's a local girl. We met in Sunday school and I've always known she's The One – always.

I took the feather home; Mam cried, Dad was angry and used words that he would never say in chapel. Annie Maude sobbed when I told her. In fact, I didn't have to tell her; she knew. It was time for me to go.

I joined the 10th Battalion South Wales Borderers and went to war. A war that would be over by Christmas.

I wrote to Annie Maude and she wrote back. We tried to keep it light, but the pain of separation soaked into every line on the page.

I wrote to my father: *I need you to keep a secret. When I get home, I want to ask Annie Maude to marry me. Will you buy me a ring so when I return, I need waste no time*? And that's what he did.

We received orders that we were off to pastures new – a place they called the Somme. We marched south from St. Pol and arrived at the fifteen-mile front, burrowing ourselves in the mud. The rain had turned the chalky soil to glue; it didn't take long before we all looked the same.

Then, on the 1st July, all hell broke loose.

But not for us, our objective lay elsewhere, and we weren't part of the nineteen thousand men who died that day. We were destined for two hundred acres of dense forest called Mametz Wood.

We joined the other regiments of the 38th Welsh Division to form an eighteen thousand strong, Welsh volunteer army. Three hundred yards away were the Prussian Guard, one of the best trained forces in the world.

The top brass told us we would clear the wood in a matter of hours and at a quarter past two in the afternoon of July seventh, we engaged the enemy. It was our first taste of battle. Their heavy machine guns cut us down like corn.

The Welsh Borderers took one hundred and eighteen casualties that day including our commanding officer – but I survived – as I did the next day, and the next.

The top brass payed us another visit, frustrated with our lack of progress. They relieved our Major General of his command and called for an all-out assault… that was when my luck ran out.

I died on Monday, 10th July 1916, joining the ranks of the five hundred and eighty-four soldiers who never made it out of Mametz Wood and were never found. I'm still there, somewhere. Annie Maude cried for a month, and the following month and the one after that. My brother George befriended her as much to salve his own grief as to comfort hers. As time went by, their friendship turned to love and seven years later they were married.

Children followed and they moved into the house on Cwm Cottage Road. The course of family life took Annie Maude into old age, when she died aged seventy-two. My brother George joined her in the afterlife eight years later.

My name is Fredrick Snellgrove, Private 23208, I'm not here to tell my story but I promise every word I've said is true… every word.

My name is inscribed on the Thiepval Memorial – one of the seventy-two thousand, three hundred and thirty-seven men who died at the Somme and have no known grave. My name is also cast in steel on the cenotaph in Abertillery, and where I fell in Mametz Woods, a Welsh dragon now stands in our honour. It would seem, there's some corner of a foreign field that is also forever Wales. It's good to be remembered.

The engagement ring my father bought now lies in the jewellery box of my great-great-niece, her name is Gemma. The man who put pen to paper and brought me back for this commemoration is my great-nephew. Annie Maude was his grandmother and the young woman who keeps safe my ring is his daughter.

His name is Rob Ashman, he writes books or something. I told him my story so he could share it with you.

My name is Fredrick Snellgrove, Private 23208, and I promise, every word I've said is true… every word.

# Four Seasons by Robert Scragg

# WINTER

Life is a just series of moments, each connected to the last, but we still make our own choices. No disrespect to my devout catholic mother, God rest her soul, but they're not stitched together by whatever cosmic embroidery design your chosen deity chooses to follow. There's no one whispering in your ear. Any voices we hear in our moments of indecision are just our own, with a slight change in tone or timbre to mask the fact we're going to choose what we really wanted all along; the good, the bad, and the ugly.

Sometimes they can be so intense, so all encompassing, that when you close your eyes a lifetime later, you're back there, in that moment, the colours, smells, sounds. You remember them fondly. You remember the parts you want to see again. Tunnel vision focussing in on her lips as they form the words.

I

Love

You

I inhale deeply, eyelids come down, and behind them I can feel everything again. I still feel the tectonic plates of my world shift with every word, words only my wife has spoken to me before, but she hasn't uttered them for an eternity. A chain reaction of such moments has gotten me to where I am today, but if I have to choose just one on which my life truly pivoted, it would be that night in the bar, long before she spoke those words. Without it, all that followed would never have come to pass.

# SPRING

Her eyes flick my way again. That's three times in as many minutes. My thumb reaches subconsciously for my wedding ring, stroking the underside, rotating it around my finger. I glance down at it, half expecting to see it working its way up towards freedom like a nut on a bolt. When I look up again, she's gone. I tell myself she probably wouldn't be interested even if I was in the mood to try my luck.

I check my watch. Hannah isn't expecting me back for another hour. Time for one last nightcap. I make eye contact with the barman, tilting my bottle towards him with a hopeful smile. He nods, turning away to put the finishing touches on a pair of mojitos, half an iceberg poking out of the top of each glass.

I sense her before I see her. A waft of perfume teases me, and I turn to see her next to me, looking up through lashes that flicker like butterfly wings. She reminds me of a young Audrey Hepburn, hypnotic hazel eyes returning my stare with a hint of amusement. I know this woman, or at least her face. She works with Hannah. I've seen her at the school. I stutter my way through a clumsy hello, annoyed at how unsure of myself I sound, but regain my composure by the time we're onto our third drink. She asks if we can try a cocktail, laughing at the innuendo laced menu, pointing at *Sex on the Beach*, then heads off to the Ladies bathroom. I watch her until she disappears, then check my watch. The hour I had to play with ended long ago. The three missed calls on my muted phone promise a frosty welcome back home, and I tuck it back inside my jacket. Why deal with today what I can put off 'til tomorrow.

She glides back minutes later. I open my mouth to make another poor joke about the lewd concoctions we've ordered, but before I can speak her lips are on mine. I swear the music has been muted and the earth has stopped turning, for in that moment all that exists is her. When she pulls back, I smile, dumbstruck for the first time in a long time. She smiles back, reaches for her glass, and fires off a wink before sucking hungrily at twin straws.

I tell myself that I didn't encourage this; that *she* came on to *me*. I tell myself it can't happen again. Won't happen again. She moves closer again, and I'm lost.

## SUMMER

What I remember most is her thumb tracing a slow, almost sensuous outline across the back of my hand while she cups it between hers. It should have been comforting; usually was comforting, but I just find it an irritant, like sandpaper on my skin; the world's slowest Chinese burn.

Her attempts at affections seem so incongruous with her words. Not the three that she captured my heart with. This time just two.

'For us,' she whispers now, but the softening of her tone does nothing to soften the meaning of her words. 'For our future.'

She threads her fingers though mine, drawing me closer, sitting up against the headboard.

'You do still want a future for us, don't you?'

What can I do? I nod until I find my voice. I tell her she is my future. I tell her I'll leave Hannah. I tell her I just need time, as I have on

15

countless nights before. And I mean it, in my heart I do. Imprisoned in a bitter excuse of a marriage for ten years, the prospect of escape breathes colour back into my world. But what she's asking of me goes beyond love. She has danced around the issue several times before tonight, but what she's suggesting now is crossing a line with no hope of retracing my steps.

She recounts stories of how Hannah has manipulated me, belittled me. I know every word by heart already, having told her the same stories lying wrapped in her arms in a stolen moment. What I know, and what she doesn't, is that almost all of them are lies. Lies designed to get my way, to have my way. With her. Like all the others before her, Lily has fallen for the man I've constructed for her. The hard-working family man, with a wife who doesn't appreciate him, with kids whose mother has turned them against him.

I am hard-working. That much is true. Whether Hannah appreciates me or not, I couldn't honestly say. The marriage, already balanced on a knife-edge, has never recovered from one night of indiscretion from her, one hand raised in anger that same night from me, the countless others that followed since then. I hate myself that little bit more each time, repeating the mantra – *never again, never again*. We've drifted through the years since like sleepwalkers, waking only to score cheap points off each other, wearing a mask of happiness for the kids in between the flare-ups.

Does she deserve what Lily is proposing? Probably not. Certainly not. Do I deserve a future with Lily? Maybe. Possibly. I can't think straight, a cocktail of her perfume and whispered promises fogs my mind.

'I couldn't hurt her. Not like that.' I hear a tremor in my voice as my words trip over themselves on my tongue, the air thick with irony after all the hurt I've already caused.

'Who said anything about hurt? There're ways to do it so she wouldn't feel a thing.'

I should be alarmed that she sounds knowledgeable, quietly confident, but that little voice, *my* inner voice, curiosity piqued, counsels patience. She starts to talk, and as she paints a picture of a world without Hannah, I start to believe in the possibilities, but doubt deep down that I have the resolve to do anything about it. I'm caught between the proverbial rock and hard place. If I do nothing, Lily will leave. Not today, not next week, but eventually. Any number of other men will be waiting to offer her what she so desperately wants from me; a happily ever after.

The prospect of losing Lily sickens me almost as much as the idea of doing anything to Hannah. It's a fine line as to which one makes me break out in the colder sweat. Both feet still firmly on the one side of the line, the morally correct side of the line. The urge to cross it comes in waves, I feel myself swaying, but I'm too much of a coward to move, let alone move with conviction.

Lily looks at me, eyes widening, urging me to commit. She scans my face, searching for a sign of the strength, or weakness depending on your point of view, that I would need to go through with it. The disappointment on her face is almost more than I can bear, but the fear of action and relief at lack of it, paralyse me as she rises and heads for the bathroom. She shakes her head as she goes, and I wonder if any chance we have goes with her.

# AUTUMN

I shift nervously in my seat. Hannah is late. She's never late. The candles weep waxy tears and I find myself staring into the flame, hypnotised by its dance. The room fades around me and the flame seems to intensify. My cheeks redden, not from the glow of the candle, but from the thought of what I must do. The surreal paradox paralyses me; what I will do tonight. I don't want to, but am so compelled, so driven by promises made and futures planned, that I know I'll go through with it, no matter how unpalatable.

The small plastic pouch in my pocket weighs less than an ounce but it pins me to my seat. I can't do it here in the restaurant, not with just the two of us. Later, in the bar, there'll be an opportunity. Her work crowd will be out, endless rounds of drinks, a window of opportunity between the bar and the table.

I blink, the ghost of the flame imprints her face when I look up. Hannah apologises as she sits, something about preparing for a parents' evening next week. Surely, she can read it in my face, see what I'm going to do? Apparently not. She smiles demurely and starts giving me a download of her day. I smile and nod at what I hope are the right places, making my share of the effort we promised each other we would make to fix things; a fresh start.

Tonight will be a fresh start of sorts, although it might take some time, a period of adjustment, before I can truly enjoy it. Dinner is bland, tasteless. I catch myself absentmindedly touching the almost invisible bump against my trouser leg. I wish I'd taken the time to google it, find out what it is, what it will do to Hannah, but as with many things these days, I trust Lily.

Hannah seems different, energised somehow, excited. I put it down to a steady stream of vodka and lemonade. I pay the bill and we step outside onto the slippery streets, slick with slush. She links her arm in mine and I turn towards her, surprised. It's been so long since she even held my hand. She locks her arm tight onto mine as we pick our way through the dirty trampled remnants of this morning's snowfall.

I assume there's a collective noun for a group of teachers? A class of teachers, an education of teachers or something equally twee. Whatever it is, there's a gathering of them over by the bar. I recognise a few faces from previous nights out, but one is noticeable by its absence. Lily has made herself scarce tonight. She wanted to come, to be here with me, but I couldn't risk Hannah picking up on any of the glances that she would surely have shot my way.

Hannah introduces me to an older couple, both English teachers, and the three of them fall into the comfort of talking shop. I head to the bar to get us drinks, digging in my pocket for change as I do, feeling the coarseness of the powder in my pocket, even through the plastic. I pull my hand back out a little too quickly, and glance back at Hannah. She's oblivious, wrapped up in conversation, and I push my way through to the bar. I tell myself it's too early, that there aren't enough people around to provide the cover I need. I add a straight vodka to the drinks order, just the one, I tell myself. One for courage, not that what I'm doing is courageous, but any more and I might back out, or worse still, make a mistake.

One drink blurs into the next. I make sure I'm not the only one visiting the bar. It wouldn't do to be the only one who makes that journey all night. Every time it's my round, I order a Coke minus the whisky, so Hannah pulls unwittingly ahead of me in the booze stakes, although I feel as light-headed as if I'd had a few too many. A few times I get caught out when people ask me a question, my mind a million miles away. My round comes around again with alarming speed, and I excuse myself to go to the Gents first. I don't recognise the man looking back at me from the mirror. His eyes are wider than mine, his forehead more creased. A quick splash of water and a blast of the hand drier and it's show time.

*A bottle of Bud, a Coke, a vodka lemonade, and a white wine.*

I mutter it under my breath as I wait my turn. When it comes, Hannah's drink is the second from last to be mixed. I slide it from the counter with my left hand, holding it below the surface of the bar. My right hand fumbles with the packet, tipping its contents into the glass. At least I hope I have. I daren't look down as I stuff the now empty pouch back deep into my pocket. It looks like a snow globe when I lift it back up, fine particles swirling in a liquid storm.

*Shit! What if it doesn't dissolve?*

It hadn't even occurred to me that it might not. I stir as calmly as I can with the trembling straw and exhale louder than I should when I see the grains start to vanish. A new problem presents itself. Four drinks, two hands. I quickly shuttle the beer and wine over to where the group stand and come back for the remaining two. That's when I see her. Ten feet beyond Hannah with a look of surprise on her face. Lily. The way she's standing looks like her head is part of Hannah's shoulder. Past, present, and future overlapping for a brief moment.

Hannah turns, sees me looking, and follows my stare. She turns and the world stops turning. The vodka in my hand weighs me down and I'm rooted to the spot. Hannah waves to Lily and beckons her to join the group. I force myself to start walking again, the world's falsest smile fixed firmly in place. They give each other the obligatory peck on the cheek. Lily's surprise has changed to confusion.

'Nice to see you again, Jack,' she says to me. 'Glad you're feeling better.' Why would she say that? I don't know what to say.

'Yeah, I'm good thanks. Nice to see you too.'

Hannah reaches out for her drink. I hand it to her, fixing my eyes on her. Anywhere but Lily. I don't trust myself to look at Lily. Why has she come?

'You've just missed the round,' she says to Lily. 'Here, hold this a second, let me get you a drink.' She passes her glass to Lily, her other hand reaching into her handbag. As Lily's hand reaches out, Hannah looks down. The hand holding the glass opens, releasing its grip before Lily takes hold, and the glass smashes into a thousand shards by our feet. Everyone gets at least a few drops on their shoes, Lily most of all. Her black suede heels are ruined. Hannah gasps an apology and goes to the bar to ask for someone to clean up the mess. Lily disappears to the Ladies without as much as a glance at me.

I stare at the liquid pooled at my feet, half expecting it to corrode the soles of my shoes, and step back, feeling glass crunch underfoot. Lily and Hannah come back at the same time, Hannah with two drinks, one of which is passed to Lily. Hannah smiles, apologising again. She raises her glass.

'Now we've all got something to toast with, here's to a new term and new classes. To new beginnings.'

Glasses raise in unison, overlapping voices echo her words. I look at Hannah as I raise my own and catch a fleeting flash of something in her eyes. I swear she just looked from me to Lily and back again.

*Don't be so bloody paranoid.*

Everyone drinks, smiles all round. A barmaid scuttles over with a dustpan and brush and whisks the glass away. I catch Lily's eye and shake my head ever so slightly. She looks away, expressionless but I can see she's tense. My heart hammers out a rhythm as loud in my ears as the bass from the speakers. Can I go through this again? I genuinely have no idea. Everyone is lost in conversation but me. The two women in my life ignore me for the next ten minutes, and I've never felt so alone in a room full of people.

# WINTER

The walls are slate grey. I stare out of the window at a sky of the same shade. The world outside is devoid of any other colour. I'm sure there's a joke about Mother Nature's version of *Fifty Shades* but I'm not in the mood for humour. Three months. Three fucking months and I still can't work it out. I have my theories, but I can't prove anything.

Hannah's face had given away nothing. No anger, no sadness; nothing. Only her eyes had moved as I was marched past her seat, the words fresh in my mind and heavy in my heart.

*We*

*Find*

*The*

*Defendant*

*Guilty*

Lily is gone, and any future I have with her. I was mercifully spared of watching it happen, watching her suffer the same fate I would readily have bestowed on Hannah. Poor Lily, alone in her flat, twitching in a puddle of her own bile, poison coursing through her veins, while I'd gone home with Hannah that night. Spared then, but not during the trial when they trotted out the glossy ten by eights to show me my supposed handiwork. What defence could I possibly have mounted?

*Not guilty, your Honour. I was trying to kill my wife, not my mistress.*

A dull clang, like a bell, sounds from behind the door as another is shut behind it. The door at the end of the room opens and in walks my chance to get the answers I've been looking for. Hannah dressed immaculately in a beige trouser suit. I'm cuffed to the table so can't rise to meet her. She approaches until she is standing opposite me, silent, waiting until she hears the click of the door closing behind the guard. I don't know what to say to her, where to begin. She saves me the trouble.

'Don't get comfortable. I'm not staying long.' She leans down, within earshot but out of reach.

'Hannah,' I begin, 'I didn't do this. You have to believe me I didn't—'

'I know,' she says, her voice barely above a whisper. 'I know you didn't.'

In that moment I know. I know it was her. I don't know how, and know she'll never tell me. Her tongue darts out to wet her lower lip. Colour rises to her cheeks. This is why she came. She wants me to know it was her, to have this moment of triumph, of redemption.

She turns without saying another word and breezes out of the door and out of my life for the last time. From somewhere a chuckle escapes. It grows, morphs into a laugh, an animal like bellow, and finally tears by the time they come to take me back to my cell.

I sit alone on my bunk now, the tear tracks cool where they dry on my cheeks, and I can't figure out who the hell they're for. Not Hannah, after what she did. Not me for what I planned to do. Not even Lily for what she ignited and incited in me. I stare at the wall, unblinking, wondering if I'll ever have anyone or anything worth crying over again. I put myself here. Me. Here, where every day is déjà vu. No moments of joy, excitement, love. Just one, never-ending cycle of grey walls and greyer days.

# The Close Encounter by Gordon Bickerstaff

It was a cold and dark Thursday evening when Gavin Shawlens and Emma Patersun sat in her Ford Mondeo waiting for the engine to heat up. It was less than a week before Christmas and an inch of snow had fallen on frozen ground. Snowflakes drifted past their windscreen in the wind-free evening air. Gavin was anxious to drive off, but Emma knew her car and its quirky behaviour in winter months. If it wasn't warm enough, it would stall.

A black Mercedes raced up the driveway to Emma Patersun's house, swerved to block their path and screeched to a halt. Gavin gaped at the passenger in the car. He was the gunman who'd stormed into his laboratory earlier today and shot at him. Gavin froze.

The Merc driver opened his door and put his foot onto the wet snow. The gunman slid out of the passenger's side.

Grateful he'd decided to drive tonight, Gavin revved the engine.

The gunman shouted, 'Doctor Shawlens, stop!'

Gavin stepped on the accelerator and the Mondeo's wheels skidded on the compacted snow until they grabbed traction and lurched them forward, ramming the Merc, and crushing the driver's foot between the door and sill. He screamed a piercing screech as his shin bones shattered.

'It's *them*!' Gavin shouted at Emma as he steered the car through shrubs lining the drive. Panic and turmoil filled the evening air as the driver howled like a banshee.

The gunman hurried around the front of the Merc while Gavin made violent manoeuvres to get the car moving through snow-covered shrubs. The gunman ran to Emma's side, slid on an ice patch and hit the window with the butt of his gun. The glass shattered into hundreds of tiny fragments. Emma turned away and covered her eyes, but the broken glass scratched across the back of her hand as the gun followed through and collided with her hand.

The shrubs yielded, tyres gripped, and Gavin accelerated violently. The Mondeo's wheels screamed as Gavin sped recklessly down the driveway.

The gunman rebounded from the Mondeo and fell to his knees. He recovered, took aim, and fired three shots. The first bullet missed the car, the second pierced the rear bumper making a neat hole, and the third hit the cluster of indicator lights.

At first, Emma wasn't conscious of the blood on her hand. She stared at the gunman through the rear window.

Gavin swept the Mondeo out of the drive and onto the main road, narrowly missing a white van travelling in the opposite direction. Cold December air rushed through the broken window and made them shiver.

The shattered glass had cut a vein on the back of Emma's hand. She clamped her fingers over the cut and her hands were soon covered in blood.

Ten minutes later, Gavin merged the Mondeo into the busy Glasgow city traffic. He planned to drive her to the main police HQ but when he turned into Argyle Street, the Mondeo ran out of fuel, so he pulled over to the kerb and they continued on foot.

Gavin pulled a handkerchief from his pocket and Emma wrapped it around her hand.

'How bad is it?'

'It's fine. Look, Gavin, I'm sorry I doubted you when you told me I was in danger. If you hadn't come to my house, I don't know what would have happened.'

'They came to the lab this afternoon demanding I hand over details of your company's new technology. I refused and they got violent. In the scuffle, one of them fired a shot at me before I escaped. I knew I had to come here to warn you.'

Gavin's handkerchief hadn't stopped the bleeding. Emma pulled tissues from her bag and used them to stem the flow of blood. Stinging pain fuelled her anxiety as they hurried away from the Mondeo and joined a crowd of people heading west. Many of them returning from late-night shopping and carrying Christmas parcels.

Before they turned a corner, Gavin looked back and saw the Merc drawing up behind the Mondeo. 'They're at your car.'

Gavin and Emma hurried along a street lined with tall, red sandstone tenement buildings on both sides with cars parked tightly. Gavin felt safer and they could dart into an entrance if the Merc followed.

While looking back, Gavin collided with an old lady waiting to enter a tenement close. She was loaded with Christmas presents in three carrier bags.

He held on to her and stopped her falling over but the presents fell into the slush on the pavement. He apologised profusely as he picked up her bags and wiped off some of the slush.

The woman was more concerned with the blood on Emma's hands.

'Pet. You're bleeding,' she said.

Emma's pale face grimaced with pain. 'I'm fine, really.'

'Let me treat that for you,' she said confidently.

'We're all right, thanks,' Gavin said as he looked up and down the street.

'Don't be silly I live just here. You can sit for a minute while I see to your hand,' she insisted.

Emma's heart raced… the thought of sitting down for a few minutes was welcome.

The lady led them through the entrance close of her tenement flat.

'It's on the third floor, middle door,' she said.

'My name's Emma and he's Gavin.'

'I'm Sadie, and I'm pleased to meet you, Emma.'

Emma helped Sadie on the final few steps of the stairs.

Gavin waited for them at the door.

'It's open, son. Go on inside.'

*Open! That's asking for trouble,* he thought as he stepped into her living room. The room reminded Gavin of his grandmother's house, cluttered with old furniture, and old photographs covering every wall. The tops of her cabinets bulged with brass ornaments and figurines.

She didn't have a TV or radio in the room, but she did have lots of newspapers stacked neatly in one corner. Her traditional furniture reflected a time long past.

Although overweight, she seemed fit for her age. Climbing the stairs hadn't sapped her energy. Her silver-grey hair was pinned back in a small bun. With a wonderful chubby smile, Emma felt a warm family presence.

She led the way through to her kitchen and Emma sat down, resting her arm on the kitchen table. Sadie sat beside her and gently took control of the bloody wound.

Emma looked away as Sadie removed the blood-soaked tissues and put on her spectacles to examine it more closely. The one-inch cut had exposed underlying tissues.

'Luckily, pet, it's only a small vein. I can heal this for you. Before I retired, I worked as a nurse you know, at the Southern General,' she said confidently.

Sadie placed the damaged hand firmly in her left hand and covered the wound with the palm of her right hand. Sadie's warm hands compressed firmly.

Emma swooned as if she might faint and she had a strong urge to withdraw her hand, but Sadie had a firm grip. For almost a minute, they stared in silence at each other.

'Blood and cuts don't bother you?' Emma asked.

'I've seen much worse, pet. Last month, when I walked through the old part of the park, a silly seven-year-old boy had tried to climb over the metal fence. He slipped and a railing spike stuck into his side.'

'Oh my God!'

'A man and his wife scurried around, shouting for someone to call an ambulance. They couldn't bear to touch him. I lifted him off the spike, sat him down, and stopped the bleeding,' she said proudly.

'It might have been safer to leave him on the spike to stem the blood loss,' Gavin said.

Sadie shot him an annoyed look. 'He wouldn't stop wriggling about. The railing moved further into his body and could have touched a major organ.'

Emma shuddered at the thought. She looked at Gavin and he frowned.

A fierce itch grew in her wounded hand and just as Emma thought it was unbearable, Sadie unclamped her hands. Sadie's hands and Emma's wrist were covered in dark red blood, but the cut had stopped bleeding. Emma ran her finger over the wound.

Sadie lightly smacked Emma's good hand. 'Don't rub it.'

She washed her hands in the sink and then fetched some gauze and warm water to clean the wound. Emma flexed and exercised her fingers to ease the stiffness in her hand.

'Do you have a bandage?' Emma asked.

'Fresh air is the best, pet.'

Emma watched as she gently dried the area around the wound. Sadie had wonderful hands and Emma felt comfortable... as if she'd known Sadie all her life.

'I won't need an ambulance then,' Emma said.

Sadie looked slightly confused. 'An ambulance, pet? Not for you,' she said with concern.

Gavin checked his watch while he paced anxiously back and forth.

'I'd keep an eye on him. He might need an ambulance,' Sadie said, and they both smiled.

Sadie reached into a large fruit bowl and picked up a small pineapple. Holding it in one hand she rotated it back and forth.

'This has healing powers. The flesh will help to heal your wound. Old ways are the best, you know,' she said with authority. She called to Gavin, 'Son, cut a slice of pineapple for me. Knives in the drawer. Be careful – they're sharp.'

*No kidding,* Gavin thought as he collected the pineapple and cut off a large piece.

Sadie squeezed it gently between clean towels then laid the pineapple flesh against the wound and pressed it gently.

Emma flinched as the acid stung sharply and a tortured expression showed she was hurting.

'This is an old remedy. Passed down through countless generations,' Sadie explained.

Gavin smiled at the old lady using pineapple to heal wounds. 'I'm impressed. Fresh pineapple contains an enzyme called bromelain that will kill bacteria and clean the cut.'

'I don't know about that, son. People around here think it's a magic potion.'

Gavin said to Emma, 'It's a remedy that dates back to Christopher Columbus. After a battle, he observed native Indians rub pineapple flesh into their battle wounds.'

'Really?'

Gavin nodded and smiled.

'You sit there, and I'll make some tea. Camomile soothes the nerves. It will help calm you down,' she said while she gave a cursory look at the scratches on Gavin's face. 'Have you been fighting?'

'I was…' he started and then decided not to explain how he'd been attacked and chased. '…a slight accident.'

The three of them sat around the kitchen table. Gavin hadn't tasted camomile tea before. He took a few sips and no more. He didn't drink tea without milk, and he didn't like tea with leaves floating in the cup. Emma enjoyed hers.

Sadie took the pineapple from Emma's cut. 'There, doesn't that look much better. Keep it clean and fresh air will do the rest.'

Gavin asked, 'Do you mind if I go through to the bedroom and have a look at what's happening on the street?'

'Not at all, on you go.'

In the cold bedroom, Gavin stood in the dark, and peered through the curtains to the street below. No sign of the Merc or its occupants. He slipped into the space between the curtains and the window for a look further along the street.

He sensed Emma behind him, looking over his shoulder then he felt her hand on his arm as a soft voice whispered, 'Everything OK?'

Gavin kept his focus on the street. He didn't whisper. 'I don't think they'll hear you up here,' he snapped then turned around to apologise for his abruptness.

'Huh?' he gasped. There was no one else in the room. He froze, and for a moment he wasn't sure if his legs would move. He stood between the curtains and felt trapped. He pushed the curtains behind him and hurried through to the kitchen.

Emma saw his face was white as a sheet and his hands agitating. 'Have they found us?'

He shook his head. 'No sign of the Merc or the men,' he replied then he turned to Sadie and asked, 'Do you live here alone?'

'I'm never alone, son. I always have seven bright ones with me.'

'Bright ones?' Emma asked.

'Lights, pet. They keep me safe and sound.'

Gavin sat beside Emma and rested his hand on her good hand as if to draw strength. The colour slowly returned to his face.

Sadie looked into Emma's empty cup with interest. Emma smiled and looking at Gavin said, 'Will I marry a handsome university lecturer?'

Sadie swirled the liquid in circles then allowed the leaves to stick to the inside of the cup. She placed a napkin on the table and turned the cup upside down on the napkin. She rotated the cup until the handle pointed to the north, then to the south, then to the east, and then to the west. She returned the cup to its upright position and examined the shapes formed by the leaves.

'I see you at the centre of a loving family, pet. A lovely family. I see three lively babies in your life. Quite a handful,' she said.

The words cut deeply into Emma's heart. Her face reflected a profound sadness.

'Triplets?' Gavin blurted with disbelief.

'Not identical babies, son.' Sadie looked up from the cup and smiled.

'Three individuals. Quite a handful, but you'll love them equally,' she said in a vague voice as if straining to see.

Emma's eyes welled up. A tear ran down her cheek. 'I doubt if I could cope with one baby,' Emma said to Sadie.

'There is a large hole in the leaves. Something missing in your life,' she said and looked at Emma for feedback.

Emma blinked to hold back more tears. She hoped Sadie would realise the reading had upset her. 'I lost my husband recently.'

'Of course, that's it. But he's not lost... he's... I'm so sorry. I'm getting too old. I can't see clearly. Have you consulted a medium?'

Emma shook her head. 'No.'

'I know a young woman with great ability. There is something important. I can feel it. If your husband passed recently, he might have news for you. Speak with him soon, pet.'

Emma looked unconvinced. 'I'll think about it.'

'A few years ago, I could have made contact for you. None of them told me that when I turned seventy, I'd have all sorts of physical and mental weaknesses to deal with.'

Sadie looked expectantly at Gavin. He hadn't drunk the tea so offered the palm of his hand instead. She looked impressed with his strong hands and soft skin. He half expected her to say he worked with his mind and not his hands.

'Wonderful hands, son, powerful. You know these could be healing hands. Look after them,' she said with a knowing smile.

'Just the one baby for you. Do you wish to know if it's a son or a daughter?'

'Sure,' he said in a mocking voice.

'A lovely wee boy. A son with strong blond hair, just like your own. He'll grow up to be an engineer in a large building with lots of nice people around him. There's a sweet girl there. She would be good for him. Let them get together. Don't stand in their way.'

'I'm so pleased,' he said sarcastically.

'You have a weakness in your stomach. It will cause you some trouble. See the doctor as soon as it starts. Don't delay and everything will be fine.'

Gavin drew back his hand and ran it over his dark-brown hair. His patience had drained. 'We need to go. I'll go downstairs and check the street is clear.'

Sadie looked disappointed with his rudeness.

Emma apologised for him and reached over to lift Sadie's frail wrinkled hand. She cradled it between her own. Their eyes locked together.

'I can't have children. I have a medical problem… no cure for me, sadly,' she said, and her eyes glistened as she patted Sadie's hand.

Sadie cupped the side of Emma's face in her hand. 'Pet, your young body just wasn't ready for that, then,' she said sympathetically.

Emma bowed her head and tears rolled down her cheeks.

Sadie put her hand under Emma's chin and gently raised her head until their eyes met again. 'But it is now.'

Emma felt a cold chill as if she'd stepped into a walk-in freezer.

'The older man who passed on. He's happy for you. He says you'll need to be strong for them,' Sadie said then took the cups over to the sink to wash them. She looked back at Emma and smiled.

Emma joined her at the sink. 'Thanks for everything. I feel much better now.' She put her arm around Sadie and gave her a gentle squeeze.

'Don't lose your way, pet. Your dreams can come true, but you'll need to hold on until the end.'

'I will.'

Sadie nodded to her door. 'It's a terrible shame about him.'

'Gavin?'

'He has five bright ones around him. Strong spirit lights. They'd love to pass a message to him, but they know he's too frightened.'

'Really?' Emma looked puzzled.

'Yes. His older sister had a Ouija board. Silly girl scared him witless when they were youngsters. He's been afraid ever since. They're very proud of him and love him so very much.'

Emma raised her eyebrows. 'How do you know he has an older sister?'

'His grandpa is unhappy with her for frightening him. You know his sister is a minx.'

Emma nodded. 'I do. I've been on the receiving end.'

'He doesn't remember, but you know when he was a baby, he had a mop of blond hair.'

'Oh, my—'

Emma gasped as a feeling of déjà vu slapped her mind. She recalled her first visit to Gavin's house when his mother said those exact words when she showed Emma a photograph of him as a baby.

When Emma didn't appear, Gavin hurried back up to the third-floor landing and found her waiting outside the flat.

Gavin called to her. 'We need to go.'

She nodded. 'I left my bag. Sadie's gone to get it for me.'

He rolled his eyes. 'I'll be glad to get moving. She gives me the creeps.'

Emma's mind moved elsewhere. 'Do you think she meant adoption or something? I mean, three kids? I just know I couldn't cope with three.'

'She's wrong. She's not even smart enough to make the predictions the same. How can I have one and you have three? That doesn't compute.'

She nodded her agreement. 'True, that's true.'

He shook his head. 'We don't need to consult a medium to work that one out.'

'Does Siobhan have a Ouija board?'

Surprise lit up his face. 'One of her pals had one. Don't even think about consulting one of those horrible things. It isn't a toy. I'll go back down and check the street is clear.'

'I'll be no more than a minute behind you.'

At the door to the entrance close, Gavin peered out through a glass panel until a young woman with two bags of Christmas parcels appeared and tried to push the door open. Gavin held it for her and didn't allow it to close on her.

'Thanks. Merry Christmas to you and yours,' she said.

Gavin nodded. 'Merry Christmas.'

They both heard Emma's footsteps coming down the last flight of stairs.

The young woman paused to dust snow off her coat and shake her hat.

Gavin called to Emma, 'Everything OK?'

'Yes, she found it.'

The woman approached Emma. 'Were you looking for someone?'

Emma replied, 'Sadie on the third floor? We were—'

'Sadie McCracken,' the woman interrupted then turned to address Gavin. 'You're not her eldest from Canada, are you?'

Gavin shook his head. 'No. Why do you ask?'

'I'm afraid you're too late. Her funeral was on Tuesday.'

# Believe by Mark Brownless

*You do know there's no Santa, don't you? How could there be?*

Matt had been the first to bring the subject up over school Christmas lunch nearly two weeks ago. They'd all sat around the table together eating sliced turkey and bullet-hard sprouts all drowned in terrible gravy while considering the metaphysical, and what to believe. The existence of God had just received a similar response.

*Yeah, it's your mum and dad, they just dress it up so it's magical or something.* Sam was of the same opinion. The two looking knowingly at their other friends, all of whom had been starting to wonder – *after all, there wasn't an Easter Bunny was there* – but were at the very least hedging their bets this year. Tom presumed that they wouldn't be excitedly going to bed on Christmas Eve, hoping to wake up in the morning saying *he's been, he's been*. No, they'd nonchalantly retire in the knowledge that they'd get all they'd asked for. Maybe.

Tom hadn't said anything and had just let the conversation pass him by while concentrating as hard as he could on the apple pie and custard that every school canteen on the planet seemed to get right. There had been the option of Christmas pudding that day, but who in their right mind would want that? It was like serving your nan's fruit cake warm, with a bizarre white sauce. No way.

Thoroughly confused and not a little upset with the idea of all his childhood beliefs crumbling away before him, Tom had brooded for the rest of the day. He'd tossed around the pros and cons in his head, and managed to sway his belief one way, but then it would inevitably swing back the other. Eventually he decided to ask his dad. Dad was the barometer of all things and would give him the most definitive answer, whether it was practical examples of physics or maths or getting dropped by the coach of the football team, Dad would give an issue measured consideration before providing the right answer. His response to this subject was to laugh.

'Mate. That's a really interesting idea from the boys, but think about the hours that Mum and I work – when do you think we'd get the time to sit down and think about all the stuff you might like, then go out and buy it and then wrap it all up? Actually, thinking about it, where do you think we'd keep it all – you know how we struggle with storage space at home, and have you ever seen any cupboards stuffed full of presents? Those guys have got a pretty cool imagination, I'll give them that, but no, we'd be in real trouble if there was no Santa.'

Tom had a lot of time for his friends, and throughout his young life, when he hadn't been at home with his family, he'd been with them. But that didn't mean that they couldn't get things wrong, and when they did, boy were they wrong.

****

Tom Seaton lay in bed on Christmas Eve, too excited to sleep. His Iron Man pyjamas kept getting rucked up around his chest as he tossed and turned, waiting for the Sandman who just wouldn't come. That was a weird thing – *the Sandman* – although he didn't know much more about it, or him, than in the Metallica song. He could hear the muffled sounds of the TV downstairs and wondered what his mum and dad were watching. Mum had let him stay up until half past nine tonight and then said he could read *Diary of a Wimpy Kid* in bed until ten. They both hoped that he'd be tired enough to go to sleep by then. But he wasn't.

He contemplated going downstairs but didn't want his folks knowing he was still awake, and to suffer the comments that Santa wouldn't come if he was. He decided to stay where he was and consider the universe. At eleven, in his last year of primary school, Tom was beginning to understand more of the wider world around him. Up until then it had been football and cricket, his mates and his PlayStation, his family as a given and school as an inconvenience. Now he noticed other things. He quite liked a girl in his class – Gemma – she made him feel a bit funny. She wasn't his girlfriend of course – no way, but there was something. He knew stuff, knew boys' and girls' bits and what happened when 'two people loved each other very much' as his mum would say. Or when Sam's big brother had gone out on a Friday night and brought someone home with him after having had too much to drink. Sam was pretty sure they didn't love each other that much at all – not for more than one night anyway – but despite this, Sam said they made up for the lack of affection in the noises they'd made.

He didn't know exactly *how* Gemma made him feel – a bit strange in the pit of his stomach was what it felt like – a 'funny tummy' his mum might say. But not like that either. She wasn't like his other friends. Well, of course, she *was* one of his friends, but in his little village school the boys tended to hang around together and play football in the yard and hope not to smash one of the little kids in the face with the ball, and get it confiscated by Miss Timson on yard duty. The girls just seemed to hang around.

A few times some of the girls had wanted to play football, but not very often. And that was good because none of them knew the rules and just toe-poked the ball around, running off laughing when they did. Occasionally, he'd gone off to hang around with Gemma – usually when his mates weren't watching or were doing something else, or after they'd hit a five-year-old in the chops and couldn't play anymore. She'd held his hand once – or at least she'd tried to – but he'd quickly pulled away before anyone saw.

So anyway, Gemma wasn't his girlfriend, but she was… nice.

The approach to Christmas this year had been different. Tom had found himself questioning things and not just assuming that everything would be the way it always had. He'd been pestering Mum and Dad (chiefly Mum, of course) to put the tree up from mid-November like some of the other kids in school, but they'd had none of it.

*Christmas should be special, something to remember, not around for months at a time,* they'd said. It didn't explain how the shops played Christmas music constantly from the end of September, did it? They'd had the school play, but he didn't want to think about that. He'd been a gangster in this weird story that was like a retelling of the Nativity but with the gangs, a lock-up garage, and a young couple on the run. It'd seemed quite good when they were practising and the songs were quite good fun, but he'd seen so many strange expressions in the audience at their first show that he wondered if only they'd 'got' the story and nobody else.

**\*\*\*\***

He heard his parents coming upstairs, the creaking of the steps giving away their movements and pushing down on the top of his glow-clock he saw it was nearly 11.30. Tom knew every single creak of the floorboards, knowing when to step on the far left of the third step, and when to turn his foot sideways because the inner half of the seventh step made a huge racket. He was well-drilled at going up and down the stairs in silence. Sometimes he did it as a game… a challenge to himself to see how quietly he could move around the house. It was good practice if he ever needed to come downstairs for a glass of water during the night, or if his parents had people round and he wanted to sit near the top to listen in. But if Santa was listening in to his thoughts right now, that never happened, he'd never be naughty like that – no way. If Santa was listening, he hoped he'd got the letters, he hoped he'd had a handover from the 'not the real' Santa he'd seen at the school fair, and the online imposter that did a little movie made up of things Mum had sent in like pictures, some family in-jokes, and his wish list.

The wish list.

The top of which was an Action Man. He had one already – a commando – but his joints were starting to work loose, and he wouldn't stand up on his own without having something to lean on. Commando needed a partner, needed a buddy to go on missions with, to infiltrate the enemy and get behind their lines, to go and blow up ammo dumps and escape in their Jeep. The Jeep. A new Action Man and a Jeep was what he wanted – more than anything. He hoped Santa had got the memo.

**\*\*\*\***

After the last creak of the stairs, he could hear the stage whispers from his parents, thinking they were being quiet, thinking he couldn't hear them even if he was awake. He made a point of being curled up in a ball in bed – his favourite sleeping position – for when his mum inevitably

45

checked on him. Right on cue, the hinges on his bedroom door creaked momentarily when the door was first moved and he could sense the growing brightness from the light in the hall on the other side of his eyelids, asking him to come out and play, to surprise his mum that he was awake. But he resisted, motionless, concentrating on breathing as softly as he would when asleep. After what seemed like an age, the hinges creaked again, and the brightness faded. Tom could hear muffled voices from his parents' room and heard the toilet flush. Then there was silence. He lay still, counting the seconds, listening for sounds from along the hallway.

His mind wandered from thinking about his parents and about Gemma, his non-girlfriend, and about his friends who'd tried to tell him that Santa didn't exist, and Tom decided that he would prove to everyone that he did. Fifteen minutes after the last noise, Tom climbed out of bed to go downstairs. Just in case Santa managed to get to his room first, he arranged his pillows under the duvet at right angles to each other, to make it look like someone was sleeping there. Satisfied with his work when he looked back from the doorway, he turned and headed for the stairs.

At the top, Tom gripped the banister and started down, picking every step and each creaking challenge, making his way down the curving staircase like this was *Raiders of the Lost Ark*, finally reaching the bottom as silently as he ever had, and walked into the lounge. He looked across to the window, to the closed blinds, and Mum's magnificent floor to ceiling Christmas tree – expertly decorated to such a standard that posh department stores probably modelled their display on it. Christmas tree decorating was a serious business, and certainly not for kids – are you mental – and with absolutely no room for the home-made decorations he made in school with lollipop sticks, spray paint, and glitter. That's what the little tree in his room was for. Blue and silver was the theme this year and ice blue jewels hung next to silver angels and baubles of both colours in a repeating pattern.

His eyes moved from the tree, surrounded by all the trimmings of Christmas with cards and presents packed around it, to the fireplace which was empty, dark, and foreboding. They hadn't lit the fire tonight of course – Santa may be magic in fitting down chimneys and getting around the whole world in a night, but he certainly didn't need his bum burnt to a crisp. Strange to think that the fire looked so cold and, well, spooky, when something so magical was about to happen.

Tom sat down in front of the fireplace and clicked his head torch on, the thin beam of light throwing off wild shadows and shapes which danced around the room as he moved his head, like black-clothed ghosts running along the tinsel.

Presents.

He suddenly realised the significance of there being presents laid out under the tree. There hadn't been any when he'd gone to bed. Well, there'd been a bottle of gin from Mum's boss in a bottle bag, and another one just like it from Aunty Sandra. And there were the presents all wrapped up to take round to Nan's tomorrow, but that was it.

Something had happened.

Had he missed Santa? Had he been and gone and not left him anything because he'd not been asleep?

Fuck.

Tom didn't use the F-word – he wasn't allowed – but plenty of people in school did, and, if his mum wasn't going to find out, then so did he, now. And this wasn't like the SAS show on TV where it was every second word, this was using that most mighty of swear words – he didn't know of any worse than that anyway – where it was most appropriate. This was a major situation.

He turned the light of the head torch back toward the fireplace again, remembering how he'd helped make sure the hearth was spotlessly clean so Santa wouldn't get dirty when he slid down the chimney. He saw the glass of milk and the carrots they'd left like always. Of course, they used to leave a glass of whisky or sherry, but Mum pointed out that if everyone did that Santa would be done for drink-driving just from their street. Always two carrots, which, now he looked at it, seemed like an odd number to leave for the nine reindeer. But presumably they'd share them out between them, and if only a few houses everywhere left them snacks, they'd still be spoilt rotten, wouldn't they?

The milk hadn't been touched and the carrots were where he'd left them. He *hadn't* been. Santa hadn't missed him out because he was awake. But what about the presents that hadn't been there three hours ago? His mind started to come around to an idea, a corner it didn't want to go around, some synapse connections that shouldn't be made. He was beginning to wonder if Matt and Sam had been right all along, if he was wrong just because he wanted to believe, just because he wanted there to be something magic like Santa.

Then he heard a noise. A scraping sound, like something being dragged. The noise came from up above him, and he tilted his head back, directing the head torch to the ceiling, wildly moving the column of light all around, but seeing nothing. It was like the noise was coming from the roof.

The roof! *Of course.*

Tom checked his watch – almost midnight. He was right on time. He stood and followed the direction of the sound. What must be a big sack was being dragged from somewhere near the kitchen, and was gradually moving along toward the lounge, toward the chimney. Tom followed, feeling like he was immediately beneath the sound. It got closer and closer to the fireplace and now Tom could hear the dragging sound transmitted down the chimney as well, slipping and sliding as if there was snow up on the roof. But he knew there wasn't.

The fireplace was tall, almost as tall as Tom, and they all liked to bank it up with piles of big logs on cold winter evenings – sometimes it got so hot that Dad said he could almost feel the paint peeling off the walls. Now Tom stood directly in front of the cold, dark opening, wondering what he should do. *Go to bed, probably,* the sensible side of his brain said, having already thought for a minute that he'd messed up Santa's visit because he was awake, *was it worth taking that chance again?* But he was too close, within touching distance of proving to everyone that Santa did exist, making the scientific discovery of the century. *Him!*

Sure, he'd seen some presents by the tree, so maybe mums and dads *do help* Santa out a bit with the heavy lifting – he hadn't quite had the chance to digest the mechanics of how it worked, but theories and equations were forming in his mind like he was discovering something new in particle physics. But the potential size of this discovery settled things in his mind – there was no way he was going to miss this chance. He *was* going to meet Santa.

Bending forward at the waist and putting his hand on the top of the fireplace, he leaned his head into the chimney void. The noise was clearer here, more direct, definitely the sounds of movement on the roof. Some dust drifted down and landed in his eyes, causing him to turn away and wipe his face, tears welling up as if he was crying. The dust irritated his nose and he tried to get back out into the lounge before he sneezed, but it was coming too quickly. He did his best to stifle it, grabbing his nose and covering his mouth, and when it came it was quiet and quick. After wiping his face one more time, he looked back up the chimney and saw something moving above him, he was too excited to keep still so he couldn't aim the head torch at it but something was reaching down for him, knowing it must be Santa's hand, he reached up joyfully to take it. He was grasped firmly by the wrist, a grip so tight it was almost painful, but then his bare feet left the ground as he was slowly pulled into the air and up the chimney, dust and clinker meeting him on the way down and bouncing off his head, once more stopping him from looking up. Surrounded by darkness, there was only the small cone of light in front of him from the head torch, but as it scrolled past brickwork, there was really nothing to see. The channel started to narrow and feel snug against his shoulders and he hit his head on the stone as the chimney angled away from the vertical, the arm pulling him squeezing tighter still as if he might get stuck or fall. He heard a noise on the roof, the sound of someone in the chimney and he sneaked a look up into the void, seeing something else reaching down. He reached his other arm up to be grasped firmly and now he accelerated up the chimney, being pulled toward the roof, to prove everyone wrong, to impress Gemma that he'd met the real Santa, and not an older guy from down the road who was wearing a false beard. He sensed a presence just above him and the grip on his wrists increased, becoming painful as Santa made sure that he didn't fall back down into the fireplace which wouldn't be good from this height. He could hear the sound of Santa's breath, heavy and rasping as he reached the top of the chimney. Tom wasn't an expert, but Santa didn't sound at all well. He remembered his granddad's breathing sounding like that the last time he'd seen him earlier that summer. Just before he died. Tom hoped that Santa was OK and was maybe just breathing heavily from his busy night and now from lugging nosy Tom Seaton all the way up the chimney. He started to feel bad – guilty even, and the idea of scientific discovery seemed to flee as well – what he really needed to do was to stop delaying Santa on his rounds.

Tom trained the head torch upwards once more, and he was blasted by Santa's breath – a rasping sigh causing him to squint, and wince from the foul smell. Santa had terrible breath. The beam of the head torch illuminated the shape above him, and he opened his eyes again to see a huge gaping mouth ringed with row upon row of teeth. Two long tentacles had snaked out of the cavernous hole to reach down and pick him up, and now a prehensile tongue was curving up and out of the back of its throat to grasp his arm, coiling around the little limb and dragging the boy down its throat.

Tom thought of everyone he'd wanted to know of his discovery, but who never would now.

As he was finally and completely pulled into the mouth of the creature, as Tom met Santa, all he did was scream.

# What Can Possibly Go Wrong? by Lucy Cameron

'What did you just say, you stuck up tosser?' The gorilla bends in towards Geoffrey as he speaks. Geoffrey swallows, or tries to as his throat appears to have gone terribly dry. Just moments earlier everything was going so well. Well, kind of well. OK, things were going poorly but 'well' is a very relative term.

The girl seated next to Geoffrey at the bar has taken offence to a comment he'd just made.

Geoffrey will later reflect on his comment, as he waits in the local Accident and Emergency ward, tilting his head, as instructed, to try to stop the flow of blood from his nose. It will be a momentary reflection superseded by the horror that there may be blood on his new cashmere scarf, one sent to him days earlier by his beloved Nanny. The scarf was accompanied by a smiling photo of Nanny outside the Spanish house she retired to. She wasn't wearing enough clothes for a woman of her age, but Geoffrey kept the photo, anyway.

'We must go and visit Nanny.' He'll splutter. Mother will blanch at the fine spray of blood that follows the words and lands on the sleeve of her coat.

Back in the bar the words have just escaped Geoffrey's lips, 'You remind me of my nanny, she was a rather buxom woman too.'

The words are at the end of a sentence, the beginning of which was the offer of a Pimm's No 1, or possibly a mulled wine considering the season. A sentence of pure compliment, Nanny was, and as the recent photographic evidence shows, still is a wonderfully buxom woman. 'I'll even throw in some crisps for good measure,' Geoffrey adds to his offer, upping his game the way the lad's magazines say you should if you want to impress.

The girl at the bar scowls, her lip quivers.

Geoffrey's made a massive error, forgotten he's at the local public house where the girls are different. 'Or pork scratchings if you prefer?'

A cracking sound pulls Geoffrey's attention slightly left and a long way up. Standing next to the girl is a man the size of a gorilla. The gorilla cracks his thick neck for a second time.

'What did you just say, you stuck up tosser?'

Geoffrey swallows a couple of times in a bid to lubricate his throat. 'I, erm, I asked the young lady if she would care to join me for a seasonal mulled wine.'

'No, he bloody didn't.'

'I think you'll find I did.'

'He said I was fat and just like his gran and asked if I wanted some crisps.' A high-pitched wail escapes her lips.

'You did what?' The gorilla stares down at Geoffrey.

'I said no such thing.'

The girl starts to cry.

'Who am I gonna believe?'

Geoffrey opens his mouth to reply but decides this is a rhetorical question. The gorilla cracks one set of knuckles.

'Hang on a second.' Geoffrey holds up his hands. 'There really is no need for one to get aggressive.'

'You just said my bird's fat. And old. You tried to buy her a drink, and scratchings, right in front of my nose.' The gorilla balls his fist. 'That's well out of line, mate.'

Geoffrey has no idea what the gorilla is talking about and very much doubts they'll ever be mates. The massive, hairy fist snaps back surprisingly quickly considering its size. Geoffrey is about to say as much when it springs forward and makes contact with his face.

**** 

Christmas is one of Geoffrey's favourite times of year. He'll never openly admit it, but sometimes he starts to get excited as early as September. He loves other events too of course, New Year's Eve, Easter, and Halloween, Bonfire night, birthdays of any description and national holidays, although as a student they've yet to reach their full potential. He also loves royal celebrations, watching rugby, horse racing (especially Ladies' days), West End theatre, and certain types of live music. The list goes on, but above all he loves Christmas.

The excitement starts to build openly from December with parties and dinners and the opportunity to wear all his favourite blazers. Trips to snow dusted Christmas markets where people speak strange languages and expect you to haggle over the cost of everything. He writes his Christmas list and while he no longer posts it to St Nick, he thinks really hard about all the items just in case.

Geoffrey's favourite part of the season is the trip home. Two weeks of quality time with Mother and Father plus his brother and sister, should they bother to turn up. Geoffrey was bowled over the first year Rupert decided not to join them and instead took his wife skiing. Father said it was fine but Mother was quiet for several hours. Elizabeth is a model, so even if she can find time in her schedule to 'pencil them in' she never eats Christmas pudding or partakes in any of the board games.

Geoffrey always feels his heart lift when the gates of home come into sight. This time though, it's rather different as his vision is slightly blurred and the pain in his nose throbs. Having let the driver have the evening off, Mother's in charge of the wheel and drives with slightly less caution than Geoffrey is comfortable with. He wonders quite how many sherries she'd consumed by the time he called?

The gates swing closed behind them like the arms of a massive hug.

Father's waiting as they step into the hallway which is warmed by its own small, log fire.

'Bather.' The word doesn't come out correctly, which could be due to the amount of cotton wool the rather lovely nurse has crammed up his nose. At least it stopped the bleeding as it was starting to make him feel most light-headed.

'Geoffrey.' Father extends his hand. 'We were awfully worried. Brawling in the pub?'

'A... ban took obfence, Bather, as I bistakenly offered his birlfriend a beverage.' Geoffrey wonders how long his voice will sound like this? When will it be safe to remove the cotton wool? His stomach lurches at the thought.

'Ah, the path of true love never runs smoothly.' Father places a hand on Geoffrey's shoulder and guides him through to the sitting room. 'I hope you're feeling industrious this season. Ready to give it a go?'

It always takes Geoffrey a few moments to catch-up with his father's flitting conversations. The after-effects of being punched in the face mean that this time he has no hope. He looks at his father blankly.

'Christmas?' Father throws his arms wide, a huge smile spreading across his face.

Geoffrey shrugs.

'Blimey, boy, that knock to the head has affected you more than we thought.' He guides Geoffrey to a chair.

'It bozn't a knock, Bather. A brute punched me. I've bold you how much I dislike the blocal.' For unknown reasons Geoffrey finds he winces as he lowers himself to sit. 'I should bonsider pressing barges.'

'Nonsense, boy, you have far more important things at hand.' Father has crouched down. 'Guess who's going to be in charge of the Key Events this year?'

Geoffrey's heart stops. It can't possibly be true. He hardly dares believe it. He feels sick just to say the word.

'Be?' He manages.

'Got it in one.' Father rises and continues talking, 'Of course, we shall start small, nothing as grand as the meal, not at these early stages, but…'

Geoffrey tunes out the words.

The Key Events Organiser. The overseer of Christmas in the Wellington-Jones household. The one to pull the dream day together, to, as he believes they say, *make it happen.*

Geoffrey's dreamt of this day since he was a boy, watching his father and Sam, the gamekeeper come handyman, head off into the woods, axe in hand to collect the Christmas tree. What a privilege, what unbridled joy. Rupert was the natural choice but now his absence marks a whole new chapter for Geoffrey. A coming of age. Becoming a man.

So many things to get sorted over the next ten days. The tree, the gifts, the decorations, the turkey, no, wait Father said not the food, either way there's plenty to do.

'…nice to put my feet up, let a younger man take charge.' Father's words come back. 'Celebratory sherry?'

Geoffrey nods even though he's not sure how it will react with his pain medication. This is going to be the best Christmas ever.

****

'But it's just an ordinary axe?' Geoffrey looks at Sam.

'What were you expecting?'

'I don't know. I guess I hadn't really thought about it.'

Sam shrugs.

'At least tell me it's a separate axe, that you have another one for chopping whatever else it is you chop?'

Sam shrugs.

Geoffrey feels queasy. It appears the etiquette for axes is very different to kitchen chopping knives and boards.

'Let's go.' Sam trudges to the barn door, leaving Geoffrey to grab the axe –grab in the loosest sense of the word. It appears axes weigh far more than the heroes wielding them in movies make out. Geoffrey's sweating slightly within his parka by the time he manoeuvres the axe so it rests casually over one shoulder like he's seen Father do. He smiles and marches after Sam.

Sam has paused just outside the barn. He shakes his head as Geoffrey approaches. Geoffrey's flooded with the comfort of childhood. Sam's been shaking his head at Geoffrey for as long as he can remember. Ever since the first day Geoffrey toddled waywardly into Sam's shed and knocked over a table covered in seed trays; Sam's been shaking his head. The shake makes Geoffrey feel warm and safe. He considers throwing the axe to the floor and hugging Sam, except he recalls Sam doesn't like being hugged.

Snow had started to fall overnight, so there's a fresh white blanket as far as the eye can see. Geoffrey looks back at their trail of black footprints as they head off to perform the first Key Events Organiser duty.

They move away from the house, slightly to the left and around the back of barns. Mother isn't a massive fan of birds, so the chickens and turkeys are kept out of sight. She always says if it wasn't for the way they flap and scurry and squawk they'd be fine.

No one is a fan of the chopping block, so that's also hidden away here, out of sight of dinner guests. Geoffrey shivers as first the chopping block, then the coops come into sight.

*Get a grip*, he tells himself. *You are the Key Events Organiser. The acquisition of the turkey is a key event.*

In all honesty, Geoffrey had forgotten about this part, or rather hoped it came under the 'Christmas meal' umbrella Father said he was to have no part in. It turned out what Father actually meant was he was to have no part in the planning, buying, or cooking of the food.

All bar the turkey.

'I vote we pop to Waitrose and purchase a turkey,' Geoffrey suggested. Father told him there was no need as they had a stock of perfectly good turkeys next to the chickens. Geoffrey finds his father's love of livestock incomprehensible. People that earn money don't have to rear animals for food.

Sam ducks into the coop, no pun intended.

Time to get in the zone.

Geoffrey puffs his chest. He's a hunter, leader of the pack. He's out to catch and provide for the womenfolk, well… Mother. The ability to do this task is in his caveman instinct. Thing is, he's sure he's pretty far removed from the aforementioned caveman. He considers doing a couple of warm up lunges, but the weight of the axe could prove detrimental.

Oh God, Sam's out and on his way over. That's definitely a bird under his arm. It's all got rather real. Sam comes to a stop. Up close the bird is rather…small. Do turkeys somehow get bigger in the cooking?

'That's rather a small turkey.'

'It's a chicken.'

'I thought we were having turkey for Christmas?'

'We are.'

The two men and the chicken look at each other in silence.

'So, are we just bringing the chicken along for the ride?' Is this some strange ritual Geoffrey hasn't heard of? Take a chicken to watch a turkey having its head cut off? Does it scare the chicken? Does the chicken go back and tell the other chickens what it's witnessed? Does it keep them in line? Will it lead to a bout of furious egg laying? It all seems rather extreme.

'No.' Sam looks from Geoffrey to the chicken, then back to Geoffrey. He shakes his head. 'As you've never done this before I thought we'd start small.'

'So, it's like a test chicken?'

'Suppose.'

'I'm really not so sure about this.'

'About what?'

'This.' Geoffrey nods towards the chopping block then back to the blinking chicken. 'It keeps looking at me.'

'I told your father this would happen.' Sam shakes his head.

Geoffrey feels his cheek redden. He takes a deep breath. He'll prove them all wrong. 'How do I do it?' His voice is several octaves higher than anticipated.

In smooth actions that seem to defy convention Sam manoeuvres the chicken onto the block, holds it in place, and lifts an axe.

'See?'

Geoffrey nods, having instantly forgotten every move Sam just made. Sam holds the chicken towards him.

Oh God.

'Do I have to touch it?'

Sam shakes his head but means yes.

The exchange is rather clumsy, Geoffrey half pulls Sam's glove off as he takes the bird which leads to lots of unnecessary apologising. The chicken is much heavier than expected. It makes a sudden and unexpected flapping movement. Geoffrey screams and drops it.

It takes at least ten minutes for Sam to re-catch the chicken, by which time all three of them are more than a little on edge. Geoffrey just wants it all to be over with. He's not going to cry, not in front of Sam.

'Right,' Sam speaks. Geoffrey can tell he's gritting his teeth. 'I'll hold it, you chop.'

Geoffrey finds that a brave move, all things considered. Geoffrey lifts the axe high. The chicken turns its head to look at him.

'Oh God.' Geoffrey closes his eyes.

'Stop!'

Geoffrey's eyes open at the sound of Sam's voice. He's standing, holding the chicken under one arm. 'You can't chop with your eyes closed.'

'Then we'll have to swap.'

'What?'

'I'll hold it and you chop.'

'No chance.' He nods to the trampled area of grass and snow he's just spent ten minutes re-capturing the chicken on.

'I know how strong it is now. I'll hold tighter. Promise.'

Sam sighs deeply and they do a second fumbled bird exchange. Geoffrey grips tighter this time, but not so tight as to hurt the chicken. He crouches down and holds it to the chopping block, clenches his teeth and looks away.

'Keep your eyes on the bird.'

Geoffrey looks back as Sam's axe thuds into the wood. The blood from the chicken's headless neck arcs high into the air and out across the snow. Geoffrey feels the wings give a final flap at the exact moment he passes out.

****

The fir cone, one of life's understated pleasures. The one Geoffrey has found is magnificent. It's fully open, dry, and perfectly formed. He's sure there's an analogy with himself in there somewhere. It feels so natural in his hand. He rubs his thumb across it. One mustn't forget the smell, of course. Thankfully, the shame of 'Chicken Gate' has kept him indoors for a few days allowing his nose to fully heal.

He inhales deeply. 'Ah yes, the wonderful—'

The force of his nasal passage dislodges one of the seeds hidden deep within the cone. It shoots up his nose and straight down into the back of his throat! He coughs and splutters, his eyes bulge, tears stream down his cheeks. He manages not only to drop the perfect, yet it would appear deadly, fir cone, but step on it, several times, in what could look like a deliberate act of retribution but is in fact merely a choking reflex.

Sam looks back over his shoulder, shakes his head. 'You OK?'

'Yes… Fine. Argh, yes. Fine.' Geoffrey isn't convinced the colour his face will have undoubtedly gone, nor his mad stamping action and chest thumping, will seem in favour of this statement. Sam, however, nods and trudges on towards the Land Rover allowing Geoffrey the privacy to cough up what is without a doubt the biggest fir seed he's ever seen. He considers pocketing it for later measurement, see if it could be a *Guinness Book of World Records* contender.

They're off to get the Christmas tree. Not from a shop, no sir. The Wellington-Jones family is always talked about in the village for its splendid Christmas tree. Every year they fell and decorate the finest specimen they can find on their grounds.

The test tree chopping went far better than the test chicken. Geoffrey's stomach lurches as he thinks of its beady eyes. He doubts he'll ever eat poultry again, which will be a hard one to explain.

Sam has shown him how to wield the axe to cut the V-shape near the base of the tree. Geoffrey notes it is indeed the same axe as was used to kill the chicken, shame stops him mentioning it. Sam says other things about felling, things to do with safety, maybe, but Geoffrey can't remember. Sam shows him how to rock the tree until it falls, or would that be fells, the opposite way to the V-shaped cut.

'It's all rather like that television show, isn't it, Sam? The one where the men have the most dangerous jobs in the world.' Geoffrey feels like a lumberjack in the deepest American forest.

'Keep your eyes on what you're doing,' is all Sam replies.

Now they're heading to the Land Rover to go deeper into the forest in search of their prize. This must be what Sir Edmund Hillary felt like when he set off on that first expedition. Backpacks heavy, warm furs pulled tight like…

Geoffrey is pulled sharply from the daydream by a face staring at him from within the Land Rover. He yelps. The face barks. Oh God no, not Rex the springer spaniel. He'd forgotten all about the dog.

'Sam, do we have to take the dog?'

'His name's Rex and yes.' Sam climbs in.

Geoffrey's heartbeat quickens. He's never been a fan of dogs after that time in the park when the dog was definitely jumping for his throat no matter what Nanny later said.

Geoffrey gets into the Land Rover, never taking his eyes off the hound. It stares back. Geoffrey ends up squashed against the passenger window while the dog loafs across the middle seat. It keeps staring at Geoffrey.

'Sam, tell it to stop looking at me.'

Sam shakes his head.

Geoffrey daren't take his eyes off the dog for the whole trip which does little to help his travel sickness as they bounce across the forest floor. The dog stares straight back, like it knows about the chicken.

They pull to a thankful stop among the most splendid Christmas trees Geoffrey has ever seen, at least they appear to be, nausea is making his vision swim slightly. He should have put the window down.

'I think here will be good.' Geoffrey nods as another wave of travel-induced sickness washes over him. The smell of the dog is doing little to help. He really needs some air. 'I'll get out and come around.' Geoffrey feels his mouth start to water, a pre-vomit warning.

'Don't open your door, there are still a few rogue pheasants around and if Rex gets—'

In a blur of activity, Geoffrey throws open the door and vomits onto the forest floor as Rex, smelling both pheasants and freedom, bounds across his back and tears away into the forest.

Sam swears, a lot. So much that Geoffrey wonders if he's accidentally been sick in the Land Rover.

'Bloody wait here.' Sam's blurry outline points as Geoffrey wipes the retching induced tears from his eyes. Sam jogs off in the direction the dog darted. He's surprisingly fast for an older man.

Geoffrey stands and waits. A few deep breaths and equilibrium is restored.

The fir trees are truly splendid. Geoffrey only takes a few paces and he's found *The One*. Sam still isn't back. He'll be getting really mad. While it's hardly Geoffrey's fault Sam can't control his dog, he does feel a small amount of responsibility.

He stares up at the massive tree, looks back at the axe in the Land Rover. It's time to make a start, he's the Key Events Organiser after all. Imagine Sam's face if he returns and the tree's already felled? That'll make up for letting the dog escape. Not that there's anything to make up for.

Geoffrey walks the circumference of the tree, axe in hand. In his mind's eye he visualises the V-shape incision. The axe thuds into the wood, hardly making a mark. Geoffrey removes his parka. Man versus tree, it's not a game he's prepared to lose.

Geoffrey can feel the sweat running down his back as Sam appears from the tree line with a very sheepish looking dog.

'Sam!' he shouts.

Sam stops dead.

'Look, Sam.' Geoffrey nods up to the huge tree. He's reached the final stages. Rocking the tree back and forth, weakening the opposite side to the V-shaped cut. The tree is seconds from the final crash to earth. Pride swells his chest. He's done it, done it all by himself.

'Look, Sam, I've done it!' The tree's trunk gives a final, loud cracking sound. Sam's mouth gapes, his hands go up to his face.

Geoffrey jumps back to safety as the tree falls away from him.

And crashes straight down onto the Land Rover.

****

'Lights. It's all about the lights,' Geoffrey says to Cook as they stand staring at the bare Christmas tree. It's been removed from the Land Rover and given pride of place in the reception room.

Sam's gone away for a few days, some kind of family emergency. Geoffrey isn't convinced. He's sure he overheard the words, 'Only return when that…' incredibly rude word Geoffrey cannot believe Sam used in front of Mother, '…has returned to university.'

Cook blinks up at Geoffrey. She reminds him of a mole. Perhaps that's what happens if you spend all your life working away in a basement kitchen? Geoffrey makes a mental note to ensure he opens his curtains fully once he's back on campus. Cook doesn't respond, but that's nothing new.

If Geoffrey's honest, this Key Events Organiser role isn't all it's cracked up to be. Christmas should be about fun and frivolity, not having to cut the heads off chickens and fell trees and be shouted at, a lot, by everyone. Thank goodness it's nearly over and next year he can go back to just enjoying the season.

He smiles to himself. Cook looks at him oddly then scurries back underground.

Geoffrey heads to the attic, not the main attic, but the secondary attic over the East Wing, where things are usually put to be forgotten. He's sure this is where he's seen more lights. All the ones they usually use have been festooned throughout the building and it's too late to get to the shops for more – the Land Rover situation took rather a long time to resolve.

Yes, there are the lights! Sets and sets of them knotted in a huge ball of green wire and small glass shapes. Abandoned all the way up here, waiting for him to rescue them.

It takes Geoffrey an age to wrestle them downstairs. The bulbs are a lot bigger than he remembers, but that's OK as the tree is massive. It takes additional time to find what Geoffrey thinks is electrical tape. It's hard without Sam there to tell him. Mice have chewed at the cable in places, but a bit of tape should see that right.

Geoffrey feels like a human pincushion by the time he's finished, who knew shaped light bulbs could be so prickly? But the eleven additional sets of lights are on the tree. The extension cables have all had to be plugged into each other, with offshoots to accommodate all the plugs. It also helps them stretch to the wall socket that's frustratingly far from the tree.

It's taken all day, but the tree is finally ready.

'Let there be light.' Geoffrey cries as he hammers the main plug home.

There's an almighty bang and flash from the wall.

**\*\*\*\***

Christmas Day in hospital isn't so bad. The nurse tells Geoffrey he's very lucky. The doctor tells his father he should invest in some electricity awareness courses for his son. Only Father laughs.

Mother's brought in a plate of turkey which Geoffrey can't bear to look at.

'Poor show, old chap,' says Father. 'The first year is always the hardest. It will be far smoother next year, or worst case, we can go for best out of three?' Father chuckles.

Geoffrey feels sick. 'Nurse, I think I need some more pain medication.'

# Mountain Dew by Paul T. Campbell.

The night before Christmas Eve was definitely not the time to be navigating the Mourne Mountains.

I'd been driving the dark roads for almost an hour, the rain and sleet heavier with each mile, almost horizontal as it hit the windscreen.

Apart from the poor visibility, my mind was not on my driving. The meeting I'd attended earlier in the day had not gone well which probably meant the end of my firm.

The car gave another jolt as rain seeped into the engine, the third time in as many minutes, slowing down, then shooting forward as the water cleared the carburettor. I knew if I didn't stop for shelter soon it would cut out altogether, leaving me stranded miles from nowhere.

I'd not seen any sign of life for the last ten miles. The Mountains of Mourne are the highest range of mountains in Northern Ireland.

In summer a beautiful sight, but in winter, as it was now, they lived up to what Percy French said in his famous song about them: dark, dreary, and for someone who doesn't know the roads, dangerous.

A wrong turn and you could be lost for hours. A bad bend and you could be lost for good.

I'd taken the wrong turn. I knew the mountains fairly well, this being the reason I'd decided to travel home through them. The mountains had been my shortcut home until I'd found the wrong bend. Now, between the rain and my thoughts, I searched each turn for a sign indicating where I was or where I'd come from.

Now shelter was more important, and as the headlights started to dim, I realised the water had reached the electrics.

I'd been confident before the meeting; I was sure my bid for the building contract for a new hotel was just what the owners wanted. Business had been quiet. Rises in interest rates had taken their toll on everyone. When the director of the hotel group had told me my bid had been turned down, they'd accepted a lower offer, I couldn't believe it. I'd thought my offer was as low as anyone could go without cutting corners. I couldn't see how I could keep the firm going on renovating the odd building or house.

The car gave another shudder. This time it didn't shoot forward. It started to slow down; my heart sank and then rose again as through the rain and darkness I saw a dim yellow light appear to my right. Pulling into the yard of an old stone building, I could just make out a sign above the door.

*The Mourne View Tavern, Proprietor James Murphy Esq*

The only sign of life apart from the light coming from two large, curtained windows either side of the door, was an old bicycle standing against the outside wall of the pub.

Turning off my dying engine, I made the short dash, splashing water up to my ankles, to the large wooden door of what I now regarded as my sanctuary.

Two things struck me as I entered what appeared to be the main bar, candles and peat, the smell and the smoke filling the room. The room had a yellow hue from about twenty candles placed strategically throughout the bar. Orange and red flames raced up the chimney of the large, open fireplace. The smell of candles and smoke gave the atmosphere, I imagined, an opium den quality.

73

Sitting around the fire, three men, local farmers I assumed from their dress and the lack of transport outside. They'd stopped talking when I'd entered, staring in my direction at the soaked and bedraggled stranger for a sign of acknowledgement expected in these parts to show you were friendly.

'Good evening,' I said to the room in general. I tried to smile but the coldness I felt from being soaked tightened my lips turning it to half smile, half grimace. They smiled back and in unison replied, 'Good evening.'

The man nearest me came forward and looking me up and down, shook his head and with a twinkle in his eyes, he started to laugh.

'My if you're not a sorry sight, worst I've seen in a long time. I'm Jim Murphy, the owner of this establishment. Get over to the fire, dry yourself, get some heat into ye, and I'll get you something warm to drink. I'll make it with plenty of sugar and cloves. We'll soon have you right.'

I was in no mood to argue and was glad to accept the heat offered at the fire.

'Don't worry about them two,' said Murphy indicating the men sitting either side of it already.

'They're regulars and if the weather's bad I can't get rid of them. The big fellow is Brian McClatchey and the smaller one is John Martin. Both local farmers and like myself love nothing better than a pint or wee one and a bit of a chat around the fire.'

'Pleased to meet you. My name's Cleary, Stephen Cleary,' I said.

I took up a chair, placed it directly in front of the fire and sat down in the warming glow. I knew I was shivering, looked awful, and needed the heat. I soaked it deep into me, relaxing with each flicker of flame.

'Here, get that into ye,' said Murphy.

I could hardly hold the glass as it burnt my fingers, the hot liquid doing the same to my throat and body.

'Thanks, I needed that.'

'What has you out on a night like this?' asked McClatchey.

'I was looking to get the building contract for a new hotel in Newcastle, but they gave the job to someone else. It's not going to be a good Christmas for me and my workers. With all the rain and darkness, I lost my way. My car started to stall, and I spotted the light coming from your windows. Where am I anyway?'

'About two miles from the main Hilltown to Newry Road,' said John Martin.

'If you wait a while it should soon clear.'

'This is great,' I said as I took another sip from my glass. 'What is it?'

'A drop of the mountain dew that falls in these parts, made to my own recipe, with loving care,' said Murphy smiling.

'Can I buy you gentlemen one in return for your hospitality?'

'Won't hear of it,' said Murphy. 'Your company is all the payment we need.'

'I'll make us another round and you can pay by joining us in a little conversation.'

McClatchey stoked the fire and smiled. For what only seemed a couple of hours, we huddled together in our own little world. We talked of everything, from the weather, to breeding cattle, to the problems of building a hotel, and keeping a marriage together.

I was surprised at how at ease I felt with the strangers who talked and laughed so freely and with great enthusiasm. I lost all sense of time and I could feel the problems of the last few hours lift off my shoulders. I felt completely relaxed and happy, even laughing at myself. Nothing mattered outside these walls; the only life worth living was here and now.

McClatchey brought my attention to the sun streaming through the gaps in the curtains.

'The morning's here,' he said. 'Time to be about our business.'

'Morning, have I been here all night?'

'Well, you didn't get here till late,' said Murphy.

I wished them all well and went to leave when John Martin spoke, 'Stephen, do you mind a little advice?'

'No, go ahead.'

'First, remember, if you worry you die, if you don't worry you still die, so why worry? And second, and I think most important is to remember that you never fail until you stop trying.'

I shook his hand and he smiled.

As I stepped out into the morning, the day was bright, clear, and crisp, a day you only get with mountain air, a day you only find in Ireland, a day when everything seems brand new… like the first day of time.

The engine turned first time and I drove with a clear head. What had happened in the bar had somehow cleansed me of all the unhappy and negative thoughts of the day before. Nothing could stop me now as

I resolved to myself to keep trying. I found the right road and an hour later, I was home. Margaret was waiting.

'Where have you been? I've been worried sick!'

I explained as best I could the events of the night before. I now realised how much I loved this woman who had worried so much about me, how I wanted her to stay with me forever.

'You should get lost more often. You're more relaxed than I've seen you in a long time.'

Just then, the phone rang. It was the hotel group director from yesterday's meeting.

'Ah, glad I caught you, Mr Cleary. I wanted to let you know that the board has had second thoughts and now agree that your bid is more acceptable. We want you to build our hotel. We hope you agree. I know it's Christmas Eve but if you do, I'll have the documents for your signature today. What do you say?'

I was speechless but eventually garbled, 'Yes, I agree.'

'Good. Then let's meet in my office, say two thirty?'

'Yes, OK.' Then he was gone.

Margaret had gathered from the expression on my face that the news was good. I told her what had been said and she agreed to go with me to the signing.

'We'll have to go via Murphy's and tell him the good news, it's going to be a good Christmas after all,' I said.

A few hours later, I pulled the car into the same entrance I'd been through the night before. A burnt-out shell of what had once been The Mourne View bar stood lonely and quiet in the midday sun.

'Are you sure this is the place?' asked Margaret.

The burnt lettering on the wall confirmed it.

A young man in blue overalls knocking on my car window broke my spellbound gaze from the building. I wound it down to hear him speak.

'Can I help you, are you lost?'

The accent was strong and local… like Murphy and his friends.

'What happened?' I asked looking back towards the bar.

'A terrible fire happened on Christmas Eve five years ago. The owner and two local farmers were killed.'

He could see the look of shock on my face.

'I'm sorry. Did you know any of them?'

'What were the farmers called?' I asked.

'John Martin and a big fellow McClatchey.'

'How did it happen?' asked Margaret.

'No one really knows, but most think one of them knocked over a jug of Murphy's home-made poteen, Mountain Dew. They think it landed in the fire and exploded, killing them as they sat talking. They were great talkers, so I'm told.'

'Oh, they were that all right,' I said with a smile.

I thanked him and turning the car towards the future, we left the past behind.

# The Art of War and Peace by John Carson

Harry McNeil took his cup of coffee and looked for a spare seat in the café in the bookshop on Princes Street. There was a young woman sitting at a table with an empty chair, reading a book. He went over and saw who it was.

'Is anybody sitting here?' he asked.

She looked up at him and put the book in her bag. 'DCI McNeil. Please.' DS Alex Maxwell indicated for him to sit.

'I didn't know you hang around in book shops,' he said, sitting down.

'Hardly *hanging about*. You make it sound like I'm a shoplifter.'

'I meant; I didn't take you for a reader.'

She lifted her eyebrows. 'What a surprise, eh? I've actually been reading since primary school, I just kept it secret.'

'I could call Vanessa and get less sarcasm.'

'I'm sure your ex-girlfriend would do a lot more than give you sarcasm.'

'You might have a point there.' He drank some of the hot liquid.

It was Saturday afternoon, and the shop's walls were bulging with shoppers, desperate to get out of the snow rather than a need to pick up the hottest new paperbacks.

'So, no swapping presents this year? And our first Christmas together, too,' she said. 'I already bought yours, just so you know.'

'First of all, this is not our first Christmas together. Our first Christmas *working* together, but not as… well… you know.' Harry drank some of the hot coffee, looking out of the window down onto Princes

Street. He reluctantly admitted he was glad he'd bumped into his sergeant.

'Like sugar daddy and soon-to-be trophy wife?' She grinned at him and kept her hands wrapped round her mug of coffee. There were still tiny pieces of melting snow on the ends of her blonde hair, the rest slowly dying on her woollen hat which was sitting on the wide window ledge.

'That would mean I'm a lot older than you, and I'm only ten years, if that. Hardly a sugar daddy. And besides, why would I choose a lippy woman like you?'

'Because of my charm, wit, and stunning good looks.'

'I have no words.'

She made a face at him. 'Have you even started your Christmas shopping yet?'

'Of course, I have.' He brought out a little bag from his coat pocket.

'Who's it for?'

'Well, it's a woman. I had to be careful what I bought. Something with taste, nothing too gaudy. Something she can wear without it jumping out at people.' He reached into the bag and brought out a velvet-covered box.

'Yes, Harry.'

'Yes, what?'

'Yes, of course I'll marry you.'

He shook his head. 'God knows how my predecessor lasted so long. I'm starting to buckle under, and I've only worked with you for six months.' He opened it and showed her the brooch inside.

'Who's it for then?'

'The only woman I love just now.' He held up a finger when he saw she was about to be a smartarse again. 'My mother.'

'Lucky woman. You'll have to introduce me to her one day.'

'Yeah, watch me.'

'Did Vanessa get to meet her? The ex who still lives around the corner from you and who you see every day.'

'First of all, yes, she did, because she was my girlfriend. Second, I do not see Vanessa every day. I see her occasionally in passing. Not that it's any of your business.'

'We're friends. I like to look after you.'

'I'm your boss, first, friend, second. And by friend, I mean, we sometimes get a drink with the others on a Friday night.' He looked out of the window again, at the snow falling down on the herd below. The castle could hardly be seen, sitting up on its perch looking down.

'You having Christmas dinner with your mum, then?'

'You kidding? She and her cronies are already off. They went to Tenerife for Christmas. My mum doesn't like the cold weather, but I secretly think she's looking to get her hooks into some old codger who has a boat and a healthy bank balance.'

'Women can have fun without men, you know.'

He smiled. 'What about you? Going to your parents for Christmas?'

'No. My granny's been under the weather. She lives down in Gosport, so they've gone down to be with her over Christmas. I wasn't planning to have dinner with them, anyway.'

He looked at his watch. It would be getting dark soon, and the buses would start to get crowded, people going home for their tea before getting ready to go back out on the town. Snow wouldn't stop the hardy people of Edinburgh from a night out on the lash. Some of the blokes would still wear T-shirts, no doubt.

'Tell me about the book you were reading.'

She put her coffee mug down and smiled, reaching into the bag. 'I wasn't reading it, I'd only just looked at it. There are several books here. This is a book on psychology, by Dr Martin Friedland and Dr Paul Foster. *The Art of War and Peace.*'

'Daft name for a book.'

'It's an amalgamation of *The Art of War* and *War and Peace.* Have you read any of their books?'

'I've read all of them. I meant to look out for that one.'

'Really?'

'No. I just said that to make you feel good, but now I realise I might have got your hopes up and feel bad.'

'No, you don't,' she said.

'You're right. I don't. I wish I did, but that's part of my chemical make-up.'

'In other words, you're a narcissistic sociopath who plays psychological games with his colleagues in the hope of constant mental satisfaction.'

'That's it, put a different spin on things. But you can't fool me with your big words.'

She made a face that suggested otherwise.

'Wait a minute; let me have a look at that,' Harry said.

She handed it over to him.

'This is second hand,' he said, looking at the old hardback.

'What gave it away? The generic carrier bag or the price sticker on the front? You should be a detective.'

'This is immoral. Buying a book in a charity shop and bringing it in here to read it.'

'It's not *illegal*. That's the difference. Besides, I bought a coffee.'

'It would be like taking your chippy into a restaurant and buying a glass of water.'

'Don't be so dramatic. Besides, you just jumped to a conclusion there, thinking it was mine. It isn't; it was on the table when I sat down, covered by a newspaper.'

Harry looked around to see if anybody was watching him flip through the old hardback, almost wishing he could pull on a pair of nitrile gloves so it wouldn't have his fingerprints on it.

'What's this?' he said.

'I told you, a book on—'

'No, this.' He held up what looked like a letter in an envelope.

'I don't know. I haven't looked inside. There's a card in the bag too.'

She brought it out to show him the card was unsealed and didn't have a stamp or an address on it.

He took the note out and read it. 'Check this out.' He handed it over to her.

*Dear Paul,*

*If you're reading this, then it's too late. Life for me is over, in the literal sense. I can't live without you, and to go on would be too painful. I just want you to know before I pass on to a better world, that I loved you, and will love you right up to my last breath.*

*Christine Xxx*

'A love note,' Harry said.

'A suicide note,' Alex said. 'Probably both. The poor woman. I can't believe it.'

'Did you see who was sitting there?' Harry asked.

'A red-headed woman, but there was a newspaper covering it, so I don't know if it was hers or not. The paper was there on the table when I sat down. I picked it up to have a read when I saw the carrier bag. I was going to hand it in but decided to be nosy and see what the book was. I was still going to take it up when I was finished my drink.'

'Yeah, of course you were.'

'It's true. But never mind that, what are we going to do about the letter?'

'We don't know this is genuine.'

'Oh, Harry. Trust me, this is genuine. That woman is hurting. This Paul, whoever he is, has broken her heart and now she can't see a way out.'

'There's an address sticker on this envelope. Have a look in the card and see if there's anything inside.'

There was a name on the front; *Martin*. She showed it to Harry, and he took it from her and opened it up. Inside was another note.

'Christ.'

'What is it?' Alex asked.

'It's another suicide note. Basically, the same, but instead of it being for Paul, this one's for Martin.'

'That's strange.'

'Suspicious to say the least.'

'We should go and talk to somebody about this, sir.'

'I agree. Let's go to the address that's on the sticker.'

'That's as good a place to start as any.'

They put they card back in the carrier bag and made their way out of the shop. The address was in Bruntsfield, a stone's throw from the city centre, but still a bus ride away. Snow was falling heavier now, making the pavements slick.

'You should wear a hat,' Alex said, pulling hers on.

'It's not as if my hair's thinning.'

'Of course, it's not.'

'It's not.'

'I just said that, didn't I?'

'Get on the bus.'

**\*\*\*\***

They got off in Bruntsfield Place and walked back to the street they wanted.

'You sure you know where you're going?' Alex said, grabbing a hold of his sleeve to steady herself.

'I do. With some help from my good friends, Mr Google and Mr Maps. Turn right here. Bruntsfield Terrace.'

The snow was still coming down hard and the pavement was treacherous. Alex held on tighter, despite having boots on. Bruntsfield Links was on their left, covered in a blanket of the white stuff.

'Be a while before anybody gets out there with their clubs,' Harry said, glad he was more interested in playing pool than golf. Both games involved using sticks and balls, but the similarity ended there. One meant engaging in too much exercise for Harry's liking.

The street turned right, morphing into Greenhill Gardens.

'The first house on the left,' Harry said, keeping back as a small SUV took the corner too fast. 'The *jaws of life* have his name written on them,' Harry said, crossing the road. Alex was still holding onto his arm.

'They all think, *It'll never happen to me.*'

The house was large, sitting in its own grounds behind a high stone wall. The driveway didn't have a gate on it, so they trudged through the snow to the front door and Harry rang the doorbell.

A woman answered, standing in a little vestibule, a glass door the barrier between them and the inside of the house.

'Can I help you?' she said, pulling a cardigan round herself. She was maybe around forty, Harry figured, with well-kept blonde hair.

'DCI McNeil and DS Maxwell,' he said as they both showed their warrant cards. 'We're looking for Dr Paul Foster.'

She looked at them as if she was going to do a runner, but then stepped back and opened the door to the inner sanctum. 'You better come in.'

**\*\*\*\***

The coffee was warm, as was the living room. The woman, Elaine Salisbury, had taken their coats and hung them up.

She sat down after fetching a plate of biscuits. Her eyes were red now, as if she'd gone through to the kitchen for a cry.

'Can I ask what you want with my dad?' she asked.

'We just wanted to ask him a few questions. Is he around?'

She looked at them both for a second before answering. 'He's dead.'

*That might have been the way to start things off with* Harry thought, but kept it to himself.

Alex looked at him as if she thought he was going to come out and say something upsetting. 'I'm so sorry for your loss, Ms Salisbury. Can you tell us how long ago he passed?'

'Only a few weeks ago.' Her voice quivered for a second before she composed herself again.

'Was it sudden?' Harry asked.

'Yes. He managed to hang himself from his wardrobe door. Autoeroticism, it's called. He was sixty-seven. God knows what he was doing that stuff for, but he wouldn't have done that when my mother was alive. It only started after he met *her*.'

'Who?' Harry said, putting his mug of coffee back down on the table.

'Christine.'

'Who's Christine?' Alex asked. *The same Christine who left him a suicide note in his book?*

'His girlfriend. The one he met online. A lot younger than he was. Hell, she's probably younger than me. I'm forty-two.' She looked at Harry as if she was waiting for him to say, *Forty-two? No.*

'Any idea where Christine is now?' he said instead.

'What's this all about?'

'It's something we're working on. We thought Dr Foster might have been able to help us with an enquiry.'

'I have no idea where she is. I've never met her. Dad always spoke to her on his computer. They seemed to hit it off. At first. Then they had a falling out, and my dad didn't want to speak to her again. Then the love affair was on again. She was going to come up for Christmas, but then dad died.'

'That must have been a shock for Christine.'

'I don't speak to her. I don't even know where she comes from. Somewhere down south, I think.'

'What was the post-mortem results?' Alex asked.

'A report was sent to the procurator fiscal, but it was recorded as accidental. Misadventure, something like that.'

'Has she contacted you at all?' Harry said.

'No. She came flitting into our lives and right back out again. She saw a sucker in my dad and obviously taught him some filth. My dad would never have done anything so vile when my mum was alive,' she reiterated.

'I was looking at your dad's book,' Alex said. 'And I saw he wrote a few with Martin Friedland.'

'Yes, he and Martin were good friends. They worked at the university together. They were both lecturers.'

'*Were?*' Harry said. 'Is Dr Friedland gone now too?'

'Not in the way you think; he's retired.' She looked puzzled. 'Is something wrong?'

'Was Christine a… very emotional person?' Harry asked.

'Bit of a drama queen, yes. My dad told me she was… feisty. Why? Are you going to tell me what this is all about?'

Harry looked quickly at Alex before carrying on. 'We're just following up on something that might be related.'

'I told him it wouldn't last,' Elaine said. 'I mean, did he really expect it to last? With somebody he met online?'

'It does for some people,' Alex said, and she realised her voice sounded a bit defensive.

'Maybe, but she was a lot younger than him.'

'Do you know how we can contact her?' Harry said. 'A phone number or something?'

'Sorry. Dad didn't leave any details for her. She's probably moved onto some other sucker now.'

'Do you know where Dr Friedman lives?'

'Let me go and get his address,' Elaine said, getting up and leaving the room.

'Love moves in mysterious ways,' Harry said.

'You talking from experience?' Alex asked.

'Me to know, you to find out,' he said noncommittally.

Alex dropped her voice for a moment. 'What if this Christine woman is a black widow?'

'She wasn't married to Paul Foster.'

'Only because he died before she could get her claws into him. What if she meets men online, they get married, and then boom, they're dead and she has their money?'

'I don't think I'm going to run that past Elaine,' Harry said.

After a few minutes, Elaine came back into the room with a piece of paper. 'He lives in Ethel Terrace, off Craiglea Drive.'

Harry looked blank.

'Just off Comiston Road.' She raised her eyebrows.

The two detectives stood up. 'Thank you for your help.'

'Any time.'

They walked towards the living room door, then Harry turned around. 'A quick question, if you don't mind? Did you live here with your father when he was alive?'

She looked puzzled for a moment. 'What's that got to do with anything?'

'Oh, nothing. I was just wondering.'

'If you must know, I have my own flat. I rent it out now and live here instead.'

Harry smiled and nodded. 'Thank you.'

Outside, the snow was coming down heavier. 'Did you see the look she gave me?' Harry said. 'She thought I should know where Craiglea Drive is. You would think I was a taxi driver or something.'

'I wish you were. Maybe we could get a fast black to Martin Friedland's house.'

'Back to the bus stop,' he said, ignoring her hint.

'Why did you ask if she lived there with her father?' Alex asked him.

'She has a different name. Like she's married… or was. Now she's living in her father's house. I wondered how long she'd lived there.'

Once again, she held onto her boss as they walked along the slick pavement. They only had to wait five minutes for the next bus to take them up Morningside Road and into Comiston.

'What do you think of this Christine woman?' Harry asked as they grabbed a seat at the back of the bus.

'She writes to Paul, hoping that he'll feel sorry for her, then Paul changes his mind about dumping her. She's obviously entertaining him well, if you know what I mean, then he makes up with her, decides to do that sex thing, and he accidentally kills himself. Then she finds solace in Martin Friedland.' She leaned into him as the bus pulled away from the stop. 'What about you?'

'It all seems a bit strange. This Christine doesn't get what she wants from Paul, so she immediately moves onto Martin? I'd like to hear what the good Dr Friedland has to say about that.'

'At the end of the day, we don't know any crime's been committed.'

'But it's got our interest piqued. And being detectives, it's our job to be nosy and poke into other people's business.'

'Correct. Plus, I was at a loose end this afternoon,' Alex said.

They got off on the main road and crossed over, Harry trying to walk and not fall. He was sure he'd never hear the end of it.

'If he's not in, this is going to be an anticlimactic Saturday,' Alex said.

'Sitting on a corpie bus with the great unwashed isn't exciting enough for you?'

'This is Morningside. Nothing unwashed about the passengers.'

The snow was being shoved by a vicious wind, bullied into slapping the faces of the unwary. They walked up the side street towards Martin Friedland's house. The number on the piece of paper indicated the first terraced house was his.

The front door was open.

Neither of them had their extendable batons on them, but Alex was still carrying the carrier bag with the book in it.

'If there's an intruder, you can always read them a passage,' Harry said. 'Bore them into submission.'

He gently pushed the door open, not wanting to announce himself just yet. There was a room on the right, and by the size of the TV, it was the living room. Then a man stepped into view and Harry was about to clean his clock when he saw the blood on the man's face.

'Police. Show me your hands.'

'You got here quickly. You'd better come through. I think I've killed her.'

They stepped into the living room and saw a red-haired woman lying on the floor. Alex put the bag down, rushed over, and felt for a pulse. Harry kept his eye on the older man.

'She's alive,' Alex said.

'Thank God,' the man said.

Harry looked at the man. 'What's your name?'

'Martin Friedman. Doctor.'

'And who's this woman?'

'She tried to kill me. She told me she was going to kill me and make it look like my friend Paul's death; accidental. But she'd already hanged him, so she was going to push me down, make it look different. She didn't know I used to be a boxer, so after she punched me, I ducked the second one. Then she screamed and came at me. I pushed her down and she hit her head on the coffee table. I was fearing for my life, let me tell you.'

'This woman attacked you?' Harry said.

'Yes.'

'Do you know her?'

'Yes. Her name's Christine.'

'Paul Foster's girlfriend?'

'Girlfriend? No, she wasn't his girlfriend. She's his daughter's wife.'

'Elaine Salisbury?'

'Yes. Her real name is Jessica. Christine, I mean, not Elaine.'

'And she came here and attacked you?' Harry sounded incredulous.

'Let me show you.' He walked over to a bookcase and picked up his iPhone and pressed a button. 'I filmed it.'

'Why would you film it? Wouldn't she see you putting your phone there?'

Friedland shook his head. 'No.' He played the video he had recorded, and it was exactly how he had described it, defending himself against an attacker.

'I'm confused,' Harry said. 'You said this is somebody calling herself Christine, but her name is really Jessica. Where does Paul's girlfriend come into this?'

They heard sirens outside, and few seconds later, uniforms rushed in, followed by an ambulance crew. Harry took the man aside. 'Explain.'

'Paul didn't like his daughter's lifestyle.'

'Her having a wife, you mean?'

'Yes. It doesn't bother me. Live and let live, that's what I say, but Paul's upbringing was very strict. He didn't like it. But he met somebody online and began chatting with her. Just for company, he said. He took a photo of her when they were talking on the webcam one night. He showed it to me. She's a very attractive woman called Christine. Well, what do you know? I was out shopping one day, and I saw Elaine out and about with a woman. And they were holding hands and kissing in public. Paul had never seen his daughter's wife. Never wanted to meet her or speak to her. But anyway, I looked up Elaine on Facebook, and there she was in photos with her wife. That woman there, the same woman who had been chatting with Paul, telling him how much she loved him.'

Harry nodded. 'He was being catfished.'

'What's that, son?' They were looking at the paramedics taking care of the woman, Alex standing beside them.

'Catfished. Somebody online pretending they're somebody else.' He looked at Friedland. 'Are you sure he never met Christine in person or spoke about meeting her?'

'He fell head over heels for her. He wanted to meet her. He said he was in love with her and he was going to marry her but he only spoke to her online.'

'I'm going to need you to go to the station to make a statement.' Harry spoke to a uniformed sergeant.

'Come on, DS Maxwell, we're going to pay somebody a visit. But we're not taking a bus this time.'

'That's her,' Alex said. 'The woman I was sitting next to in the bookshop when I was having a cup of coffee.'

Ten minutes in a patrol car and they were back at Elaine Salisbury's house.

'What is it this time?' she said, eyeing up the two uniforms behind Harry and Alex.

'We found Christine. And you're under arrest for the murder of your father, Dr Paul Foster. Turn around.'

**\*\*\*\***

'He was cantankerous to say the least,' Elaine Salisbury said to Harry as he sat across from her in the interview room. Alex was by his side. 'He was furious that I was in love with Jessica. He was always talking to women online, so we found out what chat rooms he was in and I got Jessica to create Christine. She spoke to him and eventually got talking about love. We thought a woman could make him change his mind about me and Jessica, but it had the opposite effect; he got even more vile. He was going to cut me out of his will. He'd never met Jessica, so he didn't know what she looked like. I got her to keep him occupied while we came up with a plan.'

'What was your plan?' Harry asked.

'Christine would talk dirty to him. He played along, but then he had cold feet and told her he didn't want anything else to do with her. That's why we wrote the suicide note. It worked. Then I killed him one night by making it look like an autoeroticism thing gone wrong. We didn't know he'd put the suicide note in a book until we found other books with other things tucked into them. We'd given them to the charity shop, so Jessica went and bought them back and the note was still there. She didn't have the common sense to take them out of the book. We wrote one for Martin. We were going to do the same thing to him. We just hadn't catfished him yet. Jessica got carried away and wrote the damn note well beforehand.'

'Why did you have Jessica try to kill him today?'

'He saw us together. I just panicked and thought it was better to get rid of him now. I called her to say you'd visited and were on your way. The snow had snarled the traffic, so she took longer to get there. Turns out the old boy knew how to look after himself.'

Harry closed the interview after more questions. 'Jessica is going to be OK, if a little sore. But she'll be just fine for Christmas dinner this year. They serve turkey in prison.'

****

'Cheers,' Alex said, clinking Harry's glass.

'Cheers.'

It was a white-ish Christmas Day. A lot of the snow was still around, but the sun was out.

They were in Harry's flat where he'd cooked the dinner. 'My mother was more than happy to supervise from Tenerife,' he said.

'She knows her stuff.' The Queen's speech was playing in the background as they ate. 'Did you go over to Vanessa's this morning?' she asked.

'She's my ex.'

'I know. But still.'

'No, I didn't go. Her boyfriend stopped by and picked her up.'

'You were at the window with your telescope again?'

'Binoculars.' He smiled at her. 'She called me to wish me a merry Christmas and just happened to tell me her boyfriend had arrived.'

Alex washed her turkey down with some more champagne. 'I think it's really over then, Harry. I'm sorry.'

'Don't be. I'm having a great time with my sergeant.'

'I know you said we weren't going to exchange gifts, but…' She reached into the colourful bag she'd brought and handed him a small box.

It was a new tie with smiley faces on it.

'Best gift I ever had from a woman.' He handed her a bag. She took the gift out and ripped the Christmas paper off it. Inside was a pair of furry dice.

'For Betty the blue Beemer,' he said, grinning.

She laughed. 'Thank you. My ex wasn't as thoughtful as you. I love them.'

Dinner finished, they sat and watched TV then Harry fell asleep on the couch for a while.

Afterwards, when they were in the kitchen cleaning up, she stood next to him. 'Let's not let this mistletoe go to waste,' she said, holding a piece above them. Then she kissed him.

# A Gift for Christmas by Kris Egleton

As Christmas approached Maria was starting to panic. She had no money, no job, and little in the way of food. She had no idea how she was going to feed her family after next week never mind at Christmas. She was on her own with the kids since Jimmy had died in Afghanistan.

Joe was looking for something that had eluded him most of his life, a family. He had lost his mum and dad as a small boy; both having died in a car crash when he was four. He barely remembered them but did remember the feeling of being loved. After they died, he lived in a succession of homes as a foster child before becoming a solider. Unfortunately, he was invalided out of the army but he'd since worked hard and was now a successful businessman, but nothing compensated him for his loss of comradeship and family.

Maria started to think of going to the food bank. She knew that would give her the basics but the shame, as she saw it, of taking handouts was weighing heavily on her mind. She would do it for the children. She would make sure they had enough and if the food bank was the only way, then so be it.

Joe wanted to do something about his situation; he wanted to spend Christmas as part of a family. He put an advert in the paper.

WANTED, FAMILY TO SPEND CHRISTMAS WITH FOR MAN WITH NO FAMILY.

He put nothing about his financial situation… just that he was single and his age.

Maria went to the food bank the week before Christmas. She'd been steeling herself to go for weeks and had finally plucked up the courage.

Joe waited for answers to his advert.

As Maria came away from the food bank, she picked up an old newspaper and read it while she waited for her bus.

There was only one answer to Joe's advert from a lady who said that she and her children didn't have much for Christmas but what they did have they were willing to share with him. He was elated.

The gift that Maria gave to Joe was precious. They didn't have a lot but to share what they had with a stranger was her way of being thankful for those people who contributed to the food bank.

Joe fulfilled his wish to be part of a family and rewarded them with everything they would need for Christmas as his way of saying thank you.

The gift they gave to each other was the gift of love from one fellow human to another.

# Free Time by Stewart Giles

# Then

'Don't open it here,' Sophie warned her younger sister, Esme, as soon as she handed her the envelope. 'Just make sure you don't open it here.'

'What is it?' Esme asked, intrigued.

'Something to brighten up our Christmas. But not something the folks will really approve of.'

'I'm thirty-one years old,' Esme reminded her. 'And you're two years older. We're not two teenagers smuggling a bottle of Thunderbird into a school disco.'

Sophie poked her head inside the living room. The television was on and their dad was sitting in his favourite armchair facing it, but from the rumbling snores and snorts, it was clear he wasn't watching. Mum was still busy in the kitchen clearing up the after-dinner mess. Sophie knew what to expect next. The afternoon would turn to evening, the light would fade outside, and their mother would join her husband in front of the television where, she too would soon fall asleep.

'What are you two conspiring?'

Sophie hadn't even heard her mum's footsteps behind her.

'We're thinking of going out, Mum,' Sophie told her. 'Just for a few drinks down the Bull.'

Esme's expression gave away that this was news to her, but her mother didn't notice it.

'That's right,' she said. 'There should be a few of the old crowd back for the holidays. It'll be nice to catch-up.'

She'd stuffed the envelope inside the back pocket of her jeans.

'Your dad will probably join you later. That's if he ever wakes up. I think I'll just have a nap in the front room. I've eaten far too much again.'

****

The Old Bull was an old haunt of Sophie's and Esme's. When they walked in, Sophie realised it hadn't changed at all since their first attempts at underage drinking all those years ago. Even the landlord was the same. Leon Hardy had known they were still at school. He had to – his kids were in the same class as Esme, but he served them alcohol, nevertheless.

'Did you bring the envelope?' Sophie asked her younger sister when they were seated at a booth opposite the bar.

'It's in my pocket,' Esme said having forgotten all about it.

'Let's open it in the Ladies so nobody sees us.'

'What's in it?' Esme asked. 'A cheque for a million pounds?'

'No, but you'll feel like you've won a million pounds a bit later. Come on.'

She got up and headed to the Ladies. Her sister reluctantly followed her.

'Open it,' Sophie ordered when she'd made sure there was nobody else in there.

Esme took the envelope out of her pocket, unfolded it, and carefully tore it open. At first, it didn't seem as though it contained anything, but then Esme spotted the two tiny square pieces of paper. On each one was a blood-red strawberry.

'You go first,' Sophie said.

'What is it?'

'What do you think it is? Something to brighten up Christmas a bit. Just stick it on your tongue and let it dissolve. In a couple of hours, we'll be up in the clouds and we'll be able to dance well into Boxing Day.'

'I don't know, Soph.' Esme looked at the squares of paper then at her sister. 'These are drugs.'

'Come on – live a little. One small tab won't kill you. I'll do it first if you like.'

Esme watched as her sister took one of the squares with the strawberries on, stuck out her tongue, and closing her eyes, placed the paper on it.

'There. Nothing to it. Stick out your tongue. Don't be a wimp.'

Esme did as she was told. Whatever it was that was on the paper tasted of nothing. She threw the empty envelope in the bin and followed her sister back into the pub.

## Now

'Free time,' that's what they called it. After six months, Esme could expect to look forward to more *free time*. What this meant in a place like that, one could only guess. She would still have to endure the compulsory exercise, the strict mealtimes, and the nausea-inducing medication. Even after six months without incident, free time was nothing like what it suggested in *that* place.

The third Saturday of the month had reared its ugly head and it was threatening to rain once again. Sophie glared at her reflection in the bathroom mirror. Yesterday it had been fine and tomorrow it would be fine too.

*Why does it always rain on the third Saturday of the month?* she thought as she scrutinised the face in front of her.

The lines around her thin mouth were more obvious now and the bags under her grey eyes seemed darker.

'Esme is making me old,' she said out loud. She walked back to her bedroom in disgust.

*Make-up or no make-up?* Sophie pondered as she dared to glance at her face again in the mirror on her dressing table. *Esme will no doubt look like hell,* she thought, *and the haggard man in the room next to hers will only pay me more attention than usual and I don't want that after what happened last time. No make-up it is then. Besides, this is my fault isn't it? It's my fault that Esme is in that godforsaken place, anyway.*

Lysergic acid diethylamide.

*One small tab won't kill you will it?*

We should have known better. Women in their thirties have no place in that kind of world.

The doctors called it a chronic psychosis due to an abnormal adverse reaction to the drug – a rare case that outlined the dangers of this kind of recreational drug. It was Sophie's fault and her punishment arrived on the third Saturday of each month. The first visit was the worst and even though the subsequent visits became more and more bearable, Sophie knew this was only because she'd learned what to expect.

She quickly dressed and went downstairs. The cat was nowhere to be seen.

'Bruce,' she shouted. 'Breakfast.'

She poured some cat food in the dish next to the washing machine. It smelled like halibut. She lit a cigarette and walked away from the smoke alarm.

The first visit had drained her completely – she'd returned home and sobbed uncontrollably. An hour before the second, she'd finished a bottle of wine. It had made the experience more tolerable but the staff at the hospital had obviously smelled the alcohol on her breath and had eyed her disapprovingly.

She took a deep breath, picked up her phone and keys and left the house. She'd given up on the cat.

## Then

'Es,' Sophie laid her hand on her sister's shoulder. 'What does it feel like?'

The drug didn't seem to be having much effect on Sophie.

'Es,' she said again. 'Has it kicked in yet?'

Esme didn't speak. She stared straight ahead at the optics behind the bar. Her pupils were dilated, and her gaze intense.

'I'll get us a Coke each,' Sophie offered and headed for the bar.

Esme hadn't moved when Sophie returned – her gaze was still fixed on the spirits behind the bar, but there was something different in her eyes now.

She looked absolutely terrified.

Something was clearly frightening the life out of her.

'Es,' Sophie said. 'Are you all right? Drink some Coke – it'll make you feel better.'

Esme wasn't listening. Her eyes widened and she turned to look at her sister. It was a gaze Sophie would never forget. It was the gaze of a wounded animal staring down the barrel of a rifle. Then her focus returned to the bottles behind the bar and she started to speak.

'They're coming.' It didn't even sound like Esme's voice. It was deeper and more guttural. 'They want to take me.'

Sophie was scared now, and the feeling that the drug was beginning to show some effects on her didn't help.

'Devils,' Esme shouted so loudly that a few people at the bar turned around and stared at her.

'Demons. Clawing at me, pinching and pulling me.'

She stood up and walked over to where a group of youths were playing darts. She plucked a dart out of the board and jabbed it in her arm with such force that she wasn't able to remove it to repeat the procedure. Sophie was there in an instant. Esme was still trying to pull the dart from her arm, but it was stuck fast. The darts players looked on with wide eyes.

'What's up with her?' one of them said.

'She's lost the plot,' another commented.

What happened next was something everybody who was in the Old Bull on Christmas Day would remember for a very long time afterwards. Esme started to headbutt the dartboard. She started off softly nodding her forehead against it, but then her pace quickened, and she was now smashing her head against the hard outer edge with greater ferocity. Sophie tried to stop her. Two of the darts players tried to help, but Esme wouldn't stop. Eventually, Sophie grabbed hold of her sister's hair and yanked her head back. Esme's face was a mess. Bruises had already formed, and her nose was bleeding badly. The wire from the dartboard had left red welts all over her skin. She fell to her knees and placed her hands over her face.

'Give her some room,' the authoritative voice of one of the paramedics boomed.

Somebody had called an ambulance.

'Please move out of the way.'

The young woman in the paramedic uniform pushed through the crowd of people and crouched down next to Esme.

'What happened, love?'

She turned to the people standing, wide-eyed. 'What happened?'

'She just lost it,' it was one of the darts players. 'Started headbutting the dartboard.'

'Come on,' the paramedic put her arm around Esme. 'Let's get you checked over. Dart's not your game is it?'

Esme allowed herself to be taken outside and into the ambulance parked on the street.

'She's my sister.' Sophie climbed in after her.

'Has she taken anything?' the paramedic asked and looked Sophie in the eyes.

Sophie could feel her stomach heating up. She was frightened she was going to be sick right there in the ambulance.

'Listen, love,' the paramedic said to her. 'I need to know. I'm not here to judge – my job is to save lives, so if she's taken anything, you need to tell me what.'

'Acid,' The word burnt Sophie's lips when it came out. 'We both took an acid tab. It was stupid. I didn't know this was going to happen.'

Esme lay still on the stretcher with her eyes wide open. The scene was quite disturbing. Sophie hardly recognised the sister she'd grown up with.

****

When their mum and dad walked into the waiting room at the hospital, Sophie stood up and approached them. The landlord at the Old Bull had phoned and told them what had happened, and they'd just finished talking to the doctor in charge. Sophie's dad nodded in acknowledgement, but her mother could barely bring herself to look at her daughter. When their eyes did finally meet, Sophie flinched. The expression on her mother's face was perfectly clear.

Disappointment.

Sophie looked away, but the chagrin in her mother's eyes remained in her mind's eye and she knew from that moment on she would never be forgiven for what she'd done.

The doctor had explained in some detail that what caused Esme's episode was a severe allergic reaction to the LSD she'd ingested. He'd also elaborated on the fact that taking LSD was akin to rolling the dice. One never knew exactly what was going to happen. It could be a racing, distorted high, or a severe paranoid low. Esme had suffered the latter, and whether she would fully recover from it was still unclear. It was going to take time, and Esme would need to be closely monitored.

# Now

St Mark's Hospital was a drab, double-storey face-brick eyesore. The grey skies and drizzle only enhanced the gloom surrounding it. Sophie parked her car in the visitor car park, turned off the engine and waited. She waited for a sign that this visit would be different. She waited for a gap in the weather but mostly, she waited to delay the inevitable. There was a faint rap on the window and Sophie jumped. A man in uniform stood there gazing at her with a combination of suspicion and sympathy in his eyes. Sophie rubbed her eyes and opened the car door.

'Are you OK?' the man asked.

'I'm fine,' she lied. 'I'm here to visit a friend.'

There was only sympathy in his eyes now.

Esme was now in ward four. It was here that she would have more *free time*. Sophie knew the way. After the informal check at reception where she was briefly searched for heavens knows what, she made her way past the entrance to the ward where Esme had spent the last six months. The man with the long greasy hair and goatee beard was sitting on a chair outside his room as usual. He was painting an imaginary masterpiece on the wall with his fingernails. The woman with the shaved head who had said that Sophie looked like Jesus on her first visit was nowhere to be seen.

*Maybe she got better*, Sophie thought.

At visiting time, it was sometimes difficult to tell the patients and visitors apart. Dr Green, Esme's first doctor had told Sophie once that everyone in the whole world is a potential lunatic. Those were his exact words. He had said that all it took was a tiny spark to set the wheels in motion: a tragedy, a traumatic event or, as in Esme's case, an adverse reaction to a mind-altering drug. He had asked Sophie out for a drink afterwards, but she'd lied and said she was spoken for.

Esme was sitting upright on her bed watching something on the television in the corner of the room when Sophie walked in. The sound was turned down.

'Hi, Esme,' Sophie said.

She waited for a response, but Esme carried on watching what appeared to be a wildlife documentary. Four warthogs were attacking a female lion. Sophie sat on the chair by the bed, but Esme still didn't move. She looked out of the window. Two wasps were racing up and down the windowpane frantically. Their incessant buzzing got louder and louder the more she watched. The larger of the two dropped to the bottom of the windowpane and stopped moving altogether.

'Shall we go outside?' Esme said eventually. Her voice was croaky. She sounded as if she had a cold.

'Sounds good.' Sophie smiled. 'It's raining though.'

'Doesn't matter. I have a raincoat.'

Esme jumped off the bed with surprising agility. She opened her cupboard and took out an old green mackintosh.

'Marius is gone,' she said as she put it on.

'Marius?' Sophie said.

'My old next-door neighbour – the one that liked you.'

'What happened to him?'

'They took him away. He stuck a fork in a nurse's neck. I watched him do it. One minute he was calmly eating his breakfast and then *bam*. Fork sticking out like a diving board. He said the nurse had been sucking out his thoughts with a brain vacuum and it had to stop.'

'My God,' Sophie exclaimed.

'He finished his breakfast using just his knife until they came and took him. Shall we go?'

The rain was falling heavily as they made their way past the security guard and outside to the patient recreation area. The whole garden was deserted because of the weather.

'Smoke?' Sophie asked as they found a bench under a tree.

'Please,' Esme replied.

Sophie lit the cigarette and handed it to Esme. Her hands were shaking quite badly.

'Did you see how that guard looked at us?' Esme asked. She took a long drag of the cigarette.

'What do you mean?' Sophie said.

'It's like he wasn't sure which of us was the nutjob. You should wear more make-up you know, you look pale.'

'Thanks a lot. I still feel bad about what happened. It doesn't feel real.'

'It's not your fault,' Esme said. She threw the cigarette butt into the bushes. 'I won't be here for much longer, anyway.'

'Are they letting you out?' Sophie asked.

'I think so. They think I'm getting better.'

'I saw Brian the other day,' Sophie said. 'He looks terrible, and he's getting so fat.'

'He's an idiot. He's always talking about himself.'

Esme looked away. A house sparrow had perched on a thin branch on the tree next to the kitchen building. It shook itself frantically. It was obviously annoyed by the rain.

'This is nice,' Esme said. 'Free time. I've missed being able to go outside. Could you get me something to drink? The drugs they make me take dry out my mouth.'

'Of course,' Sophie said. 'There's a vending machine in the canteen.'

She picked up her handbag and stood up. Esme suddenly looked agitated.

'Could you give me another smoke before you go?' she asked.

'Of course,' Sophie replied.

She took her purse from her handbag and left the bag on the bench.

'There's a full packet in there,' she said. 'I won't be long. Coke?'

'Perfect,' Esme replied.

While Sophie was getting the drinks, Esme opened her handbag and took out the cigarettes. She took one out and lit it. She found the car keys in a side pouch in the bag.

'Free time,' she said to herself and stood up. The visitor car park was on the other side of the fence to the patient recreation area. She walked quickly to the fence. She spotted Sophie's car immediately – a red Mazda. She was over the fence in two seconds. The exercise routine had paid off. She looked around but there was nobody to be seen. She ran to Sophie's car, unlocked the door, and got in. She put the key in the ignition and turned it.

The church tower was on the other side of the car park. It was part of the old building and was rarely used anymore. Esme put the car in gear, took one foot off the clutch, and slammed the other on the accelerator. She drove across the car park until she was facing the tower about three hundred metres away.

'Free time,' she cried.

She headed straight for the building… first gear, second, and then third. The speedometer read sixty-five miles per hour. Esme let go of the wheel, but the car carried on in a straight line.

Fifty metres to go.

Esme blinked a few times then kept her eyes wide open. She wanted to see it all. She smiled as the wall of the church tower roared towards her. It was her first smile in more than six months.

Twenty metres.

The speedometer now showed eighty miles per hour.

The car crashed and Esme screamed.

It was a scream of pure joy.

Now she really had free time.

# Died of Wounds by Malcolm Hollingdrake

Forgive me for taking the liberty of weaving fact with fiction. Some of this story is true and many of the places mentioned are real. It has never failed to amaze me how coincidences bring strangers' lives together and can link them to lives lost in the past; lives that were once real.

****

The spring of 1915 and the weather was improving. The winter had been particularly cruel; the summer and autumn had been the wettest anyone could remember followed by a severe frost and thick snow. The combination had closed the quarry and the soup kitchen had been opened to alleviate the hardship of the families of the quarrymen of Bolton Wood, Bradford. No work meant no wages! None of the brothers could remember a worse time but their father had shown his usual indifference. There would be a gill of ale at the local each evening, he would ensure that. The break in the weather had brought an urgency to work as many hours as daylight would allow, and the area around the quarry was a forest of grey steam as it swelled and enveloped the valley, contrasting the mill chimney black off in the distance; the warm vapour constantly fought and clashed with the cold air from the steam cranes, steam and horse-drawn wagons and the shunting trains.

William smiled at his brother, Jessie, and reflected on his misfortune. Three weeks had passed since the accident. It was a stroke of bad luck, fate and a chance word that had caused Jessie to pause, Tommy Tin containing his lunch in hand, to chat to his senior. Jack, the banker, the man responsible for finishing the stone, was putting the final touches to a gulley block; it was craftsmen's work needing strong hands and a careful chisel.

'Warm my tin on the plate, lad, I'll be in in a tick.' His lined face creased even further as a smile broke his lips.

It was then that it happened. As Jessie bent down to retrieve Jack's Tommy Tin, a shard of stone from the end of the cutting chisel flew into his left eye. The tin had immediately fallen as the pain from the punctured eye caused him to bring both hands to his face. The eye was lost. At twenty-one years of age, his future was now in doubt, he was devastated, but not for his injury alone but for his ambition. He had seen the posters and heard the call. The pending clouds of conflict seen the previous spring had brought the storm of war to France and Belgium. William, at nineteen, along with the younger sibling of the three, Walter, had taken the opportunity to join Kitchener's army. Now, considering the number of volunteers, they wouldn't want a one-eyed Tommy. It was as if the shard had hit the heart and not the eye.

The brothers had feared it would be over too soon, over by Christmas but that had been a cynical rumour to draw the youth of England to the recruiting sergeants and it had worked. The Pals had been only too eager to travel to new lands and leave behind the everyday drudgery. Even though news of casualties returning from the front had been in all the newspapers, the enthusiasm and the propaganda still stirred young spirits. The only hope for Jessie was the promise of work at the quarry but he knew that was because of labour shortages. Charity he would not tolerate, and his injury had wrought a change in his demeanour and personality.

'Out again?' Jessie looked at his brother, the black patch covering the empty socket. 'Polly?'

William winked and smiled, realising his error when his brother turned away. William had been seeing Polly Townsend for barely two months before he joined up. He did not wait to be conscripted and went against his parents' wishes. She too had mixed emotions. She liked William, he had a kind face and he worked hard. They'd not kissed but he had always brought her small stones in the shape of animals he had found or made at work, leaving them on the windowsill of her terraced house on his way from work. He was unsure if she could read but he would wrap his gift in paper containing a short note. He had no need to worry, she could read, write and sew as he had discovered when he boarded the train. She'd handed him a silk handkerchief and an envelope. He had lifted her hand and kissed it.

'I will return soon after training before they send me to France.' It was then he saw the tear.

She moved closer and rose on tiptoe. Her lips brushed his and he blushed. 'Take good care my soldier Bill.'

## Summer 1917

She sat with her tea and read the letter from Walter received the previous day. She'd tucked the dry, blue flowers that Walter had trapped between the folded sheet into the clip that held the mirror:

*My Dearest Mother,*

*I do hope all is well and work continues for Father and Jessie and that he is managing to remain positive. I have pressed these small flowers I found close to the battlefield, what with those and the song of the lark, life felt almost normal. For now, at least, they're the only gift I can send. We've moved again but at least I have had some rest and a hot bath. We are due at the front in a day or so. Our casualties are not as great as some, but we are fighting hard and unafraid of having a go.*

*Several of the villages we see have been shelled out of existence leaving myriad refugees. Many of the lads break down on seeing their plight but remain determined to beat the Bosch.*

*Hope the letter opener was useful. Received your package also. Thank you. The cigs and the snuff were well received. I'll share them with some of the lads less fortunate. Please don't leave yourself short I'm coming to no harm.*

*Haven't heard from Bill other than he's now a driver and will soon be delivering vital supplies to the boys at the front.*

*My love to you all but a dear kiss to you mother.*

*Your loving son,*

*Walter.*

She placed the letter back in the envelope, kissed it and tucked it into the pocket of her apron before going to the wash house. There were the chickens to feed and clothes to wash.

The knock on the door of 28 Mexborough Road was loud and late in the afternoon. Both men of the house were at the quarry and Annis opened the door, a coating of bread flour on her hands. A telegram boy held out an envelope and touched his cap. 'Sorry Mrs Drake, sorry.'

Wiping her hands on her apron she reluctantly took the telegram, her face now as white as the fine dusting of flour that clung to her clothing.

The boy swung the bag from his side to his back and cycled down the cobbled road. It had been the tenth telegram he had delivered that day.

121

Annis's hand trembled. Two mothers on the road had received these over the last month and she knew its content. She stared at the envelope as the faces of her two boys flooded her mind's eye… which of her boys would be mentioned. Were they injured, captured, missing or…? She picked up the letter knife Walter had made from the copper banding from a German shell. He had made it and brought it on the first leave he had been granted since joining the fight. She reflected on his arrival. He had aged, lost weight. He had talked more to his father about what he had seen, but she'd noticed the slight tremble of his hands as he collected his morning brew; the cup rattling in the saucer was clearly audible.

She looked at her hands. Her eyes were immediately drawn to the name – handwritten on the lined form – Cpl Walter Drake. A tear ran down her cheek as she put her head back and a deep animalistic wail hit her throat. The paper knife fell to the flagged floor and the dull, metallic ring sounded the death knell as she sank to her knees.

'Not my baby!'

*Deeply regret to inform you that Cpl Walter Drake, the Yorkshire Regiment died of wounds, 17th July 1917. The Army Council expresses its sympathy.*

**\*\*\*\***

William had read the letter he had received from Polly over and over again, it had contained the news of Walter's death.

*My Sweetheart, Bill,*

*Your mother asked me to write for she is heartbroken. She said that he'd died in a place she couldn't pronounce nor knew its whereabouts but it had become the final resting place of her precious child, her youngest… you must stay safe and come home to her for to lose you too would surely kill her...* William had wept like he had not cried since he was a child and for the first time he felt real fear, but not fear for himself, fear for those left behind. They were away from the fight, reading only what was allowed to be printed in the press.

To think Walter had been barely thirty miles away when he was wounded, thirty miles, that's all but it might as well have been on the other side of the world. He had told himself over and over again. He had to survive for his mother's sake and that of Polly, but the war seemed to have no end. The constant toing and froing over villages, ridges and woodland brought only needless slaughter on both sides; the stench of that slaughter was locked within his nostrils.

The following day he would be delivering petrol to the front. The tanks had shown their merit at Cambrai and had surprised not only the German troops but also the British commanders. A missed opportunity he had heard. 'Lions led by donkeys,' he muttered before folding the precious letter and tucking it inside the cover of the bible he kept within his breast pocket.

**\*\*\*\***

The day dawned bright, a change from the showers of the last few days that had made the roads difficult to pass. He was now well versed in the planning and the need to rendezvous with the motorcyclist who would guide them to the ever-changing front line. Wilkins, Bill's co-driver would accompany him and share the driving as usual. They'd moved from Albert to Bapaume with ease as new ground had been won. The mixed convoys of horses and carts and mechanised transport kept the troops, medical stations and machinery working.

There was little activity although the sound of the guns grew louder the closer to the front you travelled. The grind of the gears and the constant whine from straining axles was usually their only distraction. The occasional ambulance, some horse-drawn others mechanical passed, leaving the medical station.

Wilkins looked at the red cross on the canvas tilt of the wagon. 'Bloody hell, Bill. Know what the lads call the Royal Army Corps?'

Bill had heard it so often – 'Rob All Your Comrades?'

'Surprising how many lads have lost their possessions from the moment they're put on the stretcher to arriving at the medical post. Funny that unless all that jiggling about causes it all to fall onto the fields of Flanders.' He turned to Bill. 'Remind me not to get shot.'

All too frequently the wagons carrying the dead were seen, the tarpaulin shroud protecting those stacked within. You just knew they were there... boys and men. Bill would touch his cap.

'These lads lost more than their ha'penny, poor bastards.'

Now when he touched his cap he thought about his brother and offered up a small prayer. He watched as the cart pulled past, the boots of the piled dead just visible. These men would be buried together, fallen for king and country and laid to rest in the corner of a foreign field. A steadying hand moved onto the wheel.

'Steady, Bill. Eyes on the road.'

The motorcycle led the convoy towards the new line as a gaggle of troops slogged along the side of the road. On arrival at the collection point, the wagons unloaded, and the soldiers would congregate round the canteen wagon. A brew was in order. A group of soldiers crowded the wagon eager for food and a hot drink, their battledress still clogged with mud.

'What regiment, soldier?' Bill asked, allowing one to go before him.

'West Yorkshire but I'm a Harrogate lad.' He smiled; the enthusiasm of youth still fresh in his eyes. 'Been a tough one today, thought we'd secured the position but the Bosch had different ideas. We're still here. The grace of God thought I should fight the good fight for another day!'

The irony struck Bill like the shrapnel that had taken so many. He smiled.

'Bill Drake. Bolton Woods, Bradford.'

'Knew there was something right about you. A fellow Yorkshireman. Archie, Archie Eagin is the name. Never thought I'd see the fighting. Thought it would be over and done with before I got here, prayed it wouldn't be. Be careful what you wish for as my old teacher used to say!'

They both laughed and Bill patted him on the back.

'Been in long?'

'I've done me whack, Archie, and will be doing more.' He leaned over and collected the enamelled mug. 'You keep safe, young Archie.' Bill smiled and moved back to the convoy. The journey back passed without incident.

# July 1918

For some reason Bill felt more nervous than he had done driving near the front line. Butterflies bounced in his chest as the train rattled towards Bradford Forster Square Station. The square was busy with horse-drawn carts loaded with wool bales. The tram rattled by; Player's Navy Mixture emblazed along the upper open deck. He felt in his pocket… his fags were safe. Ten days after all the time in France, he had but ten days.

'And where do you think you're going without me, Bill Drake?'

He turned to see Polly. She'd been waiting on the island beneath the statue of William Edward Forster and on seeing him emerge she'd followed him towards Canal Road. Dropping his kit bag, he grabbed her and picked her up while swinging her round. She squealed. They kissed.

'Goodness, Bill, not here in the very centre of town!'

Bolton Woods was quiet. Steam still rose from the quarry on the hill and the occasional whistle could be heard. Polly insisted he go home alone; his mother would be waiting, and she was right. The table was already set with the best crockery. There was a smell of fresh bread and cakes and there she was. She looked smaller than he remembered but the warm smile brought tears as he hugged her.

'I'm safe, I'm safe.' He lifted her face and kissed her forehead. 'I have ten days. Ten whole days.'

'Your father and Jessie are at the quarry. He has a glass eye now. Very handsome he looks too. Go on, run up there. They'll be finishing soon, and you can say hello to the others. Mostly youths but doing fine jobs.'

Bill looked at his things spread on the floor. He smiled and left. Mexborough Road was just as he remembered. The cobbles and the horse shit. He paused and turned to look over the valley and Lister's Mill; a huge, stone leviathan demonstrated the strength of Bradford's industrial power. Within three minutes he reached the quarry gates. The cranes belched out smoke and steam and the men, diminutive beneath, worked in groups. It was then Bill saw Jessie.

'Jessie!' He waved as his brother turned before dropping his tools and running towards him.

'Little brother!' They stopped a yard apart and simply looked at each other. 'Quite the soldier my brave Bill.' The gap was quickly closed, and they hugged. Their father walked down. He shook Bill by the hand and smiled.

'Good to see you home, son. Your mother frets. Come on Jessie, another forty minutes. No time for this now. There'll be plenty of time to catch-up at home.'

Bill turned and walked back towards the row of terraced houses. He had not even noticed the eye!

He thought he would be able to rest once in his own bed, but sleep evaded him. The lads said it would. He felt alien and not part of his place of birth as if it had moved on, as if he too, like Walter, had passed away and although not forgotten, he was not there and it was not real. If it had not been for Polly...

Ten days passed in the blink of an eye. He had managed to spend time with Polly and had proposed on the second day. She'd bubbled with excitement and they would marry on his next leave. Jessie and Polly had gone to the station with him. The brothers parted like they'd met. Jessie moved away leaving Polly and Bill to their farewells. They both waved as he boarded the train and Bill's words rang in his ears. 'Look after Polly for me and look after Mother. It shouldn't be long, maybe another year.'

Smoke billowed from the engine and the whistle reverberated around the station. Pigeons scattered as the train pulled away.

**** 

On returning, the lads of the Service Corps greeted him like a long-lost brother. 'Missed all the bloody whiz-bangs. Had to fight the Germans with our bare hands while you were seeing all the Yorkshire lasses.'

He did not like to admit it, but it was good to be back. He felt welcome, a true brother in arms.

'Bloody hell! Look who's come back!' Wilkins slapped him on the back. 'Thank goodness you're here. The driver they replaced you with scared the shit out of me. I thought you were bad, Bill, but…'

The convoys to the front taking supplies and men continued through the summer of 1918. There seemed to be a greater urgency and optimism that the war would soon end and that made the transportation of the dead and seriously wounded even more futile. The waste, the cost was only visible to those moving the bodies which were only a small proportion as many had been turned to vapour.

The letter had arrived in the early afternoon of 26th September, but he knew from whom it came. He could almost smell Polly's perfume on the paper. He wouldn't open it until he was alone, Wilkins would only pull his leg and try to snatch it. Alone, he would pretend that she was reading to him while wrapped in his arms.

'Drivers, we've not got all bloody day standing round gossiping. Get these bloody things moving… there's men to move!'

A major push was being organised at Flesquières, a village that had changed hands many times. The ridge on which the village was perched was critical to both sides. Considering the men being brought forward it was a do or die battle.

Bill watched the men climb into the back of the wagon. Some knew their destination, they'd been before but others…? However, the majority were quiet and simply moved along the benches to the side and the centre. The green-grey canvas tilt flapped and snapped. It was then that Bill saw someone he recognised. He pointed. 'Archie?'

Archie Eagin smiled. 'Well, well, well, Bill Drake… we're in safe hands lads. Big show coming up and they need Yorkshire riflemen with a keen eye to get the job done.'

'I'll get you there and if needs be, I'll come back for thee.' Bill exaggerated his Yorkshire accent. 'You keep your bloody head down young Archie. How've you been?'

'Awarded a Military Medal last time out, Bill. My father was so proud. Victoria Cross next if it doesn't end too soon!' They both laughed.

A shiver ran down Bill's back as he looked into the face of the smiling Tommy. 'You're not listening to me – keep this down.' He tapped his metal bowler.

The artillery bombardment commenced as soon as the convoy left the front and it seemed to pursue them. Bill took a turn off the main road away from the village of Bertincourt which seemed to be targeted although it was not on the front line. A few other wagons had broken ranks too as shells displaced huge fountains of soil, rock and clay. Wilkins held on as Bill took the wagon towards a large barn. Cordite hung in the now cloudy air, stinging eyes. Horses could be heard, panic and fear were setting in.

'Jesus, Bill. Have we gone the wrong bloody ro…?' Wilkins did not finish the sentence.

Neither man heard the shell that struck the masonry of the side of the barn, but they did briefly see the fragments of stone before they struck the wagon penetrating the windscreen and then the two men. It took a shard of stone to travel through Bill's neck killing him instantly. He slumped sideways. Wilkins was less fortunate. The glass from the screen had punctured both lungs and it would take minutes for him to die; to drown in his own blood.

****

The letter was found as they lay both men on the ground and began the search for personal items and their handstamped dog tags. It was unopened but added to William Drake's belongings. It would take two weeks for the telegram to arrive and a further two for the death letter, addressed to Jessie. The unopened letter from Polly also arrived bound with it.

Jessie left the house and headed for the moor between the village and the quarry, a place they'd all played as kids. The wind blew the coarse grass bringing with it a chill. He needed the air. He slit the envelope addressed to him using Walter's letter knife and placed the opener on the grass before reading the letter out loud:

*My dearest brother,*

*If you are reading this then you will already know that I have not come through this conflict. Like Walter, I have paid the ultimate price in defending my king and my country at a time of great need. If it means Mother and Father are safe and proud of their son then that's all I can ask, but how I wish for a life we had when we were together. I cannot miss what I've not had but I know my life with Polly would have been the best. She's so kind and caring. You're all that's left, and I beg that you look after not only Mother and Father, but that you also look out for Polly for me. Keep her from harm's way.*

*I did what I had to do the best way I could. I hope I was brave when I needed to be and that my actions will make you all proud. Please give Mother a special hug as she's been the best that any son could ask for.*

*Keep me in your hearts and think of me. They say the war is so close to ending. It is for me.*

*Your dearest brother and true friend.*

*Bill.*

The final words drifted away on the breeze as Jessie returned the death letter to the envelope and kissed it. He handled the brown stained envelope addressed to Bill from Polly. The knife slit the top and he withdrew it from the envelope. He read, his hands shaking before pausing at one sentence:... *I wanted you to know straight away my darling Billy... I'm in the family way and I'm so thrilled. Come home to me safe and sound for now it's not only for my sake but also for the sake of our child.*

'He didn't know! Bill never knew.' The scream reverberated but no one heard.

## 27 September 1918

Flesquières was a maelstrom and had witnessed some of the heaviest fighting of the war. Rifleman Archie Eagin was one of the first to die that day, only minutes after the whistle had sounded to move forward, one of the many who would pay the ultimate sacrifice so close to the end of hostilities.

## Harrogate, September 2018

William Drake, the great-nephew of his namesake, completed preparations for the commemoration organised for the centenary of the conclusion of WWI. He collected posters and took them to local shops before finally calling into the Tourist Information Office. The receptionist smiled.

'We're commemorating the centenary of the ending of WWI and I hope you might add a poster to your window. I had a great-uncle who was killed close to the armistice and I want to honour him.'

Ruth smiled. 'I too had a great-uncle who died towards the end. He's buried in the cemetery at Flesquières… I think it's in Belgium.'

William Drake paused. Had he heard her correctly? 'It's in France. Do you know the date?'

'27th September 1918. I hope to visit the grave with my brother later this year.'

'My great-uncle died the day before and is buried at Bertincourt Chateau cemetery which is a mile or so from Flesquières.'

Ruth simply stared at William and then began to cry.

'I'll be there on the day, the centenary of my uncle William Drake's death, and if you would like me to place a small token of remembrance on your great-uncle's grave, I would be honoured to do that. What's his name?'

She blew her nose and wiped her eyes. 'Archibald Edgar Eagin MM. He was known as Archie.'

# The Christmas Killer by
# Louise Jensen

Christmas Eve just wasn't the same. Once a time for joy and warmth, Bill would have arrived home from his annual stint at playing Santa at his local hospital to the scent of mince pies drifting from the oven, the album of carols crackling from the stereo. Now, it was a day much like any other.

Bill shivers and pulls the itchy grey blanket up to his chin. It smells of stale smoke and cabbage. Laundry was always Maureen's domain, and it's another one of the many things he hasn't got to grips with. He really should put the gas fire on – his hands are tinged blue – but he can't afford to. One pension doesn't go far at all.

He couldn't afford any new decorations; he almost didn't put any up at all but he knew that Maureen would be disappointed in him if he didn't at least try. The aging plastic pine tree that has lost most of its needles over the years stands forlornly, thin silver tinsel twisted around its middle. Bill has tried to conjure goodwill and cheer even though nobody will visit.

In the corner, the TV glows and flickers. The newsreader has a solemn expression as he reports on last night's brutal murder of a local girl, comparing it to a spate of crimes years before – the Christmas Killer they dubbed the beast responsible. But as horrific as that is, it's the following story that makes Bill's insides turn to liquid, just like they did the first time he tried to cook a roast after Maureen passed. How was he to know how long to leave a chicken in for?

It's happened again.

Another pensioner has been terrorised in their own home. Beaten and robbed. The third one this month – and just around the corner this time. Bill shudders. What's the world coming to when you're not safe inside your own home? When he hears things like this, a tiny part of Bill is relieved Maureen isn't here to witness society plummeting to new lows. Anxiety wraps itself around him like a second skin, just like it did during Maureen's first brush with cancer, but Bill can't seem to calm himself down as easily nowadays.

There's a thud. Did that come from inside his flat, or outside? Bill's heart beats a little faster, his breath comes a little quicker. He hoists himself out of his armchair. His knees creak and he winces in pain as he hobbles to the lounge door and peers out into the hallway.

There's a bang. Bill's blood pounds in his ears. Did he remember to lock the door when he came home? His memory is full of dark spaces lately. He screws his eyes up and remembers coming home after his evening visit to the supermarket where his habit is to hover around the reduced shelf, waiting for them to mark down the perishables. The handles of the carrier bags were slicing grooves into his hands and he banged the door shut with his hip; but did he come back to lock it?

Edging down the darkened passageway, wishing he hadn't had to choose between a new light bulb and a loaf of bread, he reaches the door and presses his ear against it. Footsteps. The sound of a throat clearing. Slowly the handle begins to move. Fear turns Bill to stone, and he can only watch in horror… But the door doesn't open, and Bill lets out the breath he'd been holding as he realises he must have locked it. With a shaking hand he draws the chain across and leans his forehead against the door, imagining someone doing the same on the other side, their hot breath against his neck. There's a stillness. A heavy silence.

Retreating to the lounge, Bill huddles in his armchair once more. The air is thick with the scent of his own fear and to distract himself he aims the remote with a hand that trembles and scans the channels. Television – such a wonder when he was a boy – now there are a hundred choices of nothing. Girls and boys locked in a house, on a beach, in a jungle. He jumps as music blasts and the thump-thump-thump of bass seeps through the paper-thin walls, causing the small china figures depicting the Nativity to shiver and shake on the shelf. Baby Jesus rocking in his crib. Another party next door. Perhaps this one won't go on too late. Bill's eyes are gritty with tiredness but he daren't complain. People can be so aggressive nowadays.

Bill's stomach growls, loud and fierce, and he places a hand over it as if to reassure it food will come. There's some liver in the fridge he could fry with an onion although he had been saving that for his Christmas dinner. There was no use buying a turkey for one. If he cooks, it might get rid of the stench in the flat. The lift was out of order again last Thursday and he couldn't take his rubbish down into the communal area. 'The Courtyard' they call it, but it's always littered with needles and condoms, and chills creep up Bill's spine whenever he has to go there.

He is thankful he doesn't generate much rubbish. He was a war baby – *waste not, want not*. Each teabag is meticulously squeezed, dried, and used again, and he always clears his plate.

In the tiny kitchen, Bill scoops the rubbish spewing from the overflowing pedal bin into a plastic bag, but his arthritic fingers can't tie a knot, and as the bag slumps onto its side a cracked eggshell tumbles out. It would be nice if that pretty social worker would call again this week. It's been a long time since he's seen her. He can't remember her name and he screws up his face as he tries. He's getting more and more forgetful. There are half-started lists everywhere but the words, written in spidery handwriting he barely recognises, don't mean anything to him when he reads them back.

From his friend Ethel's flat upstairs, there's a crash... a scream? Bill's hearing isn't what it used to be, and he stands still, ears straining. A chair scrapes across the floor. Another scream... muffled this time, and the sound of something being dragged. Images of Ethel being beaten flit across Bill's mind, and he presses the heels of his hands against his eyes as though he can force them away. It's them. He knows it is, but he can't ring the police, he just can't. He doesn't want to be next and he swallows hard, tasting shame as there's a smash. The sound of pleading.

Outside the window there's a shriek and Bill shuffles across the room. His bony fingers are like hooks as he scoops back the curtain and peers down into the inky blackness. There's a girl, a slip of a thing, glossy blonde hair shimmering under the street light. Her beauty almost makes him weep. If he and Maureen had been blessed with a daughter, this is what he thinks she'd have looked like.

The girl shouts into one of those mobile thingies all the youngsters seem to be glued to and waves her hand around as if making a point. She stops talking and slumps on the bench at the bus stop. Her breath billows out in icy clouds as she jabs at her phone, frowning at the screen. A sprinkling of snow begins to fall, dusting the ground. There isn't a bus due for forty-five minutes and Bill worries she'll get cold. She looks like an angel in her silver sparkly dress, but she should have worn a jacket. Some tights at least. Bill has a vision of himself covering the girl with his blanket, warming her. She shouldn't be alone. It's not safe out there. You only have to watch the news to know that.

He has time, if she waits for the bus. He could go down if he wanted to. He can't help Ethel, but this? This he can do. But what if whoever is in Ethel's flat comes down and grabs him? It doesn't bear thinking about — but the girl turns and her profile in the orange street light is so much like Maureen's. It's an effort to wrench himself away from the window but he must hurry if he wants to catch her, and he does. He can't go outside in his pyjamas.

Bill moves as fast as he can towards the bedroom, but his slipper catches on the faded Chinese rug and he almost falls. He freezes for a moment. He can't imagine what would happen if he broke something. Who would find him? He shuffles forward, carefully this time, splaying out his fingers for balance.

The doors of the mahogany wardrobe creak open and a fusty smell hits his nostrils. As Bill reaches inside to pull out his clothes he spots, tucked at the back, the red Santa jacket, sleeves circled with white fur. He feels a pang of nostalgia for simpler times. The children on the ward grateful for his wooden toys, jigsaws, educational games, none of the iPad whatsits you got nowadays. If he wears this outfit, he won't scare the girl. He might even bring some Christmas joy. It has been a long time since he made anyone smile.

*Maureen.*

Swallowing back his tears he pulls out the costume. It's been so long since he wore it there's a foul smell, but he thinks that's probably him. It always seems so pointless showering every day. He hesitates. A quick rinse? But he doesn't have time. He struggles out of his pyjamas and into the crimson jacket. The buttons are tricky and by the time he's finished sweat beads on his top lip. He swings the empty sack over his shoulder.

'Ho. Ho. Ho.' And for a fleeting moment he feels something close to happy.

His wristwatch shows eight. He only has ten minutes and cold panic bolts through him as he thinks he may not make it. But will he make it anyway, with those thugs in the flat above him doing God knows what to Ethel? Is this worth the risk? He thinks of them getting hold of this girl who looks so much like his darling Maureen and he knows he has to try to reach her at least.

He opens up Santa's sack and drops his door key inside along with his heart pills: you can't be too careful.

The drawer of the dresser is stiff. Bill yanks the handles as hard as he can. He pulls out a roll of gaffer tape, checks it's still sticky and pops it into his sack. His hunting knife is next. He holds it to the light and his heart quickens as he studies the serrated blade, shiny and sharp. He zips up his bag and snaps on leather gloves. It's time.

He hopes the young girl is still there. He'll tell her he needs to get to his daughter's house on Green Street to play Santa for his grandchildren but he's feeling wobbly. She'll help him, he's sure of it. She looks kind. They'll cut down the alley off Gilmore Way. It will be quiet and if he surprises her, she shouldn't struggle too much.

Bill thought he'd put all this business behind him, he really did, but that was before all the attacks on the elderly. He wishes something else could calm his anxiety, but he's found nothing like the utter terror in someone else's eyes to alleviate his own fear.

It's harder than it was all those years ago – he's not as strong – but last night's victim was smaller, weaker and he hadn't had such a good night's sleep in ages. But when he woke, the calmness didn't last. It never does.

The lift judders towards the ground floor. Bill closes his eyes. He can almost hear the knife slicing through the air. Feel the resistance as it strains against flesh before popping open the skin. Can almost taste the blood.

The doors ping open and, as he steps out into the cool night air, he wonders if she'll scream. He does hope so.

Perhaps it will be a merry Christmas after all.

# The Village Hotel by Alex Kane

The crisp, white snow lay on the ground, twinkling under the still light of the moon. She could just about make out the top of the Christmas tree from the village in the distance, as it peaked above the one and two-storey cottages.

*If only I could make it to that tree, to the centre of that village then maybe I'd stand a chance of survival.*

Looking behind her, her bloodied footsteps are visible, disrupting that winter's first snow fall. There would be no way of covering them, no way to hide the trail she's left behind. Her attacker wasn't stupid, or blind. He'd see the blood, know which way she was moving… leading him right to her.

Dragging her left leg, she felt the blood trickle down… her feet numb under the snow. She'd removed her shoes so she could run faster.

The hotel on the outskirts of the village had put on a Christmas party for the company she worked for. She regretted her choice of heels but couldn't have foreseen what she would face later that night. Everyone back at the hotel would be dead, she knew that for sure. Her worry now was that if she did make it to the village, anyone who tried to help her could end up dead too. She had so much blood on her hands, so many lives lost because of her. He said it himself, but she couldn't remember what she'd done, what terrible act she'd committed to cause such tragedy.

Her own hometown was a five-mile journey away, the nearest twenty-four-hour police station almost ten. The village up ahead would likely have one officer on through the night. This kind of massacre wasn't to be imagined, never mind expected in this kind of place. There was no way she would get through this alive. But she had to try.

'Urgh,' she cried out, pain shooting through her leg. She'd hoped the cold would numb the pain, but on some level, it was making it worse.

DONG, DONG, DONG.

The church bells rang out at midnight, in time with the throbs in her legs and feet. Christmas Eve Mass. People. There would be help. She clung to the hope that her attacker would tire of chasing her and give up.

Tears pricked her eyes as the frozen air bit her skin, blood rushing in her ears made it difficult to listen for an approach. The skin on her back prickled at the thought of who could be behind her, how close they could be.

Taking a deep breath and holding it in her lungs, she tried to pick up the pace. It was no use, like running from something in a nightmare. Fast for the first step, painfully slow or even backwards for the rest.

What had she done to have so many people killed? How could she have caused someone so much pain that she was responsible for this?

DONG, DONG, DONG.

She looked up, saw the top of the church emerge from the trees as she inched closer to the village. God, help me. The bell swung from side to side, the chimes ringing in her ears, vibrating in her chest. Thinking back to the party, the beginning of the night. They'd sat down for dinner, had a few glasses of wine. A few more.

'Fancy a dance?' She remembered someone asking her. They knew her name. 'Sophia.'

Had she declined? Her memory was fuzzy, unwilling to show her who had asked her to dance. More wine, a bottle of bubbly. 'Come on, it's Christmas,' someone else had said to her.

She knew she shouldn't drink too much, shouldn't overdo it. But it was Christmas, people were right. The office party had been in full swing. She did remember the lead up, getting ready at a friend's house. Kirsty had invited her over for a girly pampering session. Hair, nails, make-up. Have to look perfect. 'He might be there.'

Could it be him? Her office crush? A crush at her age sounded ridiculous, but it was real. No, he wouldn't do something like this, would he? He had no reason to kill his colleagues. Especially since he'd only been working there for three months. Rumour had it he liked her too. Kirsty had told her. But she wouldn't pursue it, she couldn't have a relationship with someone from work, among other reasons.

DONG, DONG, DONG.

The sound was getting louder, which meant she was closer to the village. The street lights now visible, the Christmas lights twinkling as they dangle from one post to the next. Voices, distant conversations. Laughter. Joyful Christmas laughter doesn't fill her with happiness, it fills her with dread, wondering if that would be the last sound she hears before she fell into the thick and deepening snow. Pushing the thought from her mind, she continues on.

The snow is starting to fall again, thick, fluffy flakes landed in her hair, on her skin. The black and sparkling dress clings to her skin, a blue tinge forming all over her. She takes another breath, the sharpness of the cold slicing at her throat.

*Don't cry. Don't cry. You're not dead yet.*

DONG. DONG. DONG.

Reaching the outskirts of the village, she struggles but climbs over the fence, escaping the snowy field. Ignoring the sharp barbs in the wire fence, she lands on her feet, wobbling as she tries to stand. She reads the welcome sign.

*Welcome to Gartnohara, please drive safely*

Hoping for a car to pass her, she turns to face the main road. Nothing but darkness meets her gaze and she almost cries out in despair. Holding it in, she makes her way along the road, the concrete through the snow piercing at the skin on the soles of her feet. Her teeth chatter together as she keeps her eyes on the main road towards the village.

'You fancy him, don't you?' The words vibrate in her memory.

'No, I don't have time at work to do anything other than work.' She'd lied. Of course she'd lied. It wouldn't be the best of ideas to admit to her partner that she fancied a colleague. Again, at this age it was pathetic.

'If you're lying, I'll find out. If you go near him, I'll find out.'

The words settle in her memory and she shakes her head.

'Do you want to dance, Sophia?'

He had been there, Andy. It was *him* who asked her to dance. She remembered now, as if her memory was beginning to thaw out. She had more time to concentrate, more time to think about it as she fought her way through the snow, along the edge of the forest separating the village from the hotel on the other side.

'I shouldn't,' she'd replied, disappointment resting on her shoulders. He was a lovely guy. Friendly.

'You're married?' he'd asked. She shook her head. 'Then let's dance?' Andy had laughed.

Poor Andy. He wasn't laughing now. He was dead. They were all dead. Except for her.

*Keep moving, keep going.*

Reaching the edge of the village, lights twinkled in the windows of the cottages and the shops. A pop-up Christmas market was set up in the centre of the village, selling beautiful decorative scenes. Santa's workshops, the Nativity, little model villages which lit up inside. It was the kind of thing she loved as a child. She reached the market and stared down at one of the village set-ups. It was just like the centre of Gartnohara. Looking down, she spotted the place where she was standing now. She could almost see herself, in that tiny version, screaming for help. No one came. No one noticed.

As she looked up from the twinkling lights, the bell rang out above her. This time she felt the vibration in her chest, nerves rattling with fear. He'd be upon her soon.

People gathered around the Christmas tree in the centre of the village and sang some hymns she hadn't heard since she was at school. Dragging her leg behind her, she approached the group.

'Can someone help me? Please? I need an ambulance,' she said. The sound of voices in harmony drowned out her voice, her words unheard by the Christmas Eve celebrations. Standing behind one woman, she placed a hand on her shoulder and gave it a shake. The woman didn't respond. Didn't turn around. She shook a little harder but the woman moved away around the tree.

She screamed, a loud and desperate sound escaping her throat. 'Someone, please help me. I'm going to die. We're all going to die.'

Nothing. It was as if she wasn't there. The crowd grew, the volume of voices increased, the bells chimed, and the lights sparkled so brightly that she had to cover her eyes.

'You caused this,' she heard in her head. 'This is your fault. If you'd just been honest, just been faithful.'

The voice in her head echoed around her and she spun, trying to see where it was coming from. No one she recognised stood beside her. No one she knew spoke to her. The voice was familiar. Her attacker, he was here in the village.

The church doors opened, and light flooded the snow which lay on the steps. She moved towards it, hoping that someone would hear her, see her. Why couldn't people see her? She wasn't exactly camouflaged. The blood that dripped from her leg was now a constant stream and it stained the perfectly white snow on the ground. A rush of wind passed her ears, whipping her hair into a swirl around her face. People were moving from the tree towards the church. She turned, faced them all. Something is wrong. The faces, they were contorted, like her vision was blurred.

Lifting a hand, she rubbed at her eyes. The sound of voices rushed past her and her legs began to crumble beneath her.

'Help,' she said. Barely a whisper escaped her lips. She turned to face the open door, to follow the crowd going inside. Elbows nudged her as she half pushed, half dragged her way through the door and into the church. Somehow it was colder inside than it was outside. Or was that because the adrenaline was wearing off, her life was leaving her?

'Oh dear, you poor thing. Let me help you up,' a voice said into her ear. She tried to open her eyes, tried to see who was talking to her. 'Let's have a look at that leg, shall we?'

Pain surged in her knee, her calf as hands pulled at her. Was it him? She tried to struggle, tried to break away from his grip.

As she fought back the tears, the bleariness in her eyes cleared. Looking around, she was shocked by the scene which surrounded her. Darkness consumed her and every other person in the vicinity. *Lie low*, she thought. *Play dead.*

She'd been unconscious, dreaming. Nightmare induced sleep from the fall, when she'd banged her head trying to take cover amidst the reign of terror. She couldn't remember how she'd gotten to her hiding place. Crawled perhaps?

Footsteps near her, slow and cautious.

She turned to her right. Kirsty was lying on the floor, eyes wide with terror, shaking her head. 'Don't speak,' she mouthed. 'Be quiet.'

She turned to her left. Andy. Staring eyes bored into her, but he was dead. Stifling a scream, she turned back to Kirsty, who was in the same position.

'What's going on?'

All that had happened before was a nightmare, all that she'd seen, the forest, the snow, the woodland. It had all been a nightmare, her brain continuing on from the reality. Her brain showing her hope of escape, knowing that it was unrealistic.

'You had to lie to me, didn't you? You had to pretend I was going insane. But really, you were lying to me all the time. You spend so much time with them. You're never with me, never give me your time.'

The wind howled outside the hotel, the snow rushing past the windows, her eyes darting back and forth, looking for anything she could use to defend herself.

'Why can't you just give me your time?'

That voice, the one she hadn't heard in a long time.

The ex, he'd come back.

After all this time, he still couldn't let go of the fact that she'd ended it. Now, he'd come to end her and anyone in her life that took up her time.

She looked down at Kirsty, whose hands trembled against the floor. They'd crammed themselves into a small space behind the bar. Heart beating so hard she thought it might kill her, she spied a glass bottle behind Kirsty. Full, unopened. Heavy.

Footsteps approached, then moved away again. Kirsty's eyes filled with tears and she moved her hand up to her mouth, covering it as she squeezed her eyes shut.

*No one should have to suffer because my ex can't accept we're done.*

She reached across Kirsty and wrapped her fingers around the bottle. Whisky, she noted. Not her first-choice tipple but it would do. Propping herself up onto her elbow, she opened it and took a large mouthful. Dutch courage, they call it. It burnt the back of her throat, but she took another to settle her nerves.

She heard him sit down somewhere on the other side of the bar. It was now or never. If she didn't face him, there was a chance no one else would get out alive. She pulled herself up onto her knees and Kirsty began shaking her head furiously at her. 'No,' she mouthed. 'He'll kill you.'

*No, he won't. He doesn't want me dead. He just wants me.*

Still gripping the bottle in her right hand, she got to her feet and stood up. She is separated from him by the bar. Her legs tremble beneath her and she looks down, checking her leg. It's not bleeding, like in the nightmare.

'Ah, there you are,' he says.

'What are you doing here, Simon?' she asks. 'We broke up a long time ago.'

'You haven't replied to my letters, haven't thanked me for the flowers. You didn't return my phone messages. I wanted us to start again. So, I went to your house. Your tenants told me that you'd left, moved here to Gartnohara. So, I came. I've been watching you. You've been spending a lot of time with these people, with that one.' His eyes move to Andy and she shivers.

'You're in trouble, you know that don't you? You've killed him.'

'I've killed them all. All except you. You and me, we don't need anyone else,' Simon says. She eyes the knife on the table. He's placed it down.

Her stomach rolls, the thought that all her co-workers were dead because of her making her feel physically sick. She held back the tears because she knew getting emotional would just make him angry. He'd

151

think she was trying to make him feel bad. That wasn't a good idea and one of the reasons she left him in the first place.

Swallowing hard and still tasting the whisky on the back of her tongue, she said, 'Drink?'

Waggling the bottle in her hand, she kept her eyes on him. She could feel Kirsty tugging at the bottom of her dress, desperately trying to stop her from what she was doing.

'Ah, whisky. The drink to numb all the pain. It's what I drank after you left. Then I realised I wasn't going to find you if I was roaring drunk every night of the week. You didn't make it too difficult at all, really. Your tenants gave you up very quickly.'

*Of course, they did*, she thought. They were likely terrified.

Simon approached the bar and placed two hands on the surface, shoulder width apart. She shivered inside. He'd left the knife on the table behind him. He didn't want to kill her. But that didn't mean he wouldn't hurt her to get what he wanted.

She pulled a glass out from under the bar, and another. Pouring whisky into each tumbler, she thought about how she was going to get out of this. Why couldn't he just accept that they were over? She didn't want him and that was final?

Lifting the tumbler, she handed it to him, and he rested it on his lips before drinking, all the while keeping his eyes on her. He swallowed loudly.

Slight movement from the far corner of the room caught her eye, but she didn't move, her eyes only flickered. He didn't seem to notice. Bodies everywhere, all dead except Kirsty who was below her. Simon hadn't seemed to notice. Of course, the person at the back of the room wasn't dead, but she wasn't about to let that slip.

'It's beautiful outside, isn't it? Deadly if you were to go out in it, especially dressed like that,' Simon said, eyes moving between the window and Sophia's dress.

'It's a good thing I'm staying inside with you then, isn't it?' she replied.

'Ha, like you have a choice. I can see it in you, you're too terrified to move. The only reason you came out from there was because you knew you couldn't stay in there forever. That you would have to face me at some point.'

*He was right*, she thought. But gripping fear fuelled her need to survive, to help at least one other person live through this.

'Will you let me out of here?' she asked.

'Not if you're going to leave again, get into dealings with people like that Andy one. You belong to me, Sophia.'

The truth in his words almost knocked her over. He was being so honest it scared her. If she didn't do something, she would be his, forever.

A groan from the back of the room, a slight movement.

*Shit, no don't do that. He'll hear you.*

Simon smiled; his eyes narrow as he turned from her. Moving away from the bar, he starts towards the victim in the corner. She doesn't even know who it is, but she has to save them. Slipping out of her shoes, her bare feet settle on the cold floor. Lifting the bottle, she slides out from behind the bar and rushes towards him. Just as he reaches the table, fingers curling around the knife, Sophia let out a scream as she raised the bottle and brought it crashing down over Simon's head. It didn't smash, just made a clonking sound against his skull. He stumbled, turned, and the knife dropped from his grip. Without thinking, she rammed the bottom of the bottle into his face and blood spurted out. He fell, pulling down a chair as he hit the floor.

Staring up at her, his eyes began to roll in his head. He couldn't survive this; he had to go. She moved the chair away and brought the bottle down over his head one more time.

His eyes continue to stare up at her, but the light has gone from them.

He is dead.

Slumping down onto the chair beside him, she opens the bottle and takes another mouthful.

'Merry fucking Christmas.'

# A Present of Presence by H.R. Kemp

I step through the black double-doors into the first-floor ballroom. Festive silver and purple decorations hang from the ceiling and adorn each white tablecloth-topped table. The Christmas tree in the corner sparkles with tinsel and glittering baubles. Rows of various sized tables radiate out from a small stage and a TV overwhelms the back wall. An excited buzz fills the air with large boisterous family groups, kissing, shaking hands, laughing, and joking, as they take their seats.

An attendant approaches and smiles at Jamie who grips my hand tightly and pulls in close against my leg. His eyes still glisten from this morning, he'd preferred to stay home and play with his toys, but I'd insisted. Adam's parents, Bernard and Shirley, arranged a family Christmas lunch and we had to be here regardless of how we feel.

After I married Adam, Christmas became difficult for me. Shirley, sometimes known as Shirl, tried to make me welcome but Bernard, never called Bernie, is a difficult man to please. I'm sure both believe Adam could have married better. With Adam gone, Shirley and Bernard are the only family Jamie and I have in Adelaide. I would gladly leave them out of our lives, after all, who needs that kind of stress, but Jamie ties us together and now we're stuck in this uncomfortable family unit.

We sit, and behind us, a young voice laughs loudly with the kind of excitement I'd hoped Jamie would show.

'Look at that tree, Mum, isn't it beautiful?' the young boy squeals. 'Who are all those presents for, Mum?'

I order Jamie an orange juice and the waiter pours me a glass of red wine. I'd only taken two sips when Shirley bobs towards us, smiles weakly at me and encloses Jamie in an awkward but warm hug. She explodes with details about the difficulties of finding a close parking space. Bernard nods hello then shakes Jamie's hand. He sits beside Jamie, his rigidly upright posture broadcasting his stoicism and superior ability to cope. He glances at my glass of wine and frowns.

Shirley passes Jamie two presents wrapped in brightly coloured reindeer paper and I'm proud of the way he smiles and thanks them. He opens them carefully revealing a pair of pants, two cricket T-shirts, and a football. He shows me, then dutifully kisses Shirley. Bernard nods. For my non-sporty son, the present says more about what Shirley and Bernard hope than what Jamie likes but he smiles, anyway.

A waiter pours Shirley a glass of white wine and Bernard orders a Coke. I study the arrivals, women in cocktail dresses, sparkling jewellery, and carefully coiffed hair, are accompanied by men in suits or, in the Australian casual tradition, men in shorts and T-shirts.

A woman and young boy of similar age to Jamie sit at the table behind us, talking and laughing loudly. I watch enviously at their comfort and joy. Her nose ring glistens in the light as she speaks and her untidy black hair flops down over one eye, draining the colour from her face. A dark tattoo curls up her arm and disappears under the short sleeve. The little boy's face screws up as he giggles, energy oozing from every pore. They tug at each Christmas cracker and he squeals with delight as he gathers the plastic trinkets – a large paper clip and a tiny plastic dog – and stows them in his pocket. I look away as the mother and son don their paper hats and I catch Bernard's frown.

I'm a traditional girl, I've never been a rebel and always followed the rules, yet my in-laws never warmed to me. I admire this woman, in her faded floral dress and bulky army-issue boots, her obvious confidence and the way she ignores the stares and whispers. Her apparent rebellious stance also frightens me. Her boisterous son wears neat and clean clothes, but his shirt is too small, and his pants are frayed at the hem. A brown sock has worked its way out through a hole in the side of his shoe.

Shirley bombards Jamie with questions; how was school this year? What class is he in next year? What sports is he going to play? But he withdraws more with each question. She shakes her head and glances at me. Jamie is too much like me; quiet, unsure, and he avoids conflict, unlike her extroverted and sports-mad Adam.

I drown in the quietness of our table while surrounded by chatter and background music. Bernard complains about the noise, even laughter annoys him, and his disapproval infects us all. Shirley eventually gives up trying to be cheerful and sits silently, smiling weakly whenever our eyes meet.

I escape and take Jamie on a tour of the buffet, highlighting the children's table and suggesting he try new foods. Jamie picks at the selection and I load my plate with foods I can't often buy.

'Oh, Jamie, is that the best you could do?' Shirley moans when she sees his meagre arrangement of cucumber, a slice of cheese, and rice.

My heart aches as I watch Jamie move food around his plate, the joy and love in the room makes it worse. Thankfully, a children's movie on the big screen draws his attention and I let the live musicians, playing Christmas carols and old-style music, distract me. Lunch passes with regular painful silence.

I sip my wine and Shirley sips hers too. She relaxes and chats although Bernard stays stiff and unbending. After our fill of savoury dishes and bounteous dessert, Father Christmas arrives and the excitement level in the room lifts. Even Jamie sits up and watches intently. He wriggles in his chair, watching in an agony of impatience, as Santa starts at the opposite end of the room, talking with each group, 'Ho Ho Hoing' and distributing lollies. When he finally arrives at our table, Jamie nods mutely, accepts the lollies, smiles and whispers, 'Thank you.' Then Father Christmas mounts the stage and sits in his special chair ready to hand out presents.

I clasp Jamie's hand and tug him towards the already growing line. Behind us, the little boy grabs his mother's hand and pulls her forward. He navigates the aisles while his mother follows, at times losing her balance and bumping into tables as they go. They beat us there and line up before us.

Jamie's grip tightens as each child mounts the stage and he watches intently. The other boy cranes his neck and squirms to see what's being unwrapped.

'How great the kids get presents,' the woman says. Her accent is rough, and her words run together.

I agree.

When it's his turn, her son races up on stage, sits on Santa's knee, and launches into a long list of wishes.

'I've been real good,' he says loudly. 'I got a Star Wars Lego kit from Grandma in Sydney.'

Father Christmas hands him a present and he barely says thank you before hurtling off the stage to show his mother. I gently push Jamie onto the stage, and he stands awkwardly beside Santa, listening and nodding as Santa quietly asks questions. My heart aches at his shyness and how withdrawn he's become since his father died. He's never been boisterous, but he used to be more confident. Jamie grins as he accepts the present, waves it high then races down to hug me.

We walk back alongside the other mother and son.

'I'm Sherri, this is Jamie,' I say. I'm not sure why, we seem to have nothing in common.

'I'm Riva and this is Chet,' Riva responds. She tugs at the side of her short skirt as she rounds a large table and I think I detect a touch of self-consciousness after all.

'I got a Spider-Man. I always wanted one,' Chet squeals. 'What did you get?' he asks Jamie.

'Captain America.'

'C'mon, let's play heroes,' Chet suggests.

'How do you play that?' Jamie asks. The worried look on his face tugs at my heart, but I urge him forward.

'I'll show you.' Chet laughs.

Back at our table, Shirley admires Jamie's present and Bernard says it's 'very nice.' The boys, after a slightly awkward start, play with their superheroes. Their game evolves as they make up rules and roll on the floor in the space beside our table. Riva sits alone. She watches the boys and fidgets with the tablecloth. I feel an overwhelming pity. I hate that I'm alone. Maybe she does too. On impulse, I invite her to join us.

'Nah, I couldn't.' Riva shakes her head.

I almost leave it there, but I see Bernard scowl and I try again.

'You're on your own.'

'I'm used to it,' Riva says.

'You don't need to be, and I could use the company.' I point at my glum companions.

'But…' Riva hesitates, obviously not getting my hint but I insist.

Riva reluctantly agrees. She carries her wine and glass to our table and an attendant moves her chair. Bernard glares at me and Shirley frowns but I don't care. I want today to pass quickly and now there'll be some conversation. We talk about how nice lunch was, especially the dessert, how nicely the room has been decorated, the size of the crowd and how unexpected it is, nothing substantial but better than silence.

Beside us, Chet bounces into action while Jamie moves his Captain America into varying poses while speaking in a superhero voice. They roll on the floor beside Bernard who frowns and shakes his head at me. I choose to ignore it.

'We've never done anything like this before. I can't afford—' Riva starts to explain then adds, 'We moved here three months ago. My family are in Sydney and my dad gave us this lunch as a Christmas present.'

'That was nice of him. It's definitely better than Christmas alone.' My life has contracted without Adam. His job in the army, all the constant moving, was isolating and I'm not good at making friends.

'I couldn't face Christmas at home, without Adam,' Shirley admits.

Riva looks at her and then at me and I explain, 'My husband died last February—'

'Adam is… was… our only child. He was a brave soldier in the SAS and served in Afghanistan. He survived those dangers only to be killed in a car crash while on leave. It makes no sense. He was our lovely son,' Shirley interrupts.

Both Shirley and Bernard sink into their chairs, the explanation exhausting her and mortifying him.

'I'm sorry,' Riva says quietly.

'Adam was everything to us. He was so full of life and energy.' Shirley glances at Jamie quietly playing on the floor. 'I miss him. As a little boy he ran everywhere, he had so much energy and a love of life. He was always outside with a ball. Adam talked to everyone, he was always chattering, he wasn't shy or timid. He—'

'For God's sake woman, enough,' Bernard snarls.

Chet startles and dashes to his mother's side, knocking the table and a glass of wine crashes to the floor. Shirley bursts into tears.

Riva peers over Chet's head and whispers, 'Shouting frightens him.'

'That was unnecessary,' I snarl too; my own guilt coming to the surface. I'd wanted Shirley to stop too.

Jamie stares open-mouthed and finally edges over to wrap his arms around his grandmother.

'I don't want to talk about… can't talk about…' Bernard stutters. He's usually a controlled and cold man and this is the most emotional I've seen him since February.

'He refuses to talk about Adam. I'm not allowed to talk about him either,' Shirley sobs.

Bernard growls, throws down his napkin, stands abruptly, and storms out.

I'd thought they'd closed ranks to shut me out, but now, I realise, I'd shut them out too. I never talk about Adam to Shirley; I bear my loss alone.

People at nearby tables watch Bernard flee, not disguising their stares. An attendant begins to clear the broken glass, dabbing at the spill and covering the stain. I wish our family could be mended so easily.

I'm not sure what to do. Chet clings to his mother and has calmed in her arms. Jamie has released Shirley, who dries the last of her tears. I reach across and touch her arm. Her sincere smile almost brings tears to my eyes.

Instead of seeing Bernard and Shirley's pain, I've been lost in my own grief. Adam was the love of my life, the man I was going to grow old with. We were going to have a big family but now it's just Jamie and me.

'I'll check on Bernard,' I say although I'm not sure why.

I find Bernard wringing his hands while sitting on a padded bench in the foyer. His eyes are glassy.

'Are you all right?' I ask. We've never really talked, and it seems a strange time to start.

He nods.

'I miss him too,' I say. I'm not sure why I choose those words, but they seem right.

Again, he nods, and I'm emboldened.

'I love remembering Adam and the good times we had together, but it hurts.' I'm sick of crying and trying but I have to carry on, for Jamie.

'I can't believe… he's gone.' Bernard slumps in his seat, his grief visible, his whole body laden with a sorrow so suffocating I can't breathe.

I miss Adam more than I can say, especially today, but I haven't felt able to talk to his parents about it before.

'Neither can I. Jamie misses him so much too. I'm worried he's so young that he'll forget him.'

Bernard looks up, his eyes glistening, and another frown creases his forehead.

I add, 'We can't let that happen, can we?'

He nods then mutters, 'No, we can't.'

We walk back together, side by side without touching, having made a truce of sorts. Shirley's face glows and her eyes shine with unshed tears while talking to Riva. Chet and Jamie are playing a quieter version of their previous game and they watch warily as we approach.

We sit. Chet and Jamie resume their game although Chet regularly casts a cautious eye at our group. Bernard sits quietly and withdrawn but finally turns to Jamie and reaches out a hand towards the Captain America figure.

'Can I have a look?' he asks.

Jamie tentatively hands it to him and Chet watches from a distance. Jamie carefully explains what his toy can do and the rules of their game. Then Bernard invites Chet to show him the Spider-Man and with Riva's persuasion, Chet approaches and launches into an excited explanation, with elaborate demonstrations of what his toy can do.

'I thought it would be better to celebrate Christmas among other families. I've enjoyed it, but it reminds me of what's missing,' Shirley says sadly.

'You're alone too?' I ask Riva, not wanting to pry but I'm curious.

A tear forms at the corner of her eye. 'My mum's in a home, she doesn't even recognise us anymore and my dad is too sick to travel.'

'You can't travel there for Christmas?' Shirley asks.

Riva grimaces. 'It's complicated. Chet's dad is… We've been on our own for a couple of years now and try to stay out of his… way.'

I understand but Shirley frowns.

'It's tough being a single parent. Being responsible without support,' I say.

Shirley frowns again then slowly nods.

'Chet misses his father despite everything,' Riva explains.

We talk quietly, brushing over difficult topics but touching them enough to understand. We share stories and eventually, we laugh, and conversation fills the lonely space in my heart. The afternoon passes quickly. As we're leaving, I give Riva my contact details and suggest we set up a play date for the boys.

I don't know if we will become friends, we are so different, but I hope she rings. Bernard and Shirley have softened after this lunch and I suppose so have I. Perhaps we can also forge a new connection now. I'd like that, for me and for Jamie.

# The Invitation by Billy McLaughlin

In his mind's eye, Terry King was marching along the snow-laden road. The reality, he knew, was very different. His ailing legs, now ninety-two, carried him slowly through the drift. The shrapnel that had exploded into his leg remained and hindered his walking on the left side. Much worse though was the fear; fear that he didn't belong where he was headed, that the invitation had come from curiosity rather than a genuine interest in knowing him.

He stopped to catch his breath, caught sight of the ill-fitting army suit and the medals of honour and he suddenly felt like a sham. What right did he have to wear those medals? To parade himself a hero, when everything he'd done since made him anything but heroic. Maybe this trip was his penance, his old soul answerable for the sins of a much younger man.

He crossed the abandoned road, the avenue lined with the twinkle of a hundred colours. Every window shimmered, every light an entrance to the gateway of a different Christmas. He wondered what door to knock on as he pulled the letter from his pocket and squinted his eyes just enough to read it.

His mind travelled back six months. That's when the girl had found him. He'd spent three months mulling over the contact, another two resisting it until two weeks ago he'd received the letter inviting him to dinner. An invitation from a young woman he barely remembered.

His granddaughter.

Now, on Christmas Day he was hobbling to meet a family he didn't know, hadn't reared, and didn't feel entitled to call his own.

He thought of the nightmares. Sometimes the same repetitive occurrence, sometimes something new and altogether more frightening. They'd been his one solid companion, so much so he didn't know if he could exist without them. Could a person be so dependent on the long-buried mental scars they owned? He didn't know because he'd never been forced to live without them.

Then there was the reality; a cold, lonely existence that he padded with a few old fair-weather buddies. Most of his real friends were either dead or in a nursing home. Terry hadn't been given an early escape. His mind was the sharpest asset he had left; a punishment, he surmised, for the wars of the past. Lest he never forget.

He knocked on the door, heard the happy shriek of a baby and instantly felt like a stranger. Three generations of grandchildren, Gillian Walker had said when she'd insisted he spend Christmas with his family. He'd brought gifts. Nothing spectacular nor expensive, mere tokens that could never offset the balance of forty years absence.

The door opened, a middle-aged woman appeared and smiled broadly. No hint of animosity or bitterness. She was the living image of the wife he had upped and abandoned when the trauma had become so deep-set that he had stood on the edge of a bridge. Trauma wasn't publicised then. Nobody talked about it. They either survived it or lived by it. Terry had done neither. He had taken to the streets, hit the bottle and then, after catching pneumonia, found himself with an unyielding desire to live. By then, the empty years had drifted by like flakes in the wind. There was no turning back.

For almost thirty years he'd been sober, living in a cottage in a village that was close enough to the city that Terry still felt part of the world, but far enough that he could embrace tranquillity should it be required. He lived a simple life and he attributed that to his long survival. There were friends, even a girlfriend once or twice but there were few of them left now.

'Grandpa?' Gillian held her arms out as if calling the world home. The word startled Terry. She was the only grandchild he'd met, but she hadn't been able to speak forty years ago when he left. He barely even remembered being a dad. He had been wondering about Elspeth, his only daughter and the person he'd disappointed most. He had always imagined her deep-rooted anger and wasn't sure he could ever face her. There had been no mention of her in any of the letters.

He stepped into the hallway and it was like stepping into Santa's grotto. Lights and ornaments adorned every nook and cranny, each corner thematically littered with a different look.

Terry realised he was shaking. Nerves? He wasn't sure, but it was the first time in years he desired a drink. He wouldn't though. Not today. Instead he allowed his granddaughter to hug him and limped slowly to her lounge.

The noise grew, the happy voices stalling when he entered the room. He froze. He shouldn't have come. He had told his old pal, Archie, it would be a mistake. Archie had called him a miserable old fool and sent him on his way. So he was here, staring at the suddenly silent.

A real fire, something he missed in his cottage, crackled at the centre of a tall oak fireplace. The scent of cinnamon wafted across the room. Red beads and bows covered a tall bulbous Christmas tree which seemed to draw his eyes away from the sight of his silenced grandchildren.

'Hello,' he said, taking a deep breath and swallowing his awkwardness.

Gillian put her hand on his back. 'Kids, this is my grandfather.' Even when her lip shivered slightly, her smile never wavered. 'These are my three children, Lucy, Georgia, and Ben. Though Lucy's not really a child anymore, are you, sweetheart? This is my grandson, Jack.'

Terry eyed the room. In addition to his three great-grandchildren and his great-great-grandson there were two men. No other women, though. No Elspeth. His heart sank. Had he really expected her to be here, her hand held out in forgiveness, her mind bereft of all the pain he must have poured over her? Until that moment though, he hadn't known how big his desire to see her had grown. He wanted to ask about her, but allowed himself to stay in the moment because he feared what he might hear should he dare to mention his beloved Elspeth.

'This is my husband, Bill and Lucy's partner, Tim. There, I think that's everyone,' she continued.

Terry stepped forward, saw the thin wisps of milk white hair in a glittered mirror and held out the arm from his good side. He handed the small bag of gifts to the youngest child, Ben. 'It's not much. Just something for the kids.'

Gillian rubbed his shoulder. 'Having you here is present enough. You didn't have to get them anything.'

Suddenly overwhelmed, Terry growled, 'I'm their grandfather, aren't I?'

Gillian smiled, apologetically. It was the first time her lips had dipped. It didn't last though, and she pulled them back again to reveal a set of perfectly straight white veneers. 'Of course. I'm sorry. I didn't mean to sound ungrateful. Say thank you, kids.'

Terry felt ashamed. A young woman, who owed him less than nothing, had invited him, a cantankerous old man into her home for Christmas and he'd been rude.

'I'm sorry, Gillian. You can imagine an old goat like me doesn't get invited anywhere fancy very often. My nerves aren't used to it.' He flushed at his own candour. He was no more used to baring his feelings than he was being invited to dinner.

Gillian took his jacket, continuing to smile emphatically, and rushed away to hang it up.

'Does she always smile like the Cheshire cat?' Terry moved into the lounge and thumbed his hand at her. The young woman with the baby in her lap, Lucy, burst into laughter.

His great-grandson, Ben simply shrugged. 'I think she wants to be one of them desperate housewives off the telly. Dad told her once that her face looked like one of those creepy porcelain dolls.'

'Ben,' snapped the man hovering in the corner. 'That was a joke.'

Ben shrugged and dipped his eyes to whatever handheld device he'd been given for Christmas. 'I don't think she found it funny.'

Lucy smacked his leg. 'Don't be mean. This is a big thing for Mum. Dad, you should make an effort as well.' She lifted her eyes and assessed the old man now hovering over her. 'We never even knew you existed until recently. Obviously, Mum knew. She's waited her whole life for this. If she seems weird, it's probably because she's not as prepared as she thought she was.'

He snickered. 'Young lady, you don't get to be prepared for this.' There was a solemn tone to his words, and it made him return his thoughts to Elspeth. He searched the assortment of pictures in a corner unit for her face but only saw images of the people in the room. He dared not think the worst and dared not to ask. Gillian returned and he realised he hadn't thought of her discomfort, only his own. It hadn't occurred until now that she, safe in the bosom of her own family, could feel as terrified as he did.

'Grandpa, can I get you a drink? Something to eat? You must be starving.'

Bill moved slowly, exiting his mute exile on the sidelines. 'Yes, Terry. What can I get you?' There was mistrust in his tone, a sense of watching and waiting for the moment he could snap his fingers and call checkmate on this new arrangement.

'Can I have a black coffee, strong, no sugar?'

Bill disappeared, leaving Terry with the rest of the family.

The baby, now in a walker, screeched at him, banging a teething ring on the edge.

Terry limped to him. 'Hello, Little Jack,' he said, softly, recalling that Gillian wouldn't have been much older when he'd last seen her.

'Right, everyone to the table. I'm starving.'

They all followed Gillian through the hall to the dining room at the back of the large house.

Georgia, the middle child at fourteen; defiantly tomboyish and seemingly undisturbed by the strange presence, sidled up to him. 'So, how come we haven't met you before?'

Terry stuttered.

She held her hand up to him. 'It's OK. I'm only fourteen. I should be seen and not heard. But it would be good if you could hang around. I bet you've got some stories.'

Terry decided she was his favourite. A straight shooter like himself, no polite middle ground chat, no incessant smiles, just a look of disdain and the questions everybody else was afraid to ask.

They sat round the table and the question Terry wanted to ask slipped silently to his lips. Any minute now he might ask. He would need to prepare himself for the devastating truth. He wondered if his new-found family knew.

Gillian grabbed his hand, breaking the looming dread in his gut. 'I don't normally insist on prayer, but I think today is a special Christmas.'

'Let's hope it's still Christmas when she's finished,' whispered Georgia on the other side of him.

Gillian opened one eye, pursed her lips, and fired a warning stare.

Ben, the youngest laughed hysterically. 'Caught!'

A war of flying legs started under the table, much to Terry's amusement. Thank God for Georgia and Ben because in their childish bickering lay the truth of this family. It made him like them all the more.

'Enough,' hissed Bill.

Silence shifted across the room, allowing Gillian to continue. 'I want to say thanks to God for blessing us with this food, and with Little Jack who spends his first Christmas with us today. Also, for being together. Mostly though, I want to say thank you for my grandpa, who I've never met but feel like I've known all these years through the wonderful stories my mum used to tell me. I can't tell you what it means to me to have you here.'

Terry felt his resolve break. He'd come here determined not to cry and get caught up in any emotional family drama. Just slip in and then back out. It appeared Gillian was unwittingly battling against that. The mention of his daughter caused his lip to quiver. Still, he dared not ask. Elspeth would be sixty-five now. In the forty years since he'd seen her, he'd thought of little else. She was the light spot when everything else was dark and bleak and full of turmoil. How stupid he felt for allowing so many years to pass without having the courage to see her again. Once more, he felt unworthy of those medals on the lapel of his old jacket.

'So, Grandpa, will you be coming here all the time now that we've found you?'

Terry eyed Ben, crafty little smile upon his cherub face.

Gillian saved the day. 'Grandpa can come here anytime he likes. There's no pressure to come or not.' That smile again, too bright to be genuine but too beguiling not to keep his attention.

Terry ate a small portion of turkey and the trimmings, but the deep fear that his daughter was no longer with them kept him from really engaging or enjoying the meal. Even the tart that was offered afterwards didn't really keep his mind back on the table.

'My mum said you were in the war, Grandpa. I'm doing it at school just now. Did you really have to go into the trenches?'

He turned to face Georgia. 'We had to go into many dark places.' He shuddered and batted away a memory that he didn't want to surface.

'Did you ever meet the prime minister?'

'Nope. Can't say I did. Nor did I want to,' he replied, grinning at Georgia.

'Grandpa. You're pretty old,' affirmed Ben. 'Who is the most famous person you ever met?'

'Ben,' snapped Gillian and Bill at the same time.

'Don't be so rude,' continued Gillian, odd-looking without her flashy smile.

Ben groaned.

Terry snorted quietly. How was it possible that a ninety-two-year-old could feel more at home with two cheeky, modern children than he could with a middle-aged couple? He took a bite of a piece of the tart still on his plate.

The rest of the meal was uneventful and while Gillian and her family remained welcoming, Terry never settled. Finally, he rose and thanked everyone for the hospitality, but said he wanted to get home before it became too difficult to hail a taxi.

Gillian smiled. 'We have a spare room. Do you want to stay over?'

Terry wouldn't hear of it. He had imposed enough, he felt, and was wearing of the attention.

'Not at all. I've left the heating on and my friend Archie is coming tomorrow for Boxing Day lunch. It's a tradition.' He would never admit the tradition only existed because Archie had taken pity on an old man who sat alone at Christmas. Not that Terry had ever minded his solitary existence. He had, after all, chosen it and had lived with it for a long time. But it was nice to have some company at this time of year.

'Bill will drive you home then.' Her smile wavering once more. 'Please? We can't let you go off into the cold. Stay a while longer and Bill will take you home.' She was pleading now.

Truth be known, Terry liked her fine, but he hadn't allowed himself to warm to her. He'd found the children and their youthful truth much easier to digest. Yet he owed this woman an entire lifetime and she was asking for fifteen minutes. The guilt switch was tripped.

'All right.' He sat back down.

The kids left the table, all going their separate ways. Lucy kissed Terry on the cheek. 'I have to get Jack ready for bed. It was so nice to meet you.' She and her husband, who looked barely older than Ben, disappeared into another room with the baby. Ben waved and left with his console.

Georgia was last to go. Her face was awash with happiness, rosy cheeks ablaze in the growing heat. 'I reckon we're going to be great friends. You're just my type of bristly.' She turned to her mum, seemingly amused by her compliment and smirked. 'I'm going over to Amanda's. Her mum makes the best chocolate pie.'

Gillian cringed.

'No offence. But you're not Mary Berry. Anyway, I'm sure you'd like the time with Grandpa.'

It appeared to be the magic words because Gillian slapped her gently on the backside and pushed her on her way.

Bill went to make more coffee.

'Is he your husband or a barista?'

Gillian laughed, a genuine croak of laughter and Terry noticed her unnatural congenial smile gone now. She was young for forty-one. Dark hair curled onto her shoulders, a designer dress on her slim frame, and a sharp but attractive face that made her look so much like her mother and grandmother. 'He doesn't know what to say or do.'

'He doesn't want me here?' Terry's voice conveyed none of the melancholy of the question. It was a simple question.

Gillian must have read it deeper. 'Not at all. He's happy that I'm happy. He's just quiet. Shy even. He doesn't know what to say to you. You've become quite the legend in our house.'

Terry didn't hide his surprise. A legend? A man who had walked out on his own family, almost drunk himself to death, and spent his days and nights alone, could never be compared to the kind of man that Bill obviously was. He wanted to say as much but sensed that the shocking appraisal he had just heard would be too ingrained to waft away. There was a different question burning in Terry's mind though.

'I've missed almost all your life. How can you be so happy to see me?'

Gillian's brows furrowed in sadness. 'You must expect our entire family to hate you. That my gran wouldn't have your name mentioned in the house. Or that I would be raised on a diet of resentment from my mother.'

177

He narrowed his lips, his aged face battling confusion. 'That's not how it was?'

'No. My mum idolised you. Did you know she searched for you? For two years. Found you living in a park and tried to bring you home. Do you remember?'

Terry didn't. A tingle on the nape of his neck made his arthritic shoulders rise. 'No.' There were no words.

'She said you were too ill to know she was even there and that one day, you'd be sober, and you'd come home. She wasn't wrong.' That deep smile again, eyes twinkling with the flashing of nearby Christmas lights.

'I broke her heart,' he acknowledged, knowing no amount of forgiveness would allow him to forgive himself. The tears finally came, grey globules on the wrinkled face of an old man. He felt an ache rise in his stomach. 'My beautiful girl,' he muttered to himself and allowed the memory of her young face to penetrate behind his eyes.

'Do you want to see her?'

Terry wiped his cheeks, relieved that the moment had been reached where they could talk about Elspeth. No matter how much he wanted to love this young woman, she could never be a replacement, only an addition to the one person he had never stopped loving. 'You have pictures?'

Gillian took his hand and led him gently towards a nearby computer.

'I know what you've been thinking,' she said and clicked on an icon on the screen after he'd settled into the chair.

Terry knew nothing about computers and had no will to learn now. He just saw a screen open on the monitor and a face appear.

'Merry Christmas, darling.'

Gillian covered her mouth. 'Mum, he's here. He really came.'

Elspeth, sixty-five years old, but not a day over twenty-five to his elderly eyes.

Terry dropped into his seat.

'My dad? Wait a second. Give me one damn minute.' She fumbled impatiently around the bottom of the screen and finally slipped a pair of glasses on. Her chin shook as she stared through her end of the connection. 'Dad?'

Terry had no words. Forty years of distance between them made him crumble and all the things he might have wanted to say, to explain, disappeared into a deep sharp breath.

'Dad,' she repeated, slipping back into the twelve-year-old girl she was when he'd comfort her through bad dreams. How could she have known then that he comforted her through her nightmares just so he didn't have to face his own?

'I thought,' he paused, his body trembling with realisation.

'Thought what, Grandpa?' Gillian grabbed his hand. 'You thought Mum was dead, didn't you?' She looked at him softly, realising that she'd unwittingly added to his turmoil.

'Dead,' shrieked the woman in Alicante. 'I nearly died of shock seeing you but not quite dead yet. Wait until I get my breath back. You won't be able to get a word in.'

Terry laughed. Her personality had barely changed. She still had her mother's cackle, the glint in her eyes that he also saw in Gillian, and a sense of humour that he was sure could still turn the air blue.

Gillian stood. 'I'll let you two chat. I'll go and help with the coffee.'

Elspeth twitched nervously with her short blonde hair. 'I swear those two live on coffee. I think they'll be ground down into coffee beans when it's time for them to go.'

Terry laughed. The years had obliterated many memories of her, deliberately most likely, but they all came flooding back the moment she threw back her head and screamed with laughter. 'You came to find me? What must you have thought?' Terry resisted the urge to blubber. How many more chances would he get with his only daughter? He was not wasting a moment of it.

'Oh, Dad, that was eight hundred years ago. I don't want you to give it a second thought. You're here now.'

'I don't want you to hate me, but I don't have a good enough reason for you not to.'

'Hey, I've got one,' she said. 'It's Christmas. I'm not making any promises for Boxing Day, but for today, you've made an old woman very happy.'

He sniffed. 'Hey, you're not that old. Look at me.'

'Yeah, but you're older than God,' she hissed, and laughed a merry laugh that was instantly endearing to him.

'How can you just forgive that easily?'

'It's not about that. You think I don't know your pain. There were days I could have run away from Gillian and her father. I didn't have the excuse you did. Nothing had happened to me to warrant it. I'll never know how you felt but I know that something must have happened to you that you couldn't talk about. Mum knew it too.'

He could think of his daughter, speak to her, look her in the eye from thousands of miles away, and just about feel human. His wife was a different matter. There were no words he could hear that would ever let him down from that sin.

'Anyway,' she interrupted his silence. 'You have a lot of making up to do and, let's be honest, not a lot of time to do it in, so let's not sit here crying it out. I'm flying home next week, and I fully expect that you'll be there.'

Terry didn't know what to say, so he just allowed the conversation to carry on for another hour. Finally, his daughter announced she was having Spanish friends around for Christmas tapas. 'I can't wait to see you and please promise me we'll spend time together next week. I want to get to know you. I especially want to know the secret to a long life.'

He nodded his head and whispered humbly, 'I promise.'

The screen blanked out and returned to the original image of Gillian's three children.

Terry heard her behind him.

'Are you OK? This has been a big day for you.'

Terry couldn't speak. The three generations he'd been promised had just become four. If he could roll back time and relive all the other years, not one Christmas would come close to this.

When he finally said his goodbyes, waving to Georgia in a house across the avenue, he gave Gillian a warm hug. He then climbed into Bill's car.

Gillian leaned in the window. 'I'll see you again next week, Grandpa.'

Terry nodded tearfully. 'You most certainly will, my girl,' he whispered. He sat in silence and watched Gillian disappear in the snowy rear-view mirror.

For the last few days of his life though, Terry lived in a peace he'd never known. His very last sleep would not be a nightmare of firing bullets and rising flames. Instead, he would slip into the forever, dreaming of the all the people he had loved and who had gone before him; unaware that his one visit to his granddaughter would be his last and the meeting with his daughter he'd waited forty years for would never come.

# Brothers Forever by Paul Moore

Martin Clark pulled his coat collar higher around his neck, the cold wind was biting, snow was expected, it was certainly cold enough for it.

He stood in the heart of London's Oxford Street at its busiest time of year, but he loved it, the sparkling lights flashing from every shop, giant butterflies hung between the big stores.

There was an exciting atmosphere as Christmas was just around the corner.

Martin looked to his right and noticed a man running down the street towards him, his head down as he ran. Nobody else seemed to notice him, the shoppers too busy looking at the window displays.

A cold bead of sweat ran from the top of Martin's spine to the bottom when he saw the man's face, it was a face and person he'd never forget… the man had saved his life on more than one occasion.

'Chris!' he called out, but the man kept running, Martin felt he had no choice but to follow.

'Slow down, Chris!' he called out again, but his friend disappeared around a corner.

Martin followed him until he felt and heard a loud explosion, so he stopped running to go and investigate.

An alarm bellowed, the sound made louder as it bounced between the shops and cars.

An out of control red double-decker bus had left the road and ploughed into a shop window.

From the cascade of noise to an eerie silence, everything seemed to stop for a moment.

A couple of sparks and suddenly one of the giant electric wings from the butterfly broke off and headed straight for the window of the shop already badly damaged by the bus.

Martin kept his distance while looking to see how the passengers on the bus were, he feared they were injured as he couldn't see much movement, he reminded himself they would be in shock.

He was about to walk over to see if he could help when his arm was pulled over. Martin turned to see an elderly oriental gentleman with a camera round his neck. 'You must see big bus coming,' he said in broken English, and tried his best to smile.

Martin gave him a quizzical look. 'Saw big bus coming?' he repeated the question as he didn't have a clue what the man meant.

The man nodded quickly. 'You see big red bus coming and run. How you know bus go into building?'

'I saw my friend and followed him,' Martin replied.

The other butterfly wing snapped off and smashed to the floor with a loud bang, it was followed by a few screams.

'You not on your own?'

Again, the question confused him for a moment. 'My friend ran past and I followed him,'

It was time for the man to look confused. 'I not see no man. I video. You want see?'

All Martin could do was nod, unsure what he was about to watch.

Moments later he watched the video, he couldn't see his old mate Chris anywhere, he watched the video three times and didn't see Chris at all.

'If you no move maybe bus make you flat? You, lucky man,' the man said.

'Maybe I am,' Martin said, the sound of sirens getting louder and louder.

The police talked to him a little while later about the incident, he said nothing about seeing his old friend, he didn't want to look like a fool.

He read in the newspaper a week later that the driver had a heart attack at the wheel. He didn't survive the crash.

****

Six months later and it was a gorgeous summer's day, the heat wave at the start of its second week.

Martin was enjoying the second of his four days off. It was about the only good thing about shift work, you took four days off after working four nights. He'd worked four day shifts before that.

As far as he was concerned his job was a means to an end, he had to feed his wife and daughter. Security was his field, didn't mean he had to like it.

He sat talking to his wife as they both drank their first coffees of the day.

Sky Clark walked into the kitchen and looked anything but happy.

'What juice would you like, darling?' her mother asked.

Sky felt her stomach. 'I'm not feeling very well,' she moaned then fluttered her eyelids.

Her parents looked at each other, Martin the first to smile. 'So, what exactly is wrong with you?'

'It's, well… it's just… it's a pain,' the ten-year-old said, as she rubbed her tummy a bit faster for dramatic effect.

'What do you think, Mum?' Martin asked.

'Yes, it's hard to say, which one do you think, Dad?' Audra asked the same question back. Unbeknown to Sky her parents had already talked about this situation the evening before.

'I'll go with excitement,' he said.

Audra nodded. 'A good diagnosis, maybe with a bit of nerves thrown in. You know what this means, Sky?'

The little girl, with golden blonde hair tied back in a plait, could only shake her head slowly from side to side, a look of fear on her face.

'You've got butterflies,' Martin said with a smile.

'I agree, doctor,' his wife said with a giggle.

'I'm not a baby, you know! I've got a tummy ache and, and it keeps, it keeps moving.' Sky's lower lip started quivering.

'Oh, darling, we're not treating you like a baby but today is sports day and we know you're looking forward to it, you haven't talked about anything else for the last week. I think you'll find it's…'

'Nerves, and it's as natural as breathing, it really is. It will get better once you're on the field,' Martin finished Audra's sentence.

Again, the little girl shook her head.

'But it makes me not feel very well.'

'I remember feeling pretty much the same as you when I went for my first medal in dance. I thought my tummy might explode but as soon as I was out on the dance floor, all the panic and nerves just disappeared, the same will happen to you. As Dad says, it's natural,' her mum said then gave her a cuddle. It seemed to do the trick.

A few minutes later, Audra stood up and headed for the front door. 'I'm going to pick up your nan and we'll see you on the sports field. Don't worry, darling, you'll be perfectly fine,' Audra said before kissing her on the cheek.

'At least we have a nice day for it,' Martin said as he and Sky got in his car ten minutes later and put their seat belts on. Sky remained silent.

As she didn't reply Martin kept quiet, the last thing she needed was him winding her up. The school run rush hour meant the journey was slow. Martin had agreed to take some equipment to the sports field, a fifteen-minute drive from the school.

'You can go with your father or come with us on the bus, Sky, it's up to you,' her teacher, Miss Evans said.

'I want to go with Dad,' Sky replied, her mouth dry.

'See you on the field then,' her teacher said.

'How's the tummy now?' Martin asked once they were back on the road.

Sky shrugged her shoulders.

'As your mum said, you'll be fine once you start,' he tried to reassure her.

He got the same reaction so thought it best to keep quiet.

Five minutes later they came to a roundabout and Martin took the second exit.

'Why are we going a different way? The playing fields are that way,' Sky said pointing to the right.

Martin realised his mistake just before his daughter said anything. 'Don't worry I'll get us back on track at the next roundabout.'

Sky didn't reply, she looked left out of the window.

At the next roundabout, he knew he had to take the second exit, they pulled up behind a big lorry which shielded them from the sun.

'Not long now, Skylark, you're going to be great!' Martin said with a big smile.

The lorry pulled off and took the second exit, as Martin was about to follow, he had to slam on his brakes as a man stood in the road. He managed to get a glimpse of him: it was his old friend, Chris.

'What are you doing, Dad?' Sky asked, the engine cut out after her question.

'Well, I didn't want to hit that man that crossed in front of us.'

'What man?' she asked looking to see who he meant.

Martin tried to restart his car but after he'd turned the ignition key a few times he gave up. He couldn't understand it as the car had only been serviced three weeks before.

'We're going to be late!' Sky said, her bottom lip quivering again.

Before Martin could say anything, they heard a large bang, Martin's first thought it was a bomb. He tried turning the ignition key one more time and the car roared into life.

'Let's go and see if we can help.' He put his foot down hard on the accelerator.

Two minutes later they found the reason for the noise, an oak tree had fallen onto the carriageway. The lorry they'd been behind just moments before was parked up.

'Stay here, I'm just going to check everyone is OK, I won't be long,' Martin said, then released his seat belt.

The lorry driver stood behind his vehicle, a cigarette in his mouth.

'Everything all right? Are you hurt?' Martin asked as he approached the man.

The lorry driver nodded. 'I'm fine, bloody lucky escape. The tree came down behind my lorry, good job there was nobody behind me. I've phoned the police and they're on the way. Thanks for asking after me, appreciate that.'

Martin nodded as a cold chill went down his spine, he and his daughter were supposed to be behind that lorry.

He drove Sky to her sports day where he met his wife and mother-in-law, he told them what happened, keeping the fact they were behind the lorry and him seeing Chris out of the tale.

**** 

It was just after eight in the evening when Martin got home; his relief had arrived half an hour late which didn't impress the former soldier at all, one of his pet hates was people turning up late for no good reason.

'Hi, darling, I've put your dinner in the microwave, and Sky is in a bad mood. I've tried to ask her why, but she doesn't want to talk about it. Oh, and I've left your post on the bed for you,' his wife said.

'I hope it's not about sports day again, I thought she was over that, it's been a couple of months now; she needs to let it go,' Martin replied.

'I don't think it's that. It could be but as I said, she's not really talking about whatever it is.'

'Shall I have a word?'

'Leave it for the time being, Mart, she knows where we are if she needs us.'

'Right then, let me go and get out of this uniform and into something more comfortable. How much post is there?' Martin asked as he unclipped his dark-blue tie and undid the top button of his light blue shirt.

'It was two or three, I can't quite remember. I know one's from the bank if that helps.'

'Wanting money no doubt, right, see you in a minute.' And with that, he disappeared upstairs to the bedroom.

The bank letter was about life insurance, something he already had. The second letter looked quite official. He opened it to find an invitation to his army reunion, something he definitely wasn't expecting and wasn't sure if he should accept.

He returned to the front room where Audra was watching her soaps. It was never a good idea to interrupt her… he'd learned that early on in their relationship.

He sat in his chair thinking about the invite and some of the people who would probably go, a few of his ex-colleagues he didn't like, especially the ones with big egos.

The theme music played at the end of the soap and Audra looked over at him. 'Penny for them, but by the look on your face I might need a pound's worth. Is it work?'

'Is it that obvious? It's not work; although Calvin being half hour late didn't help. I've been sent a reunion invite, an army one.'

'Sounds good, the army invite I mean. Are you going and does it have a plus one?' she asked with a cheeky grin.

'To be honest, I didn't notice but if it does, please don't say that you need a new outfit, you've got loads of clothes,' he joked, but she could sense something wasn't quite right.

'Should be fun, though.'

'Really? I'm not sure I'd use the word *fun*. Talking about how we survived, sorry… but most people say it's a war we won. It didn't feel like a victory and I'm not sure I want to hear those stories again, survival stories that is, not bloody war stories. I'll think about it, but I don't know. Think I want to leave the Gulf War where it is, history.'

Audra didn't ask about it again. It was obvious he didn't want to talk about it.

**\*\*\*\***

'You look fabulous, darling, red is so your colour,' Martin said as Audra stood in front of the mirror looking at herself.

'You don't scrub up so bad yourself,' she replied as she turned to see him in a dark-blue suit, white shirt, and dark-blue tie. His shoes were always shiny, but they seemed to be extra shiny that evening.

Five minutes later they were sitting in a taxi on the way to the reunion venue.

'How you feeling?' Audra asked.

'I don't really know to be honest, a bit nervous I suppose. Seeing old faces should be fun though. I just hope it's not all war stories.'

'I'm sure it won't be. Are you not intrigued about what some of them are up to now?'

'Yes, of course. I do want to talk to Chris Harper, I hope he turns up.'

'So do I, it would be good to put a face to a name.'

They spent the rest of the journey talking about old colleagues.

Martin felt like a child on his first day at school as he got out of the taxi. The temperature had dropped a little, but it was still a mild evening.

The reunion was held in a small hotel in Central London. Martin showed their invite at reception and they were directed to the banquet room.

He thought back to when his daughter said she had pains in her tummy. He had the same butterflies.

The banquet room was half full but as Martin scanned the faces, he didn't recognise anyone.

A waiter offered them both a glass of wine, and as Martin took his, he heard, 'Shoes, is that you? Of course, it is, well I'll be damned you haven't changed a bit! Maybe a bit greyer but ain't we all, great to see you.'

Martin hadn't been called Shoes since he'd left the army, it didn't bother him as much as the fact he couldn't remember the man's name let alone his face.

'You're not looking so bad yourself.'

'Well, you know, I think it helps I'm going to the gym twice a week. That's where I met Penny, my wife of three years,' the man said, then took a sip of the orange juice he was holding.

'Shoes! Well bless my bald head it is you!' a man grinning from ear to ear said, a scar on his neck.

'Baz? No, it can't be,' Martin replied to the man he recognised as Barry Howard.

The men hugged then Baz turned to the other man, 'Wilks?' The man nodded and there was more hugging.

*Danny Wilkinson!* Martin thought, finally.

Wives and girlfriends were introduced.

Martin explained what he was doing for a living, the others followed suit.

Wilks excused himself while Audra spoke to Barry's wife.

'Have you kept in touch with any of the rest of them? I lost my address book when we moved about ten or fifteen years ago,' Barry asked.

'I can't say I have but I have seen Chris Connors, only in passing though.'

'Yeah, terrible shame that,' his old colleague said then took more wine on board.

'Well, I didn't talk to him, so it wasn't that bad,' Martin joked.

Barry suddenly looked very awkward.

'OK, Baz, what did I say, mate?'

'I hate to be the bearer of bad news, but Chris passed away after a motorbike accident. He collided with a bus that pulled out. The driver didn't see him by all reports. Look, I would have contacted you, but I didn't have a clue where you were, seriously,' Barry explained.

Martin was dumbfounded, he just stood trying to take the news in. Audra noticed her husband didn't look quite right and excused herself and joined him.

'Sorry, what's going on?' she asked Barry.

'I've just told him our friend and brother Chris Connors passed away.'

Audra knew the name as Martin had mentioned him a few times in the past.

'When was this exactly?'

'Three years ago. He was killed the day before my birthday. I sent a wreath from all of us. I wrote, *Brothers Forever*.'

Martin wasn't sure what to do or think so just made his way to the bar at the other end of the room where he and his wife raised a glass to Chris. The former soldier whispered a quiet 'Thank you' under his breath before downing his drink in one. It was the first of many.

# Girl in a Red Shirt by Owen Mullen

# Christmas Eve 1989

## O'Hare International Airport, Chicago

Across the barren runway, in the glare of a spotlight, the hydraulic arm of a de-icer truck sprayed clouds of fluid from wingtip to wing root on a Finnair jet scheduled to be landing in Helsinki. Billy Randall looked out of the giant windows of the overcrowded departure lounge, sipping the Coke cradled in his hands, his tired eyes following the progress of the final scattered snowflakes on their way to the tarmac. Seven hours earlier, beside the giant Christmas tree in the corner, a choir had enthusiastically reminded the waiting passengers that Santa Claus was coming to town. But as irony dawned, the singing petered out. They were probably at home now.

Someone had turned the air con up in the lounge and it was stifling. Dull-eyed people stared ahead, bludgeoned into silence by the circumstances they found themselves in.

Billy had expected to be in front of the fire, happily watching a movie he'd seen a dozen times, with his wife and kids.

God had had other ideas – but then, he usually did.

From behind him, a voice said, 'Billy? Billy Randall? Is that you?'

The last time he'd heard it was on a sunny morning at Travis AFB in Fairfield, California, almost twenty years ago. The voice belonged to a Sioux Indian he'd spent the best part of two decades trying to forget, and if Billy had spotted Danny 'Dakota' Goodpipe first, he would've avoided him.

They locked in an awkward embrace which only lasted seconds. In Vietnam, Goodpipe had been a spectacular specimen: six feet nine inches, towering over everybody in the unit. He was still tall, though there was grey in the ponytail tied with an elastic band, and lines either side of the mouth on his moon-face. The collar of his shirt was frayed, Danny Goodpipe had fallen on hard times, but he grinned, genuinely pleased.

'What the hell…'

'Chief.'

'You stranded, too, huh? Where you headed?'

'LA.'

'That home these days?'

'Yeah. You?'

'Memphis. Moved there a dozen years back.'

Billy nodded as if the words meant something to him.

Goodpipe said, 'Ain't this storm a bummer?'

'Sure is.'

'Screwed up your plans?'

'Done that, all right.'

'You got kids waitin'?'

'A boy and a girl.'

'Nice… nice.'

Billy tried to end the conversation. He stuck out his hand. 'Great running into you, Danny. Enjoy the holiday.'

The Indian smiled. 'I get it, Billy. Feel the same. But we never talked it out, did we?'

'I don't want to talk.'

Goodpipe understood. 'Me neither. So, let's do it.'

They stepped over a teenage GI in uniform, curled in a foetal position on the floor, and found a space against a wall. Through the window, an American Airlines jet was getting the same treatment as the Finnair. Billy Randall wished he was on it.

Danny Goodpipe said, 'Bad stuff happened in that damn war. Hard to get it straight in your head sometimes.'

'My head's fine.'

Goodpipe ran a disbelieving hand over his hair.

'Then you're a lucky guy, Billy.'

****

# Bac Lieu province, Mekong Delta, 1969

Morning crept up on them. A hundred shades of black melting to grey, then light – at least, as light as it would get under the canopy. Cold night air drifted away replaced by rising clouds of condensation plastering their fatigues against their bodies while the tick and hum of the jungle, the soundtrack to another subtropical sunrise, began to play.

Two days earlier, the firefight had been a scene from hell – dozens of men lost their lives in minutes. When the smoke cleared, their group had found themselves separated from the platoon. Worse news was to come: the radio had been hit and they'd lost communication with basecamp. Johansson, the blond Swede from New Jersey, had worked all night trying to repair it without success. He'd keep trying because, unless they re-established contact, they'd die here.

Danny Goodpipe sat against the broad base of a tree, his huge hands reducing the rifle he gripped to a toy. His watch was almost over. In a few minutes he'd rouse the others and day three of their patrol would begin; the big soldier was on his second tour. All told, he'd served nearly eighteen months. That made him a veteran. But the ingrained fatalism of his South Dakota heritage kept him from considering the past or the future.

Billy Randall was awake and struggling to admit it. His ancestors weren't watching over him. Nobody was watching over him. He'd lost count of the number of patrols he'd been on. It never got any better and it never would.

Some reckoned the hardest part of being in this godforsaken country on the other side of the world was the crippling tiredness that never went away and the heat, drenching your body while leeches drank their fill. For others, the constant drum of the rains dragged them to the edge of madness. Or the stench, vile enough to make men gag.

Then there was Charlie.

Charlie wasn't afraid. Charlie could see in the dark.

And everywhere the jungle.

During the endless nights of silence, demons seeped into every soul. No fear was left untested, no truth unquestioned in the battle to hold on to the half-remembered dream of life before. The rustle of a bush or the sharp crack of a twig was enough to terrify. Sometimes something slithered over you. Crying out would confirm what the enemy already knew – that you'd crossed the line, you were in his land, stumbling and sobbing, blind and afraid.

And that he would win because it was his destiny.

Family and friends, love and hope, were scoured from every mind by a thousand nightmares rolled into one. But when the first rays of a new sun found a way through the canopy and warmed your face, when your eyes opened on one more day, for Billy, that was the very worst thing.

Yards away, Goodpipe pulled the long double-edged knife from its sheath, keeping his gaze locked on a new danger. He edged forward. If the sleeping man moved, even a little, the snake tightly coiled against his back would strike, its needle-like fangs easily penetrating the layers of material until it found the body beneath and injected its poison.

Snakes: the jungle was full of them. At night when the temperature dropped, the heat from slumbering bodies offered warmth to their cold blood. The big Indian crept to within an arm's length of the reptile. In the growing light he could see part of the circular mark behind the hood: a monocled cobra, one of the Cong's many natural allies. Snakes don't hear, they sense vibration and their instinct is to attack any enemy that cannot be avoided. A bite from the cobra and private Jimmy Holden would be leaving Vietnam in a bag.

The action was deliberate, unhurried, no more than cutting a piece from a block of cheese. Danny leaned across the final few feet and sliced the head from the body in a single movement. A jet of dark blood spurted, staining the earth before becoming part of it. Holden continued to sleep. His comrade lifted the parts of the dead thing, tossed them into the bushes, and sat down against the tree. No one saw. No one would ever know. It wasn't important they did.

Zilli returned from an advanced position to report the enemy was up ahead and coming their way. Lieutenant Warner listened. 'So how many are there?'

'No idea. I saw four.'

'Then there are probably more, maybe as many as ten.'

Somebody at the back said, 'Ten? Where did that number come from?'

The lieutenant heard it but didn't answer. He gathered the men together and told them what was going to happen next.

'Zilli says Charlie's coming our way. We can take them.'

Billy Randall asked, 'How many?'

Warner took off his helmet and wiped sweat from his brow.

'He's not sure.'

Rodriguez supported Randall. 'If he's not sure, we should get out of the way.'

Warner hadn't been looking for suggestions. 'We're not here to hide. We're here to win. Least that's my understanding. Our orders are to seek and engage.'

Warner had the stripes. Nobody wanted to argue. Billy Randall did. 'But, sir, those orders were for the platoon. Shouldn't we establish force of numbers before we commit ourselves?'

The lieutenant didn't appreciate the private's persistence.

'Zilli saw four definites. My guess would be higher.'

'Your guess? Shouldn't we confirm that?'

Warner made a contemptuous noise in his throat.

'You volunteering to go get that information, soldier?'

Randall stood to attention and delivered his objection, 'Lieutenant, sir, we should confirm the strength of the enemy before we engage them. We should—'

'We already know their strength. There's nine of us. Surprise is on our side.'

Billy kept going, 'We don't have the firepower for another fight. Surely our priority is to clarify the enemy's strength and keep trying to make contact with base?'

Warner ignored him. 'Seek and engage. We'll backtrack, fan-out on both sides of the path and wait. If there're too many, we'll let them pass. If not...'

He allowed the alternative to hang in the air.

Pasternak, 'Yes, sir! Seek and engage, sir!'

Pasternak's salute was ridiculous in the circumstances. He couldn't help himself; he'd found a soulmate and wasn't about to lose him.

Warner's lips pressed together. 'Let's go.'

Zilli whispered to Rodriguez, 'Fucking nuts.'

'Ben Tre logic, variation thirteen.'

Zilli understood. The year before, a US Air Force Major had been famously quoted as saying, 'It became necessary to destroy the town to save it.' The town was Ben Tre. That thinking became 'Ben Tre logic'.

They advanced in single file. Warner had taken them to a clearing that might have been the site of a village a thousand years earlier. Billy Randall was on the left with Dakota Goodpipe and Rodriguez, the other four hidden in the trees where the knee-high elephant grass ended. The location had obvious advantages though it would be entirely possible to shoot one of their own.

But it was the best there was.

They waited.

Charlie didn't rush, he was never in a hurry. Why would he?

He knew how it would end.

Goodpipe saw them first, walking silently, rifles at the ready. He signalled to Rodriguez. Rodriguez passed the message along. They let the first go by, and the second – they'd be back if the shooting started. The two after that were close together, bodies tense, fingers on the triggers of their weapons.

Sweat rolled down Billy's face. He brushed it away. Then, a shot crashed through the silence, the third man went down and they were drowning in sound. The first two Vietcong raced back to the fighting and died without getting off a single round. Billy watched flashes of fire spit from behind the trees on the other side. There hadn't been time for him to contribute anything, it had gone off so fast. The fourth enemy soldier died in a burst from an M-16 and lay, eyes open, on the brown earth.

When the barrage ceased, it was like a blow to the head, leaving them reeling. Suddenly, Pasternak cried out, dropped his rifle, and fell to the ground, blood pouring from his chest. Shots followed without finding their mark. Goodpipe raced into the open and lifted the injured man. Shouts and gunfire echoed in the ancient rainforest. Billy heard a cry of pain but couldn't see who'd been hit.

It was Rodriguez.

Holden and Zilli picked him up and dragged him along the track into the jungle.

That had been yesterday. Since then, they hadn't halted. Fear kept pace with them, the enemy never far behind. Whenever they stopped, they heard him call to his brothers. He was always there, always with them.

Charlie didn't rush, he was never in a hurry: why would he hurry?

He knew how it would end.

Nine had become seven.

Lieutenant Warner was wrong – there were more than ten.

A lot more.

****

Billy Randall's body screamed for sleep. They'd come close to death and the emotional backlash overwhelmed him, leaving him shaken and weak. No one spoke. On the ground, the bodies of Pasternak and Rodriguez were frightening reminders of what they'd come through.

Survival brought no joy.

Next to him Holden slumped forward, head in his hands, his shoulders trembling. He might have been crying, Billy couldn't tell. But Zilli was crying – crying like a child. Tears rolled down his face, blackened and torn into a tragic mask. Lieutenant Warner looked into space, away from the dead soldiers at his feet, while the big Indian stared ahead, unmoved by what was going on around him.

Mario Zilli stood up and pointed to Rodriguez. 'Close his eyes! For Christ's sake close his eyes!'

The dead man had been his buddy from the moment they met, all their free time had been spent together drinking and whoring, playing pool, listening to football scores and trying to impress each other with exaggerated stories about women. Bravado that seemed distant now.

He sobbed. 'Close his eyes. Please, please.'

Billy rolled the dead man's eyelids down. Zilli fell against the tree he had been leaning on, exhausted by trauma.

Lieutenant Warner picked the wrong moment to speak.

'Just want to say, well done. Well done, guys.'

Holden lifted his head and looked at him in disbelief. Zilli wiped his tears away and struggled to get a hold on himself.

'I'll be mentioning all of you in my report, especially you, Goodpipe. Carrying a wounded comrade while under fire...' He shook his head. 'Bravest thing I ever saw.'

Nobody could've stopped what happened next. 'Dakota' wrapped his hands round the lieutenant's throat before anyone could move. The lieutenant's eyes bulged, his face seemed to expand, his tongue lolled in his open mouth as the pressure mangling his neck squeezed the life force from him. Outweighed, he tried to wrestle the soldier off him. One of his legs kicked against the body of Jackie Pasternak; Jackie was beyond indignity. The sun moved behind some clouds, reappeared then disappeared again, making the scene resemble the comic violence of the early cinema.

Randall and Holden only just managed to free Warner from the Indian's death grip. Billy Randall shouted in Goodpipe's ear to break the murderous spell he was under. When they finally pulled him off, Billy placed himself between them.

The lieutenant didn't get up, he couldn't, he stayed on the ground, coughing and rasping, trying to extinguish the fire in his lungs with precious air. Billy's hands pressed against Goodpipe's powerful chest, symbolically holding him back from renewing the assault.

The big man's breathing was deep and steady, the emotions that drove him to attack a superior visible only in his eyes.

Billy talked him down. 'Easy, easy, Dakota. Take it easy, buddy.'

Warner's sole supporter lay dead beside him. When he rose on unsteady legs, his voice was all but gone. What should have been a snarl was a whisper.

'Court martial! You! Court martial!' The words were lost but everyone knew what he was saying. 'Fuckin' crazy Indian! Fuckin' crazy…'

Billy stepped carefully over the forgotten fallen on the jungle floor and stood in front of him. Warner pointed to the big soldier staring at an invisible point in the dense undergrowth, detached from the fury directed at him.

'That fuck's finished!'

Billy said, 'Nobody's finished, Lieutenant. Nothing happened here.'

Warner's lips trembled in rage.

'Nobody's finished,' Billy Randall repeated. He gestured towards Pasternak and Rodriguez. 'Ten! You told us there were no more than ten of them, remember?'

Warner blinked defiantly.

'You said we'd wait to confirm their numbers. But you didn't wait, did you? You opened fire without knowing the enemy's strength, that's why these two,' he hooked his thumb at the dead men, 'are where you see them now.' He backed away from the leper in their midst. 'Nobody's finished, unless it's you.'

****

## Bac Lieu province, Mekong Delta, 1969

Billy bent back the lacquered leaf of a young rubber plant and saw the girl walking towards them, unaware she was the centre of attention, her shirt a fantastic red against the green wall of tall kunai grass at the edge of the clearing. She couldn't have been older than fourteen or fifteen – in another culture little more than a child – here, she was a woman.

The bucket bounced against the top of her thigh as she moved, her small fingers closing firmly and easily round its rope handle. Black hair hung long, and her face was unblemished, fear and pain still strangers there, yet her life was lived in the middle of a war. Behind her on the deep-brown earth stood a cluster of thatched huts on wooden stilts – protection from flood. She was on her way to the cool clear ribbon the soldiers had crossed a mile further up, a trip as familiar to her as going to a drugstore on the corner would be for any of them. That same gurgling rivulet would join with others until together they coursed and sped towards the larger flow of the Mekong and on to the South China

Sea. Here, it was no more than a shallow stream swollen by the rains, a timeless place where a village girl might gather water for her family.

The lieutenant pressed a finger to his lips.

Everyone understood. Nobody moved, a noise, any noise, would give them away and the tranquil scene could quickly change to reveal an enemy, whose patience was without limit, waiting for them.

Then the doors of hell would open.

With a few more steps the girl would be out of sight of anyone in the village. High above two birds crashed from the canopy, thrashing their wings and screeching. Billy's heart stopped. He closed his eyes. When he opened them, he saw a single leaf drift lazily to the ground and come to rest like ten million others under his boots. His breath left his body, controlled and measured. He waited for his heart to restart.

The girl hummed a tune. Without breaking her stride, she snatched at a blue and yellow butterfly that flew near her, missed it and carried on, as distracted as any teenager anywhere. The village might be as innocent as the girl herself, or it could be a Cong arsenal, booby-trapped and expecting them: the skill was in being able to tell allies from enemies. Too often, the very people the soldiers were there to assist ended up dead, casualties of mistaken identity. But that misjudgement could cut two ways and was never an easy call to make. The young beauty before them might be a pretty stalking horse chosen for her seeming artlessness to tempt them into revealing their presence.

Or a village girl collecting water.

Lieutenant Warner edged forward. Billy Randall tried to stop him and was shrugged aside. The girl didn't notice, lost in her private little song she bent to her task. The lieutenant came directly behind her, crossing the short distance between them in seconds. Her body jerked when he grabbed her. The bucket fell from her hand, she didn't see it float away on the current. Her delicate face disappeared behind the hand that blotted out light and air. With his other arm round her slender waist the soldier easily lifted her from the water's edge and spun round. Back in the trees, Holden saw the look on his face and didn't like it. Warner whispered in her ear like a confidant or a lover. Randall and the others emerged from the forest. The lieutenant dared them to intervene, grinning like a stupid schoolboy. When nobody moved to stop him, he headed for a patch of long grass twenty yards downstream, carrying the struggling girl. Through it all, the cries of the young Vietnamese were muffled by the rough hand of her attacker.

Randall and Goodpipe moved at the same time. Goodpipe dragged the lieutenant off the girl and threw him to the ground. Randall helped her to her feet, signalling her to keep quiet.

Warner growled. 'What? She's the enemy. C'mon.'

He brushed leaves from his arms, got up and spoke to Goodpipe.

'You've just assaulted your commanding officer a second time, soldier.' He turned to Zilli and Holden. 'Arrest him. When we get back to…'

Warner stopped speaking. His jaw slackened, he dropped to his knees and pitched face down on the grass. Billy Randall looked dumbly at the knife in his hand, blood dripping from the tip, unsure how it got there.

The girl sensed the confusion and tried to make a run for it. Randall dived at her, caught her ankle and had his fingers over her mouth before she could scream. She struggled, breathing hard, eyes wild in her head.

Zilli voiced what the rest were thinking.

'What the hell do we do now?'

Holden said, 'If she's Cong, we're dead men.'

Randall saw where it was going and panicked. 'We don't know that. We don't know anything.'

Danny Goodpipe stepped forward, shafts of golden light flashing off the steel in his palm.

Billy Randall looked up into his deep-brown eyes and pleaded for the girl's life.

'This isn't right. There has to be another way.'

Beads of sweat gathered like crystal tears on the Indian's massive brow.

'Like what, Billy? Let her go and send her a postcard when we get home?'

'We can tie her to a tree and be long gone before somebody from the village finds her.'

'Yeah, and she can tell the bastards chasing us exactly how many we are, how much ammo we don't have, and where we're headed. Can't take that chance.'

He looked at the girl. 'Probably understands every word.'

'Danny, please. She's just a kid.'

Goodpipe drew her head back and sliced her throat in a single stroke, wiped the knife on the grass, and put it back in its sheath, his moon-face expressionless.

**\*\*\*\***

## Christmas Eve 1989

## O'Hare International Airport, Chicago

The American Airlines jet taxied to the end of the runway in the slush-tracks of the departed Finnair. Goodpipe raised his gaze to the sky and the stars twinkling like silver stones at the bottom of a black lake, as a tinny voice announced the flight to Los Angeles was ready to board.

'That's me.'

'Looks like you're gonna make it.'

Billy had wondered a thousand times what he'd say if they met again. Now, the words wouldn't come.

'I'll walk you to the gate.'

'I'd rather you didn't.'

Around them, people gathered themselves and their belongings together.

Goodpipe said, 'Set it down, Billy. It was a long time ago.'

'I can't.'

'What choice did we have? We were lucky to get out of there.'

'We could've checked the village. We could've and we didn't. In the end, we were no better than Warner.'

'Don't accept that. It was war, for Christ's sake. We were a bunch of young guys separated from their platoon, being hunted, carrying our dead, led by a madman. Some of us hadn't slept in days. None of us were cut out for what we'd gone through. We were broken.' Goodpipe got a hold on himself. 'What I'm trying to say is, we did what we felt we had to do. The odds were high she was Cong.'

'It was wrong, and I knew it.'

'That makes you a better man than me, it doesn't make you right.'

'We should've checked.'

Goodpipe sighed and slowly shook his head. 'Don't know what to tell you, Billy. The enemy was right behind us and somebody could've come out of that village at any minute.' His deep voice cracked. 'We didn't have time to think it out better than we did. It was no different from you doing Warner. To my mind, we both made the correct call.'

'That what you tell yourself in the middle of the night?'

'No, I tell myself that was then, this is now and I'm alive to kiss my wife and wish my children and my grandchildren merry Christmas. Then, I pray none of them has to make those choices, because we already made them. And because we did, you're on your way home to your family and I'm on my way home to mine. Yesterday's yesterday, Billy. Don't judge it too hard.' Goodpipe pointed to a young GI – the one they'd stepped over earlier – heading to the departure gate. 'Think we knew any more at his age than he does? Cut yourself a break.'

Billy didn't answer. He picked up his bag and walked away.

Danny Goodpipe watched him until he was out of sight. The lies had come easily. Now, he needed a drink. A drink to forget. The truth would've been easier — that he'd lost everything, his wife, his job, even his health, because of a girl in a red shirt. But Billy Randall already knew the truth. Had always known it.

They should've checked.

# Pivotal Moments by Anna Franklin Osborne

A friend once told me that a good definition of depression was not being able to see a future.

Well I can't see a future, but I swear I'm not depressed, I'm just honest and a realist. I have no future; it has been taken away from me as surely as she felt hers had been when she was spiralling into her breakdown. Before this happened to me, before I became like this, I was a veritable dynamo. I had a career straight after leaving uni, pushed myself into starting my own business before any of my friends dared. I loved breaking new ground, I took risks which, when I look back, were breathtaking in their immensity, but I confess that many of these were taken in blissful ignorance of the consequences. I was twenty-two, it was the yuppy recession, I borrowed and bought two properties without even knowing what the words 'negative equity' meant.

Was I a discerning businesswoman who had a flair for seeing an opportunity, or did I just get lucky? I don't truly know, but I do know I loved every second of it.

My private life wasn't so lucky, although it was certainly as exciting. My ability to see opportunities in my work seemed to translate into taking crazy risks in love. Intense and passionate affairs, feeling like the world had ended each time I faced another break-up.

Now that I know what it really feels like to see your world disintegrating, those grief-stricken, vodka-fuelled collapses seem vacuous and pathetic. I had no perspective then, utterly selfish, utterly self-indulgent. Falling in love with my husband was the best and most beautiful emotion. We nearly missed our chance, nearly passed each other by. We had known each other for years, both of us racing from one broken relationship to the next, never alone, never recognising that we were meant to be. Best friends, ships in the night. It took a misunderstanding for me to realise. A mutual friend rang me up with news:

'Guess who's getting married?'

She actually meant her sister, I thought she must mean Robert and his then girlfriend. In that moment, not understanding her, I sat there feeling like the bottom had fallen out of my world. And then, when I did understand, the obvious question, why would I feel like that about my best friend? Why would I not be happy for him? The thought, and I made myself visualise it, of being a guest at his wedding, made me recoil with horror, I could never go.

I was in love with my best friend.

I walked miles that night. I walked the tow path between my village and the next town, staring at the river and thinking. My best friend. You cannot 'mess' with your best friend. If it goes wrong, if you mess it up, you have lost everything.

And then an insistent voice, telling me what I'd always believed before, what I'd always lived by in my business world. If it's worth a lot, it's worth the risk.

I told him.

It took two more nights of soul-searching before I was sure, sure that I wasn't on the rebound, sure that I was ready for commitment from the word 'go.' Sure that, just like in business, if you don't take the risk, you don't stand to gain anything. The chance will pass you by forever.

Thinking about this now, tonight when I can't see past the immediate bleakness, I decide to write down our story for our children. Christmas is coming and it is a beautiful story, and I have told it with so much happiness to so many friends, but I haven't ever shared it with them. They're young but I hope one day they'll read it and feel the love we felt.

I sleep. Because of my late-night thoughts and drifting memories, the dream is peaceful, beautiful. Then I awake, back in my nightmare. Back in reality. I lift the covers and look down. I pluck at my wasted legs ineffectually, hating them, wishing I could gather the energy and strength to move them. I press the button and call the nurse.

**** 

I open the notebook Robert brought me today. It's burgundy with creamy, thick pages, the kind of book that needs to be written on with a fountain pen.

I begin our story as the snow begins to fall outside of my clinically safe, locked window.

Holding them close in my heart, I tell the children about the night I rang their father to tell him I loved him. I was so nervous I couldn't say anything at first. Then, as always, he started griping about his girlfriend. He always used to do this, using me as a sounding board for his next move. She'd just asked to move in with him as she was losing her flat, it was a no-brainer from her point of view. From Robert's perspective, he was being pushed into another level of relationship, Robert, the man who always shied away from commitment. I told him I couldn't help him; my advice would be too biased to offer. He asked why, and I took the plunge, gabbling that I'd changed, I'd finally realised how I felt, that I loved him.

Robert laughed. He laughed incredulously, then stopped in his tracks, not believing what he was hearing. Then:

'Nice bloody timing, mate.'

Both of us shocked by my confession, both of us excited, both of us hardly daring to believe.

He asked me if I was sure. He asked if he could come and see me the next night.

I spent the day in a flurry of nerves. Afraid of what to do, what to say. When he walked through the door that night with a bottle of wine in his hand, it was plain to see he was in the same state.

We drank the wine. Our path became clear.

Weeks later, after he had ended his relationship, we moved in together. We were married in my eyes from the moment I told him how I felt, but in reality, our wedding was two years later and as special as it could have been. Many people had told me over the years 'you two should be together' and I'd always denied it, refuted it. Standing up in church and declaring our love to the world was the most amazing moment in my life.

Until I gave birth to you two, my beautiful children.

****

I look at the words I wrote yesterday and feel them lift my heart. Then I know I have to write more, more to describe my children, and I can hardly face it. My children are the future personified, it's so hard to know

219

I can't share it with them.

So important for them to know I love them. I start to write again.

My son. An easy pregnancy, a traumatic delivery. Fighting my way back from unconsciousness to the surface of a dark pool of exhaustion, asking for you, demanding that I could hold you naked, skin to skin. The midwife protested; she'd dressed you already. Forcing myself to function, determined to have some of my birth plans go my way, I insisted.

The moment you were laid in my arms is ingrained in my heart forever. I was on my back, incapable from the epidural, newly stitched from the caesarean, unable to sit up. I reached my hand down and laid it on your back. I've never felt anything so soft. I looked down and saw your downy head, your fuzzy little shoulder, and a tiny line of blond hair growing in a zigzag from your eyebrow to your forehead.

You were the most perfect creature I'd ever seen. I drank in the feel of you, the smell of you. Then you began nuzzling me, searching for milk, and feeding you felt like the most beautiful and natural thing in the world.

The next pregnancy was different. Last time we decided we wanted a baby I was pregnant within two weeks. This time, seven agonising months.

Trying not to worry… worrying incessantly. Counting days, dates, times. Then the roller coaster of emotion when my doctor broke it to me that I was unlikely ever to conceive again naturally, then discovering I was pregnant the very next day.

And then bleeding at nine weeks. The utter despair I felt that I'd lost everything. The roller coaster didn't stop there though, it wasn't done with me yet. Sitting in the hospital, unable to answer any questions, speechless with grief. Then to be told:

'Well you haven't lost this baby, this baby's fine.'

I'd lost your twin, sweetheart, they could see where another life had been, where another little life had ended. You were still clinging on tenaciously, the strength of the character that I see in you today already shining out.

I felt guilty all the way through your pregnancy, sweetheart. Your brother was just beginning to blossom, we would drive along in my car singing together, and I felt guilty that I would be diluted, that I wouldn't be able to devote all my time to him. Then I would feel guilty that I had had those treacherous thoughts, that I wasn't sending you the right energy, the right vibes.

I was so afraid I hadn't enough love to share.

Your birth was so calm, so organised. A planned caesarean because of last time.

What I hadn't bargained for, was me.

Last time, the backdrop to the caesarean was a blaze of pain and mind-numbing exhaustion, I swear they could have sliced me open without anaesthesia, plucked him from me without me feeling any further pain or distress.

This time, all was quiet, and I was compos mentis. Much too compos mentis. I coped admirably with the long, chilled needle for the spinal, but went cold inside when I saw the theatre nurse laying out the clamps, the scalpel.

Just before they began cutting, I panicked. I was so afraid of the scalpel, so afraid. I cried when they started, mortified by my own fear but paralysed by it, just the same.

Your dad was my anchor that day.

He leant over my face and talked to me throughout, I don't know what he said, but he kept me calm. Then he took you, our beautiful daughter, and laid you in my arms. In that moment I knew that love could multiply, that love was boundless. The most frightening moment was to come.

Later that day, Robert brought your brother to meet you for the first time. I heard him walking down the ward on the other side of the curtain, his little voice chattering away.

A terrible clench of fear, fear that he would reject you.

I should have known. I should have understood.

He climbed on the bed, took one look at you, then said in wonderment, 'Mummy, she has such tiny little hands.'

It was love at first sight.

Suddenly I need to shift position, go to move and remember. The paralysis is just the same as waiting for the epidural to wear off, willing your legs to move, no response beyond the feeblest, most useless twitch. This time, it won't wear off.

I can't write any more. I can't look at those beautiful memories without being destroyed by their poignancy, the knowledge that I will not, cannot, watch you grow up. That this Christmas, I will not be with you.

****

The dynamo in me rejoiced in my children, grew in strength as they grew.

I never mourned for the twin, that tiny child lost in time. My daughter, from the day she was born, was larger than life, there could never have been two of my Rachel.

Oddly, she and Harry are often mistaken for twins. They're so close, such good friends, rarely fighting like so many of our friends' children seem to.

Rachel explodes through life, organised to the point of bossiness, she is a go-getter. She does not take no for an answer, she is determined to bend the world to her will.

Harry is quieter, more reflective. He had always been a dreamer, a deep thinker, coming up with a side to the story that nobody else had seen. The role of big brother sits weightily on his shoulders, but he bears it with pride.

How can I describe those first few years? I sit with my notebook resting on my useless legs, temporarily stumped by the enormity of the task I've set for myself. But I know, deep inside, I can't stop now. My memories are flooding to the surface, I have so much to share with my children, and my time is limited. I begin to write again, black ink flowing smoothly across the page.

I sang with my children. That was our biggest joy, our strongest connection. Nursery rhymes, songs from the radio, wild whooping up and down a scale with the two of you in the back of the car copying me, word for word, note for note.

Those are probably my happiest memories.

Then the pride of seeing you both blossoming in pre-school, throwing yourselves into big school with energy and enthusiasm. Learning from other people, growing up into wonderful beings with so much talent, so much to give.

Then the recession hit. Our own little bubble burst, and with it, my dream of being a full-time mother.

I think I would have coped if I could have worked part-time. But full-time work hit me hard, relegating me to the position of mummy taxi instead of being your all, your everything, your mother.

At first, I knuckled under, and yes, I enjoyed using my brain again. I had not lost my business mind; I had not lost my edge.

A year went by. I began to struggle with the sheer relentlessness of it, but guiltily quiet because I knew that Rob had always done this.

Then a sneaking feeling of bitterness, he might have always worked, but now so was I, as well as cooking, washing, cleaning. I began to snap at the kids when they spilt food on their clothes at the table, criticising their manners because they were making more work for me. I could see mealtimes becoming anxious and tense, knew I was at fault, but seemingly unable to reach across the developing void to say I was sorry.

And I was sorry. But too tired and too dispirited to do anything about it.

One night, at the end of my tether after a trying day at work, I arrived too late at school to find a parking space. I abandoned the car and ran, got there just in time. Then rushing you both home to change for your art class, grabbing your Brownie and Cubs uniforms for afterwards.

When Rachel piped up that I'd forgotten to give you a snack, I lost it. I yelled at you both, anger burning through the shame of seeing Harry putting his arm round her to protect her from my wrath.

I threatened you. I said no more clubs, no more classes. Then I relented in the face of your tears, rushed you across the village to your class.

I sat and wept in the car that day. None of this had been your fault, I was just tired and drowning under the weight of the constant planning and rushing to make it all work, make it all fit in. I stay outside your class looking in, a fly on the wall.

After the emotional trauma caused by me, by my failure to cope, you both sat there, peaceably immersed in your work, absorbed by what you were painting. Your faces were calm, your faces were happy.

I resolved to do better. To try harder. To cope.

Another year went by.

Tears at breakfast one day when I explained I couldn't be there to see Rachel's work at school. Not her tears. Mine. Mine, when my six-year-old asked me if my work was more important than my children.

****

I wake again from the usual nightmare. Sweating, shaking with shock. The memory of the car hitting me, the feeling of being thrown bodily into the air. The nurse comes to me and offers a sedative as she usually does. I see the sympathy in her eyes, the pity, and recoiling from her kindness, this time I refuse her. The terrible irony is that I used to work here. Throughout my uni years, as so many of us did, I worked as a supply nurse as they called us then, unskilled but useful, lifting people, dressing people, putting them to bed. I used to look at these wasted bodies and think I would rather be dead.

One of the physios there became a friend of mine then. She told me that after an accident, most paraplegics would either deal with it, or, as she put it, would choose to 'opt out' early on.

So here I am. Wasted legs. Useless. A decision made.

But I have a story to tell first.

My notebook is nearly full. I read through, wondering if I've said too much, been too honest. I don't want to hurt Robert. He knew I couldn't cope any longer, did his best to lighten the load for me, both at work and at home. His face now is full of desperation as he tries to envisage our future, how we will cope with this, with my disaster.

The day of the accident, strangely, was calm. Nobody had forgotten anything; nobody was in a panic. We parked up in time, stood on the pavement chatting with friends.

I'm not sure exactly what happened next. I heard a squeal of tyres, a car going much too fast. In that instant I saw it, skidding across the rain-damp road towards our children, towards me. I remember screaming out, I remember instinctively shoving to get them out of its path. Then the feeling of it clipping me with the edge of the bonnet, spinning me in mid-air. Then seeing you both, safe, shocked, looking at me.

Looking down at me.

Then nothing.

Waking in here, downstairs actually, I've 'graduated' out of intensive care and am now in the spinal injuries 'recovery' unit. I don't see any recovery. My legs are dead. The only flicker I get to show me that they're still there is a fleeting electric shock of pain, beyond that, nothing.

And I have time now, so much time at my disposal to reflect on our whirlwind life. Art classes, dance classes, singing lessons, Cubs, Brownies, swimming. Sailing on summer weekends. Skiing in better off years, saving for it in other years.

I do not want my handicap to handicap my children's lives. I want Robert to move on, I don't want him to nurse a cripple for the rest of our days together. This is not what he signed up for, it's not what I signed up for. Those words 'in sickness and in health' seem trite and infantile in the enormity of this injury, this calamity which has befallen me, befallen us all.

I write a few more lines, saying I'm sorry. Sorry I can't be there for them. Sorry I didn't manage to dodge the car quickly enough like they did. Sorry for yelling.

I wish them luck. I wish them love in their lives. I wish them happiness for this Christmas. I wish it with all my heart.

I sign off.

****

The actual deed should be easy enough. Easier than facing the relentless, agonising, pointless task of trying to make these dead legs work for me.

I have more than enough now. I've collected the sedatives from every nightmare awakening since they began, except for the first time. The first time, I accepted the offer, then much later awoke from the deepest, most perfect, dreamless sleep. That's when I realised what I would do, my path seemed clear from that moment, and I began to plan my exit strategy.

The regular nurses go off on Fridays, to be replaced by agency nurses, just like I used to be, for the weekends. Untrained, indifferent. Not uncaring, but their minds are elsewhere, the job a means to a different end. No vigilance. Lax. Perfect. You are visiting today with the kids. I want to make it special. I ask the nurse to place the notebook in the bottom of my locker, I want you to find it, but find it last, so you can read it and read it with the kids when you're ready.

Oh, Robert, I'm so sorry. That a moment of carelessness on my part, recklessness on someone else's, should end our marriage. But, love, our marriage ended well, if you have loved me till death us do part, and I have loved you until then too.

But I don't want you to be trapped by our vows, which I know you would feel bound to keep. So, I plan to go, to set you free. To set the kids free. To set me free. Back to that dreamless, painless, deep sleep.

Then you arrive, all three of you, exploding though the door in a wave of energy. In some part of me, my heart is breaking that I can never be part of this again, yet in another part, I'm proud and happy of my tough little family, propping each other up in times of hardship.

Then Rachel climbs on my lap. I can't really feel this, but I can feel her arms locked around my neck. 'Mummy, can you read me a story?'

I laugh. 'Rachel, you can read so well, we don't do that any more!'

'But, Mummy, I want you to, just like when I was little.' I capitulate and see that she has brought me one of her baby books, an old family favourite. I start to read, my family all listening, and soon we all join in, reciting every well-worn, well-loved word.

'I can't wait till you come home, Mummy,' says Harry. 'We've put the Christmas decorations up, but we want to do the tree with you, so we're going to buy it when you're back.'

I shudder, withdraw. Home? How? The thought of ramps and wet rooms fills me with icy dread. Not me. If I cannot be me, the dynamo, then I am nobody.

'I can't wait either,' Rachel chips in. 'No more rushing, Mummy. We can just read to each other. We can sit on the floor and read. Just like when we were babies when you used to sing with us. We can just be.'

Robert smiles at me, tremulous, tears in his eyes. A question in his eyes.

With enormous effort, I focus my thoughts, harness my tangled emotions. In a moment of purest clarity I understand that they've just saved me. When they leave, they all kiss me. Robert holds me close.

I press the button and call the nurse. I hand her my carefully hoarded stash of pills.

'Someone gave me these by mistake. I don't need these. They're not meant for me.'

# Uncle Christmas by Val Portelli

'Penny for the guy?'

'Sorry, son. I haven't even got a penny.'

It had been a long while since I'd heard that expression, but what I'd told him was the absolute truth. My landlord had taken the last of my money when he'd called round with a couple of heavies this morning. I was already two months in arrears, and if I hadn't paid up, he'd have thrown me out. Once, I'd have been fit enough to take on all three of them, but the injury from when I was in service crippled me with arthritis as soon as the bad weather set in.

Although it was only three o'clock it was misty, cold, and almost dark. My feet squished through my damp socks where the rain had got in through the hole in my shoe, and my stomach rumbled in sympathy. What would have happened if I'd already left for the supermarket before they arrived? I would have had some food for my belly but no roof over my head, so at least that was something to be grateful for.

'Count your blessings,' my old mum used to say. A smile crossed my face as I remembered the last time I'd come home on leave. Never mind Facebook, I think every neighbour within a five hundred mile radius had heard all about 'My boy, Jack,' and the wonderful job he and his friends were doing 'to help those poor people in the country with the funny name.' At least I came back, more or less in one piece. Not like Johnny Jackson, or Pete Crozier. What was left of him. I was here, in good old London town, and as long as there's life, there's hope.

With a bit of luck, the next firm I applied to would take me on, or the jobcentre would find my file and send me some money. It wasn't the young slip of a girl's fault I didn't exist according to her computer. It had been nearly closing time and she was probably eager to get home or have a takeaway with her boyfriend before going clubbing. Not a good idea to think of food; it only reminded me I hadn't eaten since yesterday. I'd have to swallow my pride and try one of those food banks, but someone told me you had to have a referral. Who did the referring? It was all so complicated, and everyone told you something different. Better to keep trying for work so I could pay my own way.

'Hey, mister. You stink.'

The crowd of kids in the park looked no older than twelve. What were their parents thinking of, letting them out in the dark? They were right though. I'd always been so proud of my appearance, but the landlord was ignoring my requests to repair the hot water until I caught up the back rent. Fat chance of that. Then the washing machine broke down, and I had no money to repair it. Using the launderette was too expensive, but it was nice and warm in there. Sometimes I sneaked in when it wasn't busy and sat for a while before going back to my freezing flat. Perhaps it wasn't such a good idea as it made the weather outside feel even colder when I emerged.

Was that a flake of snow? Surely the end of November is too early, but with global warming the weather's gone crazy the last few years. Better get home before it starts in earnest. Perhaps I'll hear from the post office about the temporary delivery job tomorrow, but no one seems to send Christmas cards any more. It's all done online now, and I'm not that good with computers. If you wanted an engine stripped down, or a garden shed built, I'm your man. Daft idea. Who puts up a garden shed in the middle of winter? If I can make it through to spring, perhaps I could get a job gardening.

Have I been job hunting in the wrong place? I'm willing to do anything, but it's the wrong time to be looking. I wonder if Santa needs a little helper? That's an idea, tomorrow I'll try the department stores. With less than four weeks to Christmas they might need someone to help in the packing department. At least I'm rich for now. The £20 from the emergency fund was a godsend. I thought of putting it towards the rent, but my stomach said no. Who knew a few tins of soup and a bit of battered fruit could be so expensive? I assumed by leaving it late there might be some bargains, but with the supermarkets open 24/7 that doesn't work anymore. Still, it was good of that young chap to try to help.

Not all the kids today are selfish. He promised to let me know if something came up in the supply depot. Said I reminded him of his granddad. I wonder if I knew him? Probably not. From what he was saying his father is more my age. Money can't buy you happiness but lack of it definitely makes you look older. It was embarrassing when he asked for my mobile number. As if I could afford a phone, but he did take my address, so fingers crossed. The details of the soup kitchen might be useful too, but I'm not homeless so it wouldn't be fair to take food out of the mouths of people who need it more than me.

**\*\*\*\***

December the third and it's freezing. I don't want to get up but it's no good lazing in bed. I need to earn some money, or I won't eat next week. What's this letter on the mat? Perhaps they've sent a cheque early for

Christmas. I don't think so, it doesn't look official. They use brown envelopes and this one's white. Only one way to find out.

*Open it, you fool.*

It's a Christmas card from Luke. I don't know anyone called Luke. Wait a minute. That was the name of the young lad in the supermarket. Bless him. What a lovely thought. There's a letter with it. His spelling leaves a lot to be desired.

*Short-term work. Go to the staff entrance at the supermarket at ten o'clock and ask for Dave.*

Saturday? That's today. Better get my skates on, it's already nearly nine. Should I wear my suit? It's the only decent thing I've got left. I wonder what sort of job it is.

****

'Hey, Jack. You wanted to know when young Luke was back from his holiday. You should find him in the staff canteen around 12.30 when he has his break. Don't be too long though, we need you down here, or we'll never get this lot organised.'

'Thanks, Dave. I'll make the time up. I only wanted to thank him for getting me this job.'

'My pleasure, Jack. You've worked like a Trojan since you've been here. I've had a word with personnel to see about keeping you on after the Christmas break. No promises mind. They're a law unto themselves in the office, but I'd be delighted if they said yes.'

'You're a diamond, Dave. Back in five.'

Things were on the up. I had a job, at least for now, the promise of a future, some money coming in, and cheap food from the subsidised work canteen. The night shift wasn't popular, but it paid double, so for the moment I was doing nothing but work and sleep, but at least this month's rent would be covered. I'd had another stroke of luck, but not so good for poor Santa who had been off with flu. To save money on shaving I'd let my beard grow, and although I needed a bit of padding, for two weeks I spent my days dressed in a big red suit giving out presents to the children in the fairy grotto, before going back to my usual job in the despatch department. For once, it really felt like Christmas.

Although some of the older kids were spoilt brats, it gladdened my heart to see the joy on the faces of many of the younger ones when I gave them their brightly wrapped gift. Funny how it was the poorest parents who had the kids who were most appreciative.

'Are you really Father Christmas?' one little girl asked me, her big brown eyes enormous in her sweet elfin face. 'Can I have a present for Mummy instead of for me? We've got a tiny tree at home, and I've already got a present under it, but she hasn't got anything.'

Glancing up, I noticed tears welling in the eyes of the shabbily dressed woman waiting for her.

'Come on, darling,' she said. 'Santa has got lots of other boys and girls to see, so say *Thank you*, and we'll go home now.'

'Are you really Father Christmas?' the little girl asked again. 'Thank you for my present.'

'Shush,' I said. 'I'll tell you a little secret. Father Christmas is very busy, so he asked me to help him out. I'm *Uncle* Christmas. Tell Mummy to close her eyes for a minute.'

I remembered the small box of chocolates I'd bought with staff discount, intending to treat myself on Christmas Day. It was worth going without to see the delight on the little girl's face as I handed them over.

'Put these under the tree for Mummy, and both of you have a lovely Christmas.'

'Thank you, Uncle Christmas. We will. Thank you so much.'

I gave her mother a wink, as the youngster, a huge smile on her face, skipped off carrying her two presents.

**\*\*\*\***

'Uncle Jack. I've been looking for you all week. Mum says if you're not busy on Christmas Day, can you come over to us for lunch? She says she's bought miles too much food, but I think she just wants someone to help with the washing up.'

I'd become quite close to Luke over the previous few weeks. He was trying to rebuild his dad's old motorbike and I'd offered to give him a hand. We'd spent several afternoons working on it, and his mum always insisted I stay for her Sunday roast special, so I knew she was an excellent cook. It had been his idea to call me 'Uncle Jack,' but it made me feel part of the family.

All too soon the good life came to an end. Boxing Day was back to work for the sales, but then there was the dead period in January. As a casual worker I didn't get paid for the enforced holiday, but I was waiting to hear from Dave that I would be offered permanent employment. Money was tight as I'd splashed out on small presents for Luke and his mum; nothing extravagant but I couldn't go empty-handed when I'd enjoyed their hospitality.

It wasn't a good start to the year.

'I'm really sorry, mate,' Dave said. 'I tried my best but with everyone buying online these days, the store is cutting right back. They've even offered me redundancy. I'm only a year off retirement so I'll be all right, but I feel I've let you down.'

'Not your fault, Dave. Thanks for trying. Don't worry, I'll find something.'

With no wages coming in I was back where I started. The unemployment benefit had stopped when I was working, so I had to start again with form filling and interviews until I officially existed on their computer. By April, I'd fallen behind with the rent again, and the landlord evicted me. I was now jobless, homeless, and of no fixed abode. With no permanent address there was nowhere to send any support cheques. The third bench on the left, by the duck pond in the park blew the computer's brain.

I missed the company of Luke and his mum but didn't want to turn up on their doorstep like a charity case. The one time I plucked up courage to try to visit him at the store I was stopped by security.

'We don't want your sort in here. Push off and do your robbing somewhere else.'

I didn't really blame him. After six months surviving on the streets, I looked and felt like a tramp, so it was not surprising he assumed I was only there to steal. Autumn slipped into winter and the signs of another Christmas started to appear. This time last year I had a roof over my head, a job, money, friends, and was optimistic about a fresh start.

Now all I could look forward to was surviving the winter, and the thought crossed my mind that perhaps it was better to give up the fight.

How would I do it? I couldn't afford to buy enough pills. I was too much of a coward to throw myself under a bus. What if I was only injured or paralysed? It wouldn't be fair to cause the driver such trauma. He might lose his job or be forever wondering if it was his fault. It would shake up the Christmas shoppers, and what about the hard-working doctors and nurses trying to save me when others were more deserving? No, I couldn't be that selfish.

Although the bench was cold and uncomfortable, I must have dozed off. I woke to feel a tongue licking my face through my long, white beard which hadn't felt a razor in months. Opening my eyes, I saw a small, black bundle of fluff trying to wriggle its way into my coat.

'I'm so sorry. He's my stepdaughter's early Christmas present and it's his first proper walk. Are you all right?'

I looked up into the concerned face of a smartly dressed man as he removed the puppy from me and tried to refasten his lead.

'You're a naughty boy, Jack. No doggie treats for you if you don't behave.'

I couldn't help laughing at the bemused look on his face and felt I had to explain.

'It's OK. I'm hungry enough to eat doggie treats. By the way, my name's Jack too.'

I held out my hand to shake his, then hastily withdrew it, not wanting my grubby mitts spoiling his expensive clothes. He sensed my hesitancy but reached out and shook it firmly.

'Nice to meet you, Jack. Look, please don't take offence but could I give you something for the inconvenience? Forgive me if I'm being nosey, but are you ex-forces? You have the look of a military man, and it would be my way of saying thank you to all our heroes.'

'Uncle Christmas! Look, Mummy, it's Uncle Christmas. I told you we'd see him again.'

I recognised the little girl instantly, but the woman holding her hand looked totally different. Gone was the worried look and ragged clothes. Now her face radiated warmth and contentment as she turned to the man sitting on the bench next to me.

'She's right, Steve. You remember we told you about the Santa in the store who gave me a present last year. It brought me luck and changed my life. We were on our way home when Lucy dropped it and you helped her pick it up.'

'In which case, we owe you double thanks, Father Christmas. Not only did you help me find my beautiful wife here but also my own ready-made family with this little scamp.'

'He's not Father Christmas, Daddy,' Lucy joined in, 'he's *Uncle* Christmas. Can he come home with us? I want to give him a present.'

'Yes, why don't you?' Steve said. 'We can't leave you on your own over Christmas, and there's plenty of room at the house. What do you think, Sally?'

Although I was happy things had worked out for her, I was embarrassed Lucy had put them in that position. After all, they didn't know me, and I could have been any sort of low life or thief and taken advantage of their hospitality.

'I appreciate your offer, Steve, but I must decline. It's a busy time of year and Santa will need my help,' I said, giving him a wink. 'Perhaps we'll bump into each other again sometime. Have a lovely Christmas, and make sure you look after Little Jack properly,' I said, bending down to Lucy's height, but keeping some distance between us as I knew I didn't smell very savoury. 'Give him a lot of love and cuddles but train him to learn right from wrong so he grows into a big, strong dog. OK?'

'OK, Uncle Christmas,' Lucy said. 'We'll come and visit you in the park when we take him for a walk. Tell Father Christmas I've been a good girl and give him this from me.' Ignoring my rank clothing she gave me a hug and a kiss on the cheek, making my cheeks even redder than they already were from the bitterly cold wind which had blown up.

'One last thing, Jack,' her stepfather said as she took his hand. 'Take this and contact me when you've finished helping Santa. I'm sure I can find a job for you until he needs you again. My grateful thanks.' Hidden under the business card he pressed into my hand was a £20 note, but by the time I noticed, the family had walked away. I treated myself to the luxury of a cheap bar of chocolate but decided to save it for my Christmas dinner.

The chance meeting seemed to bring me luck as, shortly after they left, I came across a skip outside a house at the edge of the park. The smell of a still-warm pizza caught my attention and nestling below the box was a stained but thick duvet someone had thrown out. Tonight, I would dine and sleep like a lord on my trusty bench.

The afternoon of Christmas Eve the weather took a turn for the worse, and people hurried by, eager to finish their shopping as the first snowflakes began to fall. It looked as if it was going to be a white Christmas.

'Jack. Jack. Wake up. Come on, mate. I can't leave you here like this.' The snow had melted making my bedding sodden, and my teeth chattered as I opened my eyes to see Steve shaking my shoulder. 'Lucy hasn't given me a moment's peace, so I promised I would try to find you. You're spending Christmas with us. No arguments. You can decide what you want to do after the holidays, but for now, you're coming home with me. It's not far. Can you walk?'

I felt too weak to argue so followed him across the park until we reached his house. The warmth hit me as he opened the front door, making me even more aware that my damp clothes smelt worse than Little Jack's bedding.

'You found him!' Sally said as he led me through to the kitchen where the smell of the turkey roasting in the oven made my stomach rumble. 'I've made up the spare room just in case, and there's plenty of hot water if you fancy a bath, Jack. There's a lasagne keeping warm in the oven, and a few nibbles for later. Lucy's in bed but she'll be so excited to see you tomorrow. Steve, did you sort out those clothes you were talking about? I found the snowman jumper if Jack's not too embarrassed to wear it.'

That Christmas was magical. Although I slept like a log for the first time in ages in a proper bed, I was up early to see what I could do to help. Little Lucy's face was a picture when she came down to find me in the kitchen washing up, and for once I wasn't ashamed as she snuggled into me with her trademark hug. I joined the family for the traditional church service where I was introduced to everyone as 'Uncle Jack.'

That was five years ago, and it's nearly that magical time of year again. Steve is a successful businessman who gave me back my self-respect along with a job. I now manage one of his garages and have my own flat, although I spend most of my spare time at his house as part of the family. Even though Lucy started big school last autumn, she still calls me Uncle Christmas. Now, I'd better go and find my red suit for my appearance at the children's party, even if it doesn't need padding any more.

Ho! Ho! Ho!

# Time for a Barbecue by Carmen Radtke

Three months after his parents walked into the trap with him, James Potter ran for his life. He was too afraid to wait longer, even if this meant leaving Mum and Dad behind, but he figured they'd be spared awhile, even with Christmas coming up. Dad was too useful as a mechanic to be killed, and Mum helped in the bakery.

They didn't believe him anyway when he told them what he knew. 'What an imagination you have, James,' his mum said, clucking her tongue. But it was all true.

His old teacher had warned him. When James told her they'd leave Leeds to set sail for New Zealand after the summer holidays, 1951, Miss Damson gasped and clasped him to her bosom. It was like being swallowed by a duvet.

'You poor, poor boy. Whatever put an idea like that in Mr Potter's head?' She let go of James.

'Dad says as they want workers in New Zealand, and he reckons they pay good money. Lots of sunshine too, he says,' James said, shaken by her reaction.

'Oh yes, it's sunny enough in those topsy-turvy places,' Miss Damson said, her lips narrowing until they were a dark slash on the floury stuff she put on her face. 'But nothing good will ever come out of it, mark my words. Why, the whole place is riddled with heathens who tattoo their faces and eat people alive.'

James felt sick. 'They eat people? Like cannibals?' He wondered if his dad knew. No; his parents would never leave England then.

Miss Damson's eyes bored into his. She lowered her voice ominously which reminded him of the radio shows his mum forbade him to listen to, but he did it all the same. 'That's right,' she said. 'Cannibals.'

James whispered, 'I didn't know that, Miss.'

She handed him a handkerchief and dabbed away the few fat tears that trickled down his cheek. 'Tell your parents they'd better think again. England is still the best place in the world. Especially south of Hadrian's Wall.'

The bell rang. She padded off, leaving behind the smell of chalk, and a fear that was growing in James's heart.

At teatime, he felt too sick to eat a bite. His mum put her hand on his forehead. 'You're a bit clammy,' she said. 'How about I make you a nice cup of tea and some eggs and soldiers? You'll feel better when you've got something in your stomach.'

'You spoil the child,' Dad said, but without conviction. He was the kindest man in the world. Mum said that too. She always told James the bullets flew past his dad in the war because the angels watched over him. They hadn't watched over some of his mates' fathers, though.

'Mum, Dad?'

'Yes, love?' Mum smiled at him.

'I don't want to go to New Zealand.'

'Why ever not?' She looked around. 'You'll have your own room instead of sleeping on the sofa. Just imagine, you can play on the beach all summer long.'

'But—'

'No buts,' his father said. 'If you ask me, the sooner we're off, the better for all of us. It'll be a proper start for us in life again.'

James knew when he'd lost. He sipped his tea and ate his eggs and soldiers, but his fear wouldn't leave him.

Even on the ship he dreaded each morning. Otherwise the journey would have been the most exciting thing in his life, with mighty waves, bouncing whales, and freedom to run around on deck and play hide-and-seek with other children. The Potters were part of a large group of emigrants New Zealand bound.

**\*\*\*\***

The first weeks in New Zealand were almost nice. Mum spent her days fixing up the rented weatherboard cottage in Timaru that was big enough to house a soccer team. She sang and smiled all day, scrubbing already gleaming floors and planning flower beds and vegetable plots. Dad came home whistling, something he never used to do back home. Even the way he looked changed bit by bit. Where in the old days his face was like porridge, thin and pale, Dad now started to turn all pink and cheerful, like a domesticated pig.

Mum noticed too, without understanding what it meant. She simply said, 'You pile on any more meat, Bill, and I'll have to make you new shirts. I've let out what I could but that only goes so far.'

Dad punched himself in the stomach before he hung up another paperchain on the rafters over the fireplace. 'That's one thing I sure don't miss, Molly, all that rationing. Didn't I promise you we'd have plenty here?'

But James knew better what was going on, and the iron fist around his heart gripped harder and harder.

He'd seen the cannibals too. Two elderly men, with black paintings on their dark skin and muscles of iron. They'd smiled at him, baring their big, shiny teeth.

**\*\*\*\***

James bit back tears as he recalled that day. He'd tried to tell them then, but they just didn't listen. And now he would never see them again. He clutched his bundle as hard as he could, as if it could give him support. He started to feel tired and hungry, but he didn't dare to stop. He only had one water bottle, and a couple of stale sandwiches he'd managed to squirrel aside. It was a long way up north to Lyttelton, where the ships left to go back home, so he had to be careful with his rations.

James wondered what Mum and Dad were doing right now. The sun was rising, spilling its light over the red earth. It looked a bit like icing running down a Christmas pudding.

He swallowed. Mum made the best Christmas pudding ever. The cottage had been smelling of her baking for weeks, and Dad had found a spindly tree to put in the living room. Yesterday they'd trimmed it with tinsel and the red and silver baubles they'd brought in a box all the way from Leeds. And tomorrow Mum had promised them a try of one of the small Christmas puddings, to see if she got the mix right.

His mouth watered just thinking of it. But even if he had one right now, he wouldn't eat it. Not until he'd made his way to safety. There would be puddings again next Christmas for him, in England, where he belonged.

His right heel hurt. James put his bundle carefully down before he lowered himself onto the brownish stubbles that passed for grass in this wilderness. He took off his sandal to uncover a blister the size of a shilling.

He wished he'd put on his hobnailed boots from home, but Mum would have noticed. Instead, he wore sandals, with one sole already flapping, and his play shorts and shirt.

'The rod,' James said aloud, startling a bellbird into protesting flight. 'I forgot my fishing rod.' Now he really started to cry, shameful for a big eight-year-old, but there was no one around to see it. He needed the rod. Not only to prove to his parents that he had gone fishing before sunrise on a Sunday morning which is what the note on his pillow said, but he needed to catch fish to survive.

James pressed his bundle with the water, the spare clothes, and the sandwiches to his chest and cried. He'd never make it to Lyttelton. He was as good as dead.

**\*\*\*\***

Bill Potter found him there at the side of the road an hour later, curled up tight as a coil, sobbing quietly.

He squatted down and touched his son on the shoulder. 'James?' His voice sounded puzzled, and tired.

The boy rolled himself up even tighter.

'Son?'

James's whole body began to shake.

'What's wrong, James?' his father asked. 'Only we really need to get going if we want to be home before your mother worries herself half to death.'

James's breath grew so shallow his father thought the boy would faint. Bill Potter frowned. Whatever had gotten into the boy? Sure, it took some getting used to being in New Zealand instead of the council estate in Leeds, but the boy had been acting kind of strange lately.

'Son?'

James looked up at him with eyes that were black with fear. 'You go home, Dad,' he said. 'I can't. They'll eat me.'

'What on earth are you talking about?'

'I told you, again and again, you and Mum, but you didn't listen.' James stared at the ground to hide the tears that welled up in his eyes.

'Listen to what?'

'Don't you remember? Miss Damson said there's nothing but cannibals here, and she was right.' James grabbed his father's arm and tugged it frantically, as if underlining the strength of his arguments. 'Haven't you noticed, there's almost no men here with arms or legs missing, like they do back home? And everybody tells you not to go to the city where they charge you an arm and a leg for nearly everything? So, where do all these people go then?'

The tears grew from a trickle to a cascade, but James was past caring. 'And when Mum took me to school, the new teacher pinched my cheek and said, school dinners would soon fatten me up nicely, and you and Mum have both grown all bigger. They call us ten-pound Poms, Dad, do you know that? I reckon that's how much they carve off our bones.'

He wiped his nose with this grubby hand. 'I waited as long as I could, Dad, I did, but today they're going to come for me.'

'What makes you think so?'

James stared at his obtuse father. 'You must know that, Dad. There are banners everywhere.'

'Banners?'

'For the community Christmas barbecue tonight. All welcome, especially our new ten-pound Poms.'

'I see.' Bill Potter sat down next to his son and hugged him like a drowning man clinging to a raft. 'So, you've been dead scared all this time.'

'I'd have written you a letter,' James said.

'Where did you plan to go, then?'

'Home. Or maybe to Tasmania, where they beat even the devil, teacher says, so I reckon they wouldn't be afraid of cannibals, would they?'

'I reckon you're right,' said Bill, ruffling his son's curls. 'But you know something? I also reckon your Miss Damson got a few things mixed up. These things with cannibals in these parts of the world used to be a long time ago, so I think she must have gotten confused with the dates.'

He leant over to his son and whispered, in a hush-hush voice that signalled the sharing of a big secret, 'That's women for you, James. Mind you, not all of them, but they can get all mixed up when they're distracted.'

'Even teacher?'

'Cross my heart and hope to die. Why, if you don't believe me, bite my finger and see how you like it. Nobody would eat all gristly stuff like that, when you got herds and herds of cows and sheep to feast on here. So, what do you say, shall we go to the car now?' Bill winked at his son. 'I packed your fishing rod, so your mum won't smell a rat.'

'I've got a blister as big as a barn, Dad.'

'All right, then.' Dad carried him to the battered Ford Model T. He snuggled as close as possible to his father's chest. This felt even nicer and safer than Tasmania could have done.

Dad pressed a kiss on James's forehead before he lowered him onto the passenger seat. 'You'd better not ask your mum for a dance then tonight with your injured foot.'

'What dance?'

'Did I forget to mention it? We've agreed to go to the Christmas barbecue, and promised to make sure we bring you along.'

# Christmas Present by Lexi Rees

'You'll regret it,' Mandy said as they left work.

The words cut into Sarah's heart like shards of glass. 'You know I don't have a choice with the scheduling, I'll make it up to Ben. Anyway, it's only the school play, they always sell a video afterwards for £20. It's a PTA money-making scheme, but at least we can cuddle up on the sofa and watch it together. I'll bribe him with some toffee popcorn.'

'He's Tiny Tim, it's a lead role, I wouldn't miss it for the world if it was Jack. Mind you, Jack was third aardvark from the left in the *Jungle Book* and from where I was sitting in the hall, I couldn't even see him. Plus, I missed his one and only line completely, I had to pretend it was fabulous when he asked even though I didn't have a clue. But at least I was there.'

Sarah sighed. 'I know, but you're lucky, your department is fully staffed. We're so short, I daren't let anyone down, they need me.' She spotted the number 19 bus coming around the corner. 'Aargh,' she squealed, launching herself across the road. 'If I catch that, I can be home in time to read a bedtime story.' Once this week wasn't too bad, given how busy work was.

'At least think about going to the play,' Mandy called after her.

Sarah glanced back over her shoulder at her colleague. Someone screamed, then everything went black.

**\*\*\*\***

She cracked her eyes open. Too bright, she squeezed them shut again. Sarah's brain processed the situation. The car. It had shot out from behind the bus. She tried to sit up only to find a hand on her shoulder and Mandy's panic-stricken voice, 'Don't move a muscle. The ambulance will be here in a second, you're lucky we're not far from the hospital.' A wave of pain flooded through her and she sank back into the darkness.

White.

Room.

Machine.

Nurse.

Dream.

Nightmare.

*Please, Mum, you've got to come, we've got to do the three-legged race, all the other mums will be there.' Then she was running, her handbag flapping as she sprinted across the playground, grateful for her sensible work shoes.*

Sarah sat bolt upright, dripping with sweat. She tugged the cannula out of her arm and swung her legs over the edge of her bed. She had to get to sports day, Ben needed her. He hated sports day, and Sarah tended to agree; at no other point in the school year were you publicly humiliated in front of the whole school plus all their parents. It was fine for the sporty kids but cruel, she felt, for so many of the others. After all, there wasn't an enforced public display of mental arithmetic or verbal reasoning, both of which Ben excelled at.

'Where do you think you're going?' said a voice, kind but firm, as it guided her back into bed.

'Sports day,' Sarah mumbled. Her subconscious nagged her to focus on the nurse, aware that she wasn't in the right place.

'That's a very unseasonal dream, unless your school does sports day at Christmas. I guess they could, but Christmas term always seems so busy, I'd be surprised.' The nurse babbled away as Sarah lay back down. 'Don't you worry, you just rest up now and we'll do our best to have you home for Christmas.' The nurse plugged the cannula back in and replaced the bands of tape, then tucked Sarah in like a child.

'Wait, the accident, was anyone else hurt? It was all my fault; I'll feel terrible if—'

'Don't worry, everyone else is fine.'

Relieved, Sarah allowed her eyes to drift closed and the mind-movie resumed. *Ben, sitting alone to one side of the playing field, hugging his knees to his chest.*

*You missed it*, the dream-self berated her.

****

Next morning, the ward sprang into action shortly after six thirty. The flickering artificial lighting combined with all the frantic toing and froing as the hospital prepared itself for another busy day meant getting back to sleep was highly unlikely. A bright and breezy nurse tugged open the curtains around her bed. Sarah admitted defeat and adjusted the bed, so she was in a semi-upright position. She looked around the ward; her cubicle was in the middle of the room, right opposite the door. There were eight beds in the ward, all occupied. On her left was a lump, huddled under the covers. To her right was a lady who she guessed to be about the same age as her mum, putting the finishing touches to her make-up. The lady caught her staring and smiled at her.

'Hi, I'm Polly, and that's Tessa.' She pointed at the lump who rolled over and uncurled, pushing a mass of tangled dark hair back from her face.

'You were a bit out of it when they brought you back from theatre yesterday and they closed your curtains, so we didn't get a chance to say hi. It's my hip. What are you in for?'

'Don't be so nosy, Tessa.'

'It's OK, I don't mind. It was just a silly accident, my fault entirely. I got hit by a car, I was running for a bus. I feel so bad to be taking up a bed when there are other people who need it more.'

'I'm sure you'll be back on your feet in no time,' Polly said.

It felt strange to be watching everyone at work while she rested and the day dragged until her mum brought Ben in to visit after school. He produced a battered *Biff and Chip* book from his school bag. Sarah ran her finger under the lines and helped him break up a few of the more challenging words into the sounds by covering up sections at a time then signed his reading record. As they left, she called after him, 'Break a leg.'

Tessa raised an eyebrow and pointed at Sarah's own leg.

'I didn't mean literally! He's in the school play tomorrow, and I'm going to miss it. That's the last thing I remember before the accident, my friend was trying to get me to change my shift so I could go.'

Tessa laughed then yelped. 'Oh, look at the time! It's almost time for the doctor's evening round.' She grabbed a hairbrush and started to tug frantically at her hair.

Polly sat back and preened herself. 'I'm ready.'

'Hand's off, he's mine. And you're old enough to be his mother!' Tessa turned to Sarah. 'Are you married?'

'Not any more, I lost my husband last year.' She found it best just to keep the statement simple. People always got tongue-tied at first but, in the long run, it was easier. She'd tried pretending she was divorced a few times, but that always got complicated and then the real explanation took forever.

Tessa blushed. 'Oh, I'm so sorry. I didn't mean to pry.'

'It's OK. It was a relief in the end, he was very sick.' Sarah changed the topic before it got awkward. 'So, which doctor are you fighting over?'

'You'll see.'

Sarah saw.

Doctor Rae strode into the ward, followed by the house officer. Tall and dark with chiselled cheekbones, he wore the shapeless white doctor's coat like a catwalk model. She studied the way he worked his way round the ward, skipping the occasional bed allocated to a different rota. Although the curtain was drawn to give a modicum of privacy, you could hear the low voices and the occasional laugh as he chatted to each patient. She bit her lip as he approached her bed, but he carried on past. 'Bad luck,' Tessa mouthed at her.

****

Time was marked by the regular checks from the nurses, magazines were traded like currency. Slow off the mark, Sarah ended up with a choice of Christmas crafts or celebrity gossip: the crafts won hands down. Polly lent her a slushy novel about a muscular (of course) cowboy meeting a ditzy (of course) city girl. On his way home from the school play, an overexcited and overtired Ben, still in full Tiny Tim costume, delivered a melodramatic performance of his lines. After he left, Sarah yawned several times before they'd even dimmed the lighting, it was surprising how tiring being a patient could be.

*The bar was empty expect for a cowboy in hospital scrubs. She pulled up a stool and ordered a whisky, the first sip hit the back of her throat, tasting of smoke and peat. The cowboy didn't take his eyes off her as she took another sip. She shuffled awkwardly on the stool. Whether it was the whisky or the cowboy, or a bit of both, the bar felt stifling and she undid a button on her shirt. She met his gaze and a shiver ran down her spine. The way he looked at her, like he knew her.*

She reached for the glass of tepid water beside her bed, mentally prepared for the whisky burn, her body still tingling. *Serves me right for reading romance*, she thought, pushing the image of Doctor Rae in cowboy boots out of her mind.

**** 

Despite the tinsel, paper chains, and even a small Christmas tree perched on a window ledge, the pervasive smell of bleach and antiseptic instead of cloves and cinnamon meant the ward failed to throw off the sterile feel and fully embrace the festive season. Propped up behind the plastic water glass and jug was a hand-drawn Christmas card from Ben of a reindeer, at least he assured her it was a reindeer, despite an uncanny resemblance to a hedgehog. With 'Rudolph the Red-Nosed Reindeer' stuck in her head, she dozed off counting red-nosed hedgehogs.

*In her liver-spotted hands, the old lady held a drawing of a reindeer, or maybe a hedgehog. She looked at the artist, her grandson, he was the spitting image of Ben at the same age. From across the room, Ben took a breath. 'Why did you never remarry?'*

*The old lady shrugged. 'Too busy, I guess.'*

*'You know, I was so proud of you when I was growing up. I told all my friends how you were a hero at work. I know it can't have been easy after Dad died, but I wouldn't have minded if you'd gone out on a date or two, I would have understood. I used to worry that you never had any fun, I still do worry. You should make time for yourself, as well as taking care of everyone else.'*

*Sarah tried to protest, I do have fun, every moment with you is fun. But a social life? I don't have time.*

Her mouth was dry, and the words stuck in her throat.

****

Christmas was fast approaching, and Sarah's heart sank at the thought of spending it in a hospital bed. Today, Tessa was sporting a pair of large, sparkly bauble earrings. Sarah checked the white plastic clock with its threadbare tinsel trim; Doctor Rae would start his evening round soon. She twirled a strand of hair around her finger as the minutes ticked by. The ward door swung open, the gust of air dislodging the tinsel from the clock and it caught in the doors as they swung shut. She dropped the twisted lock and tucked it behind her ear. She didn't recognise the sour-faced doctor who was surveying them, presumably a reluctant locum drafted in to fill the gaps over the festive period. Anyway, it wasn't Doctor Rae. The new doctor worked her way round the ward with a clinical efficiency, not pausing for the lengthy chats that Doctor Rae always made time for. She cut short the latest instalment of the mayhem Polly's cat was causing at the cat-sitter and didn't even crack a smile at Tessa's bauble earrings.

The doctor added a few notes to the clipboard holder at the foot of her bed, her stony face giving no clues as to what she was thinking, then slotted it back into the rack. Sarah held her breath for the verdict.

'So, you've been in for three nights now—'

Three nights. Three dreams. Past, present, and future.

'—and I've got good news for you, you're going home. We'll just do the sign-off paperwork.'

'When can I go back to work?'

'Don't rush, I'm signing you off for another week.'

Sarah counted the days off on her fingers, she'd be back at work on Christmas Day.

The doctor continued, 'If you want to call someone to come and pick you up, we should be all wrapped up in half an hour.'

'I'm going to catch a taxi, but I'll let my mum know I'm on my way, she's looking after...' Sarah closed her mouth mid-sentence as the doctor turned to talk to one of the nurses.

Sarah sat on the edge of her bed, her overnight bag beside her, packed and ready to go. Despite her protests that she knew what to do, the duty nurse ran through the prescription details with her step by step before passing over the paperwork. Released, Sarah swung herself onto the floor and turned to say bye to her ward-mates.

Tessa cupped her hand to her mouth and pretended to whisper, 'Since it looks like Polly and I will be here for a while yet, you've got to promise to use your connections to smuggle in something bubbly for us on Christmas Day.'

The duty nurse overheard and chuckled. 'Don't you worry, we've got a few treats lined up for you on Christmas Day.' From under her desk, she pulled out enormous, bright red, felt reindeer antlers attached to a headband. She flicked a switch and they twinkled. 'Shhh, we're going to make Doctor Rae wear them all day. He doesn't know though, so you've got to keep it secret.'

Sarah started at his name. He was working on Christmas Day too. She'd pictured him with a mince pie in one hand and a mulled wine in the other, family singing carols around the tree, all clad in pristine Mini Boden. She shook the image away, grabbed her bag and waved at everyone.

'Don't forget the bubbles!' Tessa called after her.

****

Always a light sleeper, Sarah woke on Christmas morning to the sound of tiny footsteps padding down the stairs. The clock on her bedside table flashed 5:03. There was a squeal, swiftly followed by an elephant racing towards her room. Ben burst through the door and leapt on top of her.

'Mummy!' Bounce. 'Santa's been!' Bounce. 'Can we open our presents?' Bounce, bounce.

She managed to pull on a thick pair of socks to go with her fleecy, tartan, pyjamas before Ben dragged her downstairs. A few minutes later,

Ben, wearing a new knitted bobble hat and a pirate eyepatch, was munching on a decapitated chocolate Santa. He tipped packet after packet of Lego over the carpet, paying no attention to any instructions. *Just like his dad*, Sarah thought as a wave of sadness washed over her. 'What are you building?'

'A hospital, so you can save even more lives. That's you.' Ben pointed at a white plastic stormtrooper character. He wriggled close to her for a cuddle, clutching the stormtrooper in his fist, then slid off the sofa to play with his new toys.

She took the opportunity to make a coffee, wading through a sea of wrapping paper on the way to the kitchen. Mug in one hand she breathed in the aroma and leant back against the kitchen table to watch her son, grinning from ear to ear, play in the next room.

After a breakfast of mince pies and orange juice, the next few hours were lost to some serious Lego construction work. 'I'm sorry, I'd love to stay and play, but I have to go to work. Granny is coming around soon to look after you and we're going to have a big Christmas dinner tomorrow instead.'

Her phone buzzed; it was Mandy.

*Happy Xmas, Doc!*

She typed a quick reply and put the phone down. It pinged again straight away.

*By the way, Doctor Rae was asking after you.*

A string of winking emojis filled the rest of the message.

So much had changed in the past year and Ben was right, it was time to grab the present.

# Inside Out by KA Richardson

Everywhere seemed to have sparkly Christmas lights twinkling, people smiling and rushing along on their quests to purchase every gift available for their loved ones. Paul sighed loudly – he hated the bright lights and the amount of people filling the city at this time of year. There was a time he loved Christmas but that felt like a lifetime ago now.

He could barely focus on keeping it together, let alone braving the crowds to shop. Not that he had anyone to shop for.

Paul sighed again and rubbed a calloused hand over his eyes – deep blue eyes that swam with pain and frustration. He'd given up wanting to be normal ages ago. He was happiest outside with his blankets and the den he had in the park at the bottom of Princes Street in Edinburgh.

*Someone else will be in that den now – it's too well built for there not to be.*

Paul twisted in his seat, pissed off at the amount of anger he felt at someone else being in his den – it was his, built with his own two hands. It was well hidden too – only a select few people knew where it was.

*Then why be angry – they won't have moved in – they're your friends.*

The voice in his head made sense for once – but he still struggled to let go of the anger. It was like it was a permanent fixture now, deep down inside where the feelings had the chance to grow and fester. He was good at hiding it – years of practice meant his temper didn't blow at every opportunity.

*But damn, I feel close to it all the time.*

PTSD the doctors had said way back when he first returned from Afghanistan. He'd seen things he knew he would never talk about – not to anyone. But especially not to a shrink who'd never seen a day of combat in her perfect little life. The woman he'd been allocated 'to help him deal with his emotions and anger' on his return from that godforsaken country was always close to the front of his mind.

She was gorgeous in a girl-next-door kind of way. Long brown hair that curled naturally – she mostly wore it tied up. Tanned skin with a small mole on the side of her cheek, just where the wonderful Marilyn Monroe had hers, and a killer smile that knocked his socks off at every opportunity. He'd gone to two months' worth of sessions and eventually realised that he was falling for her without knowing anything about her. She was the epitome of professionalism – would never have crossed the line into that forbidden area of doctors seeing their patients.

So, to deal with it – like she was teaching him to do – he stopped going. His mobile rang several times, but he ignored it. Then his phone was stolen, so it was no longer a problem. He had the money to buy a new one – his bank account was OK looking for someone who lived in a den in the park. But he'd rather give the money away than spend it himself. Two-thirds of his monthly army pension went anonymously to one of the best homeless charities in Edinburgh. He knew first-hand how much they did and how much they relied on donations like his. Even he used their services from time to time – because even though he was used to being on the streets and preferred it to being inside, occasionally he needed a hot meal or a bed for the night.

The only reason he was thinking of her now was because he'd seen her at the hospital while he was a patient. Scowling, he rubbed his chest, and a sharp stab of pain reminded him why he was in this grotty bedsit in the first place. *Still can't believe I let him close enough to stab me. I must be losing it.*

Glancing around, he felt his chest tighten as the walls started to move and close in on him. Paul gritted his teeth, focussing on one item in the room as *she'd* given instructions to – the kettle didn't move – it stayed on the counter and remained still. Just like the room did. Slowly, he managed to unclench his jaw and draw in a shaky breath. Panic attack averted – this time.

*That goddamn tiny room, with its shitty clay and brick walls. No light. The constant dripping of the water in the corner.*

Paul's breath caught in his throat and his chest tightened instantly with no warning this time. He gasped for breath, but it was like his throat was frozen closed. He stared at the kettle, willing it to stay still as the walls moved again. His perception altered and the walls became a dirty brown colour – large breeze blocks overtook the faded paint and wallpaper. And in seconds, he was back inside his own personal hell.

*Faint voices outside the tiny room filtered in – Paul listened intently, only able to make out certain words of the Pashto language – 'prisoner' and 'water'. Were they going to bring him water? Or take him to their torture room. Both options made Paul shudder. He couldn't count the number of days he'd been here – the door to the tiny room was thick and stopped all light coming in. The steady drip of water in the corner by the door never ceased. It made it hell to sleep. Which he knew was what they preferred – exhaustion could make people more pliable.*

*Paul's hands were tied behind his back, had been since he'd been thrown in this hole. His shoulders had a constant ache that never let up. Actually, all of him ached – every single bone and muscle. Dried blood accumulated all over his face but especially under his nose and at the corners of his mouth. His lips were cracked and dry. His tongue swollen from lack of fluid. He would have drunk from the drip had he not been chained to a ring in the stone floor by his feet – the chain had just enough give to get him near the dripping, but not close enough to drink. Yet another torture technique. He knew all this – he'd been trained with the best to withstand everything the Taliban could throw at him. But now, being cooped up in this hole with his team God knows where, Paul felt more alone than he ever had before.*

*The door flung open, making him jump and jar his aching body once more.*

*Two men entered, both dressed in traditional garb of perahan tunban and a lungee on their heads. Paul groaned inwardly as he realised one of the men was Ahman Sakhi – Sakhi was on the intelligence his team had been provided prior to their mission. And he took great pleasure in trying to get Paul to talk.*

*It hadn't worked before however, and it wouldn't work this time. Paul steeled himself for pain as he was unlocked from the ring on the floor and dragged from the tiny cell.*

**\*\*\*\***

Dr Marcia Robinson glanced around the exterior to the building containing six bedsits – she was only visiting one, but the graffiti on the walls outside, and the fact the communal entrance door stood wide open in the dead of winter, gave her a hint as to what to expect inside.

Her nose crinkled as she entered, the smell of urine permeating the air. She made her way past the two ground floor bedsits then up the stairs to the next floor.

Pausing on the landing, she took in the hand-painted door numbers of the two doors either side of her. Choosing the one numbered '4', she knocked lightly.

No response.

She glanced back down the stairs, half expecting someone from the hospital to catch her doing something she really shouldn't be doing. Taking the allocated address from the NHS systems was frowned upon though she knew it was explainable. She wanted to check on a past patient and see how he was doing.

It had absolutely nothing to do with the fact she couldn't get the man out of her head and hadn't been able to since he'd left her waiting for him to attend his session in her office. It had even less to do with the chiselled features of his face, the body of pure steel, and the haunted dark-blue eyes that held control and emotion all at the same time. *Yeah right, keep lying to yourself.*

She sighed as she knocked again, louder this time.

Still no reply.

*Now you know it would be wrong to try the handle — it's already wrong making excuses to see him.*

Ignoring the voice of reason echoing round her brain, she tried the door handle and was surprised as it slowly opened.

'Paul, it's me, Marcia — umm I mean Dr Robinson. I just wanted to…' Pausing she saw him in the seat by the window, staring into space and not even aware she was there. Pain rippled across his face in waves — but he never let out a sound. She needed to be careful, she knew that. She wanted to rush over to him and pull him out of whatever he was seeing – but if she did that, he could very likely forget who and where he was and act in response to whatever flashback he was experiencing.

Her heart tugged as he gasped and ground his teeth together.

Knowing the only option was to bring him out slowly, she knelt in front of him, taking his big hands in hers, and started speaking softly.

**\*\*\*\***

*Paul gasped for breath as the filthy towel over his face flooded with water that had nowhere to go but into his mouth – he coughed, wondering if this would be the time they let him drown. He knew from experience that struggling was futile but still tried to thrash his head to the side to get rid of the water. Panic threatened to overwhelm – despite his training this would be an awful way to die. Suddenly the towel was ripped off his face and he was shoved into a more upright position. Gasping, each breath hurt as it battled with the water in his lungs and windpipe – he coughed again, throwing up what little there was in his stomach. His vomit hit Sakhi's shoes and he flinched, waiting for the violent response he knew was coming. Sakhi didn't disappoint – his fists flew at Paul's face in quick succession, and from the crunch that echoed round his head, and the blood that pooled under his tongue, he knew he'd lost another tooth.*

'Paul – everything's going to be OK. I need you to come back to me.'

*What the hell? Is that Dr Robinson's voice floating in the air? It makes no sense. I didn't even know her when I was here.* Still, the thought was enough to penetrate the flashback and make him think of something else, albeit for a second. That was all it took for the flashback to drag him back.

*Grimacing, he took another punch off Sakhi, felt his eye swell almost instantly. Through gritted teeth he uttered, 'Fuck... you.' Sakhi grabbed Paul's*

269

*cheeks in his bony fingers and gripped hard, knowing he'd be pressing the exact place one of his punches had landed.*

*'Fuck me? Fuck you – I have you here. I caught one of the stupidest men trying to catch me. And he spends his time in a hole – or in here with me. I could have killed you days ago. You know that. But you've yet to tell me what I want to know. So, I'll ask again – once more. Then Guhlam over there will be cutting the information from you while you squeal like a pig.' Paul understood every word – but glared at Sakhi through his one open eye.*

*'No idea what you just said, but it sounded pretty girly. Were you trying to turn me on?'*

*Sakhi made a strangled noise and launched at Paul – punching him over and over. Paul felt his consciousness start to slip – and he welcomed the incoming blackness. Nothing could touch him when he wasn't there anymore.*

'Paul – I need you to come back to me. This is just a flashback – it can't hurt you. Not anymore. You're safe.'

Marcia's voice drifted through his mind again, this time feeling stronger. If he didn't know better, he'd swear her hands were on his arms. He could almost feel the warmth of her breath on his face. Which was ridiculous considering the only time her breath had ever been that close was in his dreams.

The hairs on his arms lifted – responding to what felt like her fingers lightly stroking him. *This isn't real – no way this can be happening.* Paul felt himself pulling further out of the flashback and blinked, focussing his eyes.

Marcia came into view, her dark curly hair surrounding her face like an angel's halo. His fingers reached out of their own accord, caressing her soft cheeks which also felt real. Paul was confused. He'd never had a flashback containing the good doctor. Not once. But it couldn't be happening. He had a strong mind, but he wasn't strong enough to make her appear at whim – didn't even believe in all that crap, really.

He caught a flash of something in her eyes – something he hadn't seen in many years. Desire. He wanted to move towards her, capture her mouth with his. It was almost like an overwhelming need. *But this isn't real – she's not really here.*

It felt real though – through battling with himself, he slowly leaned forward, pausing millimetres from her lips. *I could swear I feel her breath on my lips.*

Slowly, he captured her imagined mouth with his own, his tongue sweeping across her bottom lip, coaxing her into allowing him access. *Fuck this feels so real. What the hell?* She tasted like he knew she would, undertones of honey and coffee sent his mind reeling. Her skin was soft under his fingers, and he moved them round, curling them into the thick brown waves that surrounded her face. *So fucking real. If this is what fantasies are, then bring them on.*

**\*\*\*\***

Marcia held onto Paul's arms as if her life depended on it. She knew she needed to stop the kiss; it wasn't right. She was taking advantage surely. But he tasted of caramel – the kiss drew her in, and she couldn't help but sigh against his lips. His arm muscles were toned and taut – and without thinking, she pushed herself further towards Paul.

She couldn't drag herself away from the one time in her life she'd actually get to experience a kiss that knocked all the wind out of her. She hadn't even believed they existed until now. It was all crap that people wrote in romance novels or showed on the big screen. It wasn't real... it couldn't be. But that's exactly what it felt like – electricity sparked between the two of them, and the deeper he kissed her, the more she yearned for more. It was like a drug.

Eventually, after what felt like hours, she forced herself to register her thoughts. Paul didn't need this – whatever *this* was. He needed support and guidance.

Pulling back further, she broke the kiss, feeling the loss immediately. Her breath shook as she drew a breath in, and she stared at him, unable to speak.

'Marcia? Is this real? You can't be sitting here in front of me. I'm going mad – now I'm talking to an empty room about a kiss that never happened even though it rocked my world. What the hell is going on?!'

Paul closed his eyes and rubbed both hands across them, then they opened slowly, and surprise flittered across as he realised she was still there. Tentatively he reached out and ran his fingers down her cheek. It made her shiver, every nerve ending tingling in response. She had to respond – she knew that. He thought he was going mad and that she wasn't really there. But damn if his touch wasn't distracting.

Putting her hand over his on her cheek, she said, 'I'm here – for real. I saw you in the hospital last week and wanted to check on you. But when I knocked you didn't answer – I was... worried... so I tried the handle and realised you were in the middle of a flashback. I'm sorry – I should have stopped the kiss, I know that. You were in a vulnerable position, and I shouldn't have taken advantage of you like that.'

'Taken advantage? I thought you weren't real. I should never have kissed you. That was me taking advantage – thinking you were my every fantasy come to life. I'm sorry you caught me in a flashback – it was a... tough one.'

'Will you please let me refer you to someone to talk to? Dr Wilson can help – he served too, understands what you're going through. It's ruled your life for long enough, don't you think?' She kept her voice soft and neutral on purpose, knowing from experience that this suggestion didn't always go down very well.

She could see Paul turning her words round in his mind – *he probably thinks I'm a bitch now. Soft and slow was the plan, Marcia, not throw all your hoops in the ring at once. He's got your brain addled.*

'I don't mean to imply that you're not coping – I know you're coping as best you can. When you stopped your sessions with me, I felt like we had been making some progress. But you obviously felt very differently, and I shouldn't have assumed. I'm sorry if my actions made you feel like therapy wasn't for you.'

'You? You didn't make me feel like therapy wasn't working, Doc, trust me. It was more what I wanted to work and had no chance of doing that impeded my progress.'

'Do you aim to be cryptic or does it come naturally?' Marcia smiled at him, suddenly conscious that her hand still covered his on her cheek. It felt intimate and like it belonged there, and when she moved her hand, he withdrew his, leaving her feeling bereft.

'I've been dreaming of kissing you like that since the first time I walked into your office. I had to stop the sessions because I wanted to kiss you like that and do a whole lot more and it was getting tougher to try to hide it. You didn't and don't need a broken man like me – you deserve so much better. And it's not fair for me to put anyone through me having flashbacks, or the anger that I have inside. It gets… tough to handle sometimes. Takes a lot of control. More than I have I think.'

'And yet you've managed to keep it in check as far as I know? Surely that alone means you're coping better than you think you are. Will you speak to Dr Wilson? Even just once – he might be able to give you some insights you're not aware of. Whatever you went through, he is someone you can talk to. And he's not a stalker who goes to her ex-patient's address in the hopes of catching a glimpse of the man who's been in her dreams since he first walked into her office.'

Marcia moved her hands and rested them on his forearms. 'I shouldn't have come here; I was pushing every limit there is by doing so. But I needed to see you, to know if you were OK. Hell, maybe it's me who needs to speak to Dr Wilson, because never in my life, have I ever done anything like this before. I saw you in the hospital and my world stopped spinning. Which is the weirdest stalkerish thing anyone ever said because I barely know you. Yet I *know* you if that makes sense. You don't deserve what happened to you over there – you never did. No one does. At the session you missed, I already had the referral letter typed up ready to pass to you. I knew back then that I couldn't be your therapist – because I didn't want to treat you. I just wanted you. All of you, as a whole package.'

'But I'm broken… I can't even stay inside four walls without having flashbacks.'

Paul sounded heartbroken – and in that second, she made the decision to disclose something she rarely spoke to anyone about anymore, knowing he needed to hear it. 'I'll let you into a little secret – I hate walls. I hate houses and buildings. I spend a lot of time outside – even do some sessions with patients in parks or whatever. Something happened when I was a child that made me terrified when I was inside. It still does – and I'll tell you about it one day soon.'

'But the point is, we've all got things we're dealing with – every one of us has some proverbial skeleton in the closet. But we'll all just keep trying – it's how we're programmed. The difference between us and some other people, is we're at least willing to try to get past our fears and history. We're trying not to let them control us. Some people can, and some can't but learn to adapt. Like you being in this bedsit since your release a week ago – you hate it, hate the feelings it invokes, but you know your stab wound needs to heal so you're doing it. That makes you strong, Paul Cavanagh – you are *not* broken or damaged. We're all just held together with bits of tape and plaster trying to get along in this crazy world. It's just how it is.'

**\*\*\*\***

Paul sat back in his seat, thinking about her words. They did make sense – he knew some men and women who'd returned and fallen headfirst into a bottle of Jack, or wandered the streets looking for something to numb the pain and flashbacks. He'd never done that – but he didn't blame the people that did. He understood it fully. Sometimes it was easier to give up control and force the pain away.

Could she be right? Am I strong enough to get through this? I'm still here and kicking – which is more than can be said for Sakhi and Guhlam – his team had taken those bastards out when they'd finally arrived to drag him from the hellhole that he hated. Even the army, when they'd discharged him on medical grounds, had done so with honours. He was offered everything they could offer support wise but hadn't been ready to face any of his fears. *Maybe being here in this shitty bedsit is my chance to turn it around. Maybe it's time to face it all head on and talk to someone who understands.*

'Can you put the referral in for me to see Dr Wilson? Or do I have to speak to someone else to do it?'

The smile Marcia beamed at him made him even more sure he was doing the right thing. It wasn't living when you muddled through without acknowledging the fears and lack of control – or the bad dreams that invaded your sleep. Maybe, with help from Dr Wilson, he'd be able to start living and not just try to muddle through each day. And maybe, sometime in the future, when his head was on a little straighter, he'd be able to support other people. That felt like a long way off, but it was still a possibility.

'I'm not saying it'll be easy – therapy never is. I do have experience from both sides but talking helps. And if you don't object, maybe I can support you too, in a different way. Not in an official capacity, but as a friend. We can go for coffee or dinner. Talk about normal things that people talk about. It might help us both see there's more to life than walls and open spaces.'

'There already is – I've not kissed anyone in seven years. My girlfriend at the time dumped me when I got back from Afghanistan – I get it, I was angry all the time. I couldn't be not angry – I shouted, threw things in the house. I scared her – I know that now. It was never aimed at her, but she witnessed it. And it was bad. She did the right thing by leaving me. You coming here today feels like fate, and I've never been a believer in things like that. But that's what it feels like to me. If you hadn't come over today, I'd have come out of the flashback, cursed more and then probably would have left the bedsit and not looked back. Now – because of you – I feel a little less angry and more ready to deal. Because if I do all that, I can see a future. You might be in it; you might not be. But long-term, I have a sliver of hope that it can change, that I can change. I hope you realise that. And I do want you in my future, just to be clear. As a friend yes, but later on, when my head is a bit straighter, maybe we can look at more than friends.'

'I think that sounds like a good idea. Friends first definitely. I want to get to know you properly. If it doesn't work in the future then fine, we'll deal with it. For now, though, here's the referral for Dr Wilson – he's already agreed to see you. Said to ring and he'll fit you in next week. I hope that wasn't too presumptuous of me?'

Paul smiled. 'Nope – not presumptuous. I'm grateful. Thank you.'

He leaned forward and kissed her lightly on the cheek. 'Friends are allowed to kiss on the cheek, aren't they?'

'Absolutely,' said Marcia softly, running her fingers down his arm lightly in response.

**\*\*\*\***

Three weeks later, Paul exited Dr Wilson's office. He'd just finished his fifth session and it had been helpful – he had no doubts he would continue to go. Dr Wilson had been straight with him from the start – he'd served. He'd seen similar things to what Paul had – he'd lost people. He was honest too – told Paul he still had occasional flashbacks and that he had learned to accept them as part of his own recovery. Any unease Paul had felt at the start had soon dissipated.

He knew nothing would be fixed overnight – it wasn't possible. And Dr Wilson had indicated it would likely take months. There was a lot more work to do. But for the first time in what felt like forever, Paul felt he had a purpose. The walls felt a little further set apart and didn't close in as quickly.

And he felt less inside out.

Now he needed to see Marcia. Again.

A faint blush tinged his cheeks at the thought of her. The friend stage was still ongoing. They saw each other most days, and she was the only person he texted on an evening to say goodnight to.

They had a formal dinner booked at a seafood restaurant in the city centre.

For the first time in years, the Christmas lights held joy for Paul. He felt like his eyes were finally open and taking in the vibrancy of the city at this time of year. He passed the markets on Princes Street, inhaling the smells of the food on offer before heading up Frederick Street and onto Rose Street. The evening had drawn in fast and it was dark – there was a crispness to the air that smelled of snow. And why shouldn't it snow – Christmas was only two days away now. He found himself longing for a white Christmas and for a second felt like he was ten years old again.

He entered the restaurant and glanced around, spotting Marcia seated by the open fire, the glow of which surrounded her with a flickering orange hue. The room was tastefully decorated for Christmas – gold and white tinsel and baubles throughout with a magnificent tree next to the bar.

Paul couldn't wait any longer – he leant across the table, surprising her by capturing her lips with his. He let it linger a little longer than was socially polite, then withdrew, sitting down opposite her and flashing her a smile. It was only their second real kiss, and he knew it wasn't the fireplace making her cheeks grow pinker.

Twisting, he removed his coat and pulled a small wrapped box from his inside jacket pocket.

'I know it's not Christmas for a couple of days, but I wanted you to have this.'

Grinning, she passed him a wrapped box of about the same size from her handbag.

'Ditto. Let's open them together.'

They both unwrapped the paper carefully and lifted the lid on identical boxes. Inside both, was a front door key.

'Great minds think alike.' Paul grinned. 'I got my flat keys yesterday and wanted you to have your own.'

'Ditto re the key — and for the record, if you hadn't kissed me when you entered, I was planning on doing the same. Now let's eat, then I'll treat you to a hot chocolate from the market stand. And a trip on the big wheel if you'd like.'

'I like — nothing could be more perfect that being inside while outside.'

# Penance by Jane Risdon

The man in the red suit with the white beard sighed as the last child accepted their gift and ran back to its mother, squealing with delight. Spreading a little joy was all very well but after four hours his face ached from smiling and his tolerance levels were at almost zero. Why on earth did kids, almost without exception, feel the need to tug at his beard, he'd no idea, but it was getting beyond a joke. Prematurely white, his beard and hair were his own and the constant tugging was getting too much. It was his last shift in the store for this year. He hoped he'd never have to come back again, but somehow, deep down, he feared he would. He had kept returning ever hopeful that he might see him – see them – again. But so far, he had never.

Gabriel changed into his street clothes, hung his red suit in the locker marked 'Father Christmas', and headed for the staffroom to say goodbye to his colleagues and wish them – without much conviction – a Happy Christmas and New Year, saying he'd see them all again next year, as he had done for the last five. He didn't want to stop for mince pies and mulled wine, he wanted to get home to have a quick shower and grab something to eat before going out again.

It was dark when he parked. Turning the headlights off he sat for a few moments taking in his surroundings, noting every tree and hedge, listening to the ticking of his engine and the sounds of various nocturnal creatures scurrying around in the deserted lane. After a while he reached for a duffel bag behind his seat, removed a torch from the glove compartment and quietly opened the door. He stood in the darkness, alert. No sounds of human activity reached him as he gently closed the car door. Satisfied he was alone he slung the bag over his shoulder,

The former reserve soldier moved slowly, every nerve tuned, ready to react should the need arise — old habits die hard. Silently he stepped through a break in the bushes beside him and crossed a narrow ditch into a small field, back on familiar ground once again. Luckily there weren't any farm animals to worry about as he moved quickly towards his objective.

****

The large white-washed Georgian house loomed ahead in the moonlight, silent and brooding. It had been empty some years but remained in good condition thanks to the monthly administrations of an estate management company hired by the absent owner who, Gabriel knew they believed, lived overseas and so far had never returned, thus enabling him to come and go and use the house when necessary, unobserved, ever mindful of neighbours across the lane. He supposed they'd be home entertaining visitors this time of year.

Gabriel remained cautious even though he knew an inspection was not due for another three weeks. But you could never be too sure; there had been talk of squatters in the area and the last thing he needed was to bump into any of them. Creeping along the wall of the house he made his way to the tradesman's entrance. Hesitating, listening, he eased the key from his pocket and gently teased it into the lock, turning it quickly. The door opened silently on oiled hinges and he stepped into the large, now dated, kitchen. He scanned the room for any signs of life, listening intently, before shutting the door behind him.

The kitchen looked the same as it had done on his last visit. He moved silently through the corridor to the downstairs rooms double-checking he was alone. No one had been and nothing had changed. He didn't bother checking the basement because it had long ago been blocked up and was completely inaccessible. He ran effortlessly up the grand staircase and quickly entered every room. Satisfied, he began his ascent to the attic floor – the old playroom.

**\*\*\*\***

He didn't have to wait long. He'd no sooner settled himself in the battered armchair next to the box of children's toys when she arrived. She stood gazing around the cobwebbed room and sighed as her brimming eyes found the toy box. Gabriel watched patiently. She needed to drink in her surroundings before speaking. After a while she nodded, acknowledging him at last.

'You came.'

'Of course, you knew I would.'

'I suppose so.' She smiled briefly and sat on the large wooden chest opposite Gabriel.

'I was almost late.' His eyes never left hers as she stared at him, her face determined and her jaw tight. 'Things overran. I've been working all afternoon and…'

'It's Christmas Eve. You always worked Christmas Eve. Every year it was the same. Perhaps you should've asked for at least one Christmas off to spend with us, and then you'd have had more time for the most important things,' she admonished. 'The reserves always came first.'

'You know I never meant to be late, something came up, don't you think I'd have – I mean – if I'd had any idea…' He couldn't stand her tone of voice and the look on her face each time they'd met since – so cold, so accusatory, but with stinging put-downs made to strike at his heart, his conscience. Once it had been different, her voice had been… he sighed, stopping the thought. That was long ago.

'No matter.' She ran a hand through her thick, dark, shining hair. 'You know what has to be done.' She rose and stood beside him. He smelled the familiar scent of roses and for an instant he was transported to another time – a lifetime ago. Gabriel shook his head, not wanting to go there just now.

'Do everything the same as before, but this time don't fail, just do it!' Her voice had an edge of steel. 'That place, that room…' she shuddered, 'this time, don't let us down.'

'I've never deliberately let you down, you have to believe that. I try to try but I just can't seem to make it happen. I need to make it happen too, trust me.'

The young woman's eyes closed tightly, briefly, and she winced. Nodding slowly, she placed her hand on his shoulder. 'Of course. I can trust you. I always did, Gabriel, if only you'd…'

Gabriel waited, but she didn't continue. She knew she didn't need to.

'I know, if only I'd had taken the call, had come right away – do you think I can ever forget, forgive myself?' His voice rose with emotion and he closed his eyes as the memories tormented his mind. 'Do you think you can ever forgive me?' Her hand left his shoulder and he opened his eyes to implore her, but she'd gone.

Gabriel didn't linger, couldn't bear to remain in their former home any longer. Every time it got harder.

He opened the kitchen door and crept outside. Waiting, his ears tuned and his eyes vigilant, he closed the door, turned the key and replaced it in his pocket. He'd sat for some time after she'd left, thinking about the past and how things might have been, if only – he sighed heavily – his life had become one big *if only*.

**\*\*\*\***

Parking the car some half a mile from his destination Gabriel walked purposefully, keeping to the shadows where possible. External Christmas lights decorated some terraced houses he passed, others displayed twinkling trees in festive windows and the sounds of voices and laughter drifted outside into the otherwise silent night. Gabriel hated Christmas and everything to do with it – Christmas meant only one thing to him now, and celebration wasn't any part of it.

It was gone midnight by the time he reached his objective. He stopped, checking his surroundings with an expert eye before entering the overgrown garden. Exposed tree roots and low-hanging branches caused some difficulty as he ventured towards the run-down cottage. Once, he nearly twisted his ankle on a broken paving slab, but he kept moving forward. His mind on the task ahead.

The cottage was in darkness and not showing any apparent signs of occupation. But it was occupied, he knew it was. As always, he ventured around the building from the right-hand side, following a narrow, broken brick path between the house and the line of leylandii trees marking the boundary between it and another property. He poked his head around the corner of the cottage, ears alert, eyes watchful, before moving to the French windows and peering hard through the grime. The room inside was deserted, but it showed some signs of recent occupation; a mug and plate on a side table, next to a battered sofa. He couldn't see much more. No lights were on anywhere in the house. All was still. Expectant almost.

Behind him at the end of the garden he spotted the large brick-built garden shed. He moved towards it on the balls of his feet, ready for flight if the need arose. Gabriel didn't want to engage with his enemy outside. He'd rather take cover at any signs of life and try again a little later – the element of surprise was all.

He scouted the shed and noted the windows were still blacked out. A padlock hung on the door, but it wasn't locked. His target was inside he was sure. Squatting on the ground he removed gloves from his bag and put them on, reaching inside once more for his weapon, all the time listening and evaluating his surroundings and the building he was about to enter. He prepared himself for what he imagined was to come.

Briefly, his mind went back to another Christmas Eve long ago, when his friend dressed as Father Christmas entertained his Christmas party; when their neighbour's children joined in the fun and party games. He'd loved watching the wonder in their little faces with their bright eyes. Their parents stood in the kitchen chatting and laughing until their children tired and one by one they drifted home. Later he'd tiptoed into his children's bedroom and placed gift filled sacks on the ends of their beds before sneaking back downstairs to enjoy a last drink or two and mince pies with his wife. Content in the bosom of his family. Unaware of the danger they'd invited into their home.

Gabriel took a deep breath as he stood up. Cautiously he lifted the padlock away from the door handle and gently eased the door open. It didn't creak. The air smelled of damp and kerosene – garden shed smells. The atmosphere was thick, his chest heaved at the lack of air. Taking his torch from his pocket he slowly moved the beam around. There were the usual garden implements, which was ironic considering the state of the garden. But nothing had really changed – not in the five years he'd been returning.

The room had been soundproofed long ago. It had been used briefly for the occupant's drum practices and he could see, upon closer scrutiny, that there were still sound-deadening tiles on the walls and ceiling. He noticed the windows remained sealed airtight. Gabriel tripped on the slight incline in the floor. It was a large trapdoor with an inlaid handle flat against its surface.

The determined father bent down and traced his fingers around the edges of the trap door. He bent forward, his ear to the ground, and listened. Satisfied, he stood up and reached for the handle. Not long now.

**\*\*\*\***

Cool air wafted into his face as he gingerly descended the concrete steps. A dim light glowed at the bottom and Gabriel gripped his gun tighter as he prepared for whatever he'd encounter. As he stepped off the last step he stood still, attuned to the slightest sound or movement beyond the rooms on either side of him. Nothing was detectable but the hum of the machine bringing oxygen into the basement. He moved forward cautiously, his weapon in front of him, his nerves and senses highly tuned.

A Christmas tree, lights twinkling, caught his attention in a darkened corner of the larger room. A pile of wrapped gifts surrounded the base of the artificial tree. Decorations hung from the ceiling and adorned the walls. All very cosy and normal if it had been inside a home, but inside a basement? A home – his heart jolted at the realisation. It was a home, well, it resembled a home. A home he recognised. His home. Back when. Nothing had been forgotten, even the large piece of polished stone he'd given his wife who collected such trinkets from places they'd visited, had pride of place on the garland draped sideboard. He was dumbfounded. The last time he'd ventured inside none of this was here. In fact, for the last five years he'd never got any further than the bedrooms, so perhaps it had been like this all along, but how did he miss this room before?

A sudden, unconscious awareness shook him from his reverie, and he spun round, gun ready, and adrenaline pumping, before he'd heard any sound or detected the slight movement behind him.

The older man stared at him, uncomprehending, stunned for a few moments.

'You!' he whispered, 'it can't be.' His body shook with fear. 'How…?'

Gabriel took one look at the target and fired without thinking. The man dressed in red with a white beard dropped to the floor, his last words unspoken, his flaccid and expressionless face sporting a small hole

289

in the centre of his wrinkled forehead. Gabriel cursed himself, why did he do that?

Ignoring the prone figure at his feet Gabriel moved quickly. He hurried out of the room and without a second thought burst through the bedroom door now showing the little pink sign, 'Keep out, this is Kate and Sarah's room!'

The room was empty, the girls were gone. The bedside light cast shadows over the twin beds with identical rag dolls propped up upon the pink fairy decorated pillows. Two small dolls' prams waited at the ends of the beds, Christmas paper strewn across them where excited fingers had torn the paper off, just before Christmas Day had dawned.

Gabriel's heart tightened in his chest and terror coursed his veins as he ran to the larger bedroom. The door was slightly open and once more the room was unoccupied. He cried out in anguish, 'No, no, no!' He fell upon the bed and sobbed. He was too late, again. Forever doomed.

Grief-stricken Gabriel eventually looked for and found his wife's scribbled note which he knew would be on the bedside table. He didn't read it. He'd read it a thousand times before; he knew it off by heart.

*See you later, taking the girls to the Christmas Grotto at Beale's to see Frank who is Father Christmas this year, meet us there after 5pm, we love you xxxx. PS: for once don't disappoint us, don't be late, we can all get some dinner out!!*

But he had been late, he hadn't even listened to her phone message until much later. If he had he would've been there for them. Saved them. Now he'd killed the only person who knew, he couldn't believe what he'd just done. Despair gripped him.

**\*\*\*\***

A quiet moan came from the sitting room and Gabriel ran silently to the door and peered out. Another man was leaning over the prone figure, sobbing. Gabriel was shocked.

'I don't believe it, both of you!'

The man stiffened visibly and turned his head towards Gabriel. 'You!'

Gabriel raised his gun, but the man seemed unafraid.

The familiar man remained silent, glaring at the gunman. 'Well?' Gabriel moved closer. 'Where are they? Where is my wife and daughters?'

'Don't be stupid, you know where they are. You always ask the same questions and for some stubborn reason you refuse to accept the truth.' The man slowly stood up and pointed at Gabriel.

'You were too late, too late. You're always too late, always were.'

'I don't understand, I can't stand this anymore. I need to know. What have you done to them?'

'I haven't done anything, Gabriel, don't accuse me.' His former neighbour was indignant.

'Both of you! My family, our friends, welcomed you into our home and you abused our trust!'

'Don't accuse me. I tried, really tried, but he was sick, couldn't help himself.' The man pleaded, hands on his head.

'You knew? You tried? Why didn't you warn us, protect us, tell someone?' Gabriel screamed at the top of his voice. 'Prevented him, saved them!'

'I've watched him like a hawk all our adult lives, but I got stuck in traffic. I knew it was his shift, but Frank had already seen the girls when I arrived and because you hadn't shown up, he'd offered to take them all for dinner. I couldn't find them, so I came here. He always comes here when he wants to be with his friends…'

'You should've phoned me, called the police, done something – why didn't you?'

'Gabriel, he's my brother.' Frank's twin sobbed. 'You killed him; I can't believe it!'

'Where are they? What happened to them?' Gabriel jabbed the gun in Fred's chest. He thought he might as well kill him now that Frank was dead. 'You've watched me search for them every year, watched me disappoint her, let her down. How could you?'

'You're too late, always too late. It's too late.' Fred shook his head. 'She told Frank you never put her and the girls first, always working, always away; even over Christmas.'

'If you don't tell me where they are, I'll kill you too, I've nothing to lose. I can't stand this anymore, please, please.' Gabriel shook with emotion. 'I want to take them home, be a family again.'

Fred stared at his neighbour, visibly debating what he should do. His brother was a monster, he knew that, knew Gabriel's family weren't the only ones he'd 'entertained' in their late parent's home. He'd discovered his brother's secret long ago and had tried hard to protect Frank's 'chosen' ones. He'd succeeded more than failed, but Gabriel's wife and girls were close to Frank, had confided in him and they trusted him. Fred did all he could to protect them, but he had to protect his brother too. He'd been torn and tormented for years. He'd had enough.

'I told you long ago what happened, where they are,' he said eventually. 'You must remember.'

'I don't, I know I don't, tell me.' Gabriel pushed the gun harder into Fred's chest.

'Gabriel, you came here that first Christmas Eve and you found them, with Frank, remember?'

'No, I don't, I'm sure I've never found the girls, she makes me look every year, she trusts me to find them, but I never do. She sends me here every year, wants me to save them, but when I get inside the rooms are always empty. I can't keep letting her down. I can't.'

'You found them with Frank. They were dead, Gabriel, and I found you all.'

'No, they can't be, I see her, talk to her, she wants me to find her, she can't be dead.' Gabriel's heart ached. 'You found us? What did you do to help? I don't remember any of this.'

'I found you with them, Gabriel, Frank had killed you too. You were too late; I was too late.'

'Dead? Me? Are you crazy? If I'm dead how are you talking to me, how do I play Father Christmas every year hoping to find Frank? Don't talk rubbish, take me to my family, now!'

'Is that what you really want, Gabriel, to be with them?' Fred bit his lip. Thinking.

'I'll kill you if you don't.' Gabriel waved the gun.

'So be it,' said Fred as he grabbed the gun, firing at Gabriel's heart before his friend had time to react. 'So be it.'

Fred pulled his friend over his shoulder and took him into the bedroom and placed his body on the huge double bed, beside his wife and daughters. Reunited at last.

Closing the door quietly, Fred returned to the festive room where his twin lay dead and stretched out beside him, together once more. He prayed that this was the last time he'd have to repeat everything that happened, and he'd be able to rest in peace.

Fred hoped Gabriel's penitent ghost would at last be quieted – the father's quest to find his family finally over now he was back in the bosom of his family once more.

Finally, Fred's penance was done. His own spirit could rest at last. *He needed it to be over*, he thought, as he fired into his own heart, once more.

# New Year's Resolution by Robert Scragg

Sarah always said that whisky and depression weren't a good mixture, yet here he sits, with a healthy measure of the former in his glass and an unhealthy dose of the latter in his heart. Christopher's hand hovers over the drink, fingers clutching at the rim like the claw on a 'Grab a Toy' machine at the funfair. He closes his eyes. The echo of her voice, the memory of her perfume washes over him. He remembers fragments, not entirely sure if the warm glow is the whisky or reverie.

He smiles at the remembrance of a smile, catches the eye of the blonde at the corner of the bar. He looks away, worries that she might misinterpret. He stares instead at the inch-deep amber pond in his glass, watching the lights from the dance floor behind him scatter over the bar like a kaleidoscope.

A tap on his shoulder. Breathy whispering in his ear.

'Hey, handsome, fancy a dance?'

He manages another smile but doesn't turn to show it.

'Not tonight, sis, I've got a headache.'

'Some big brother you are. You're meant to protect me from the cavemen and their mating dances out there.'

He knows without looking that she's pouting, lips like pink pillows, big brown eyes a puppy would be proud of. He turns, finally, sees hope in her eyes, and then douses it.

'Maybe later.'

She scowls, aims a playful punch at his chest, fixes him with a steely glare.

'I'll hold you to that.'

He opens his mouth to speak, but she floats away, lost in the tide of people ebbing and flowing to the music. There won't be a *Later*, but he can't tell her that. How do you break it to your baby sister that you've decided you don't want to be here anymore?

*Not here.*

*Not anywhere.*

Rhetorical question, you don't of course. Why had he come then? How could he not? He curses the sentimentality that brought him here, but knows it was one final stop he had to make. Seeing her.

He is bound to her by a promise made a decade earlier, one they'd made to each other. She needed him here, so he came. That simple. For an instance the crowd parts like the Red Sea, and there she is. She sways in time to the beat, smiling, dancing through the rejection of the idiot who has stood her up tonight. The smile won't be there tomorrow; not when she finds out he…

He drains the glass in one gulp, blaming the sting of tears on the whisky fumes. He looks again, sees her hugging two girlfriends, their arms wrapped around her from both sides like the wings of a mother hen.

She is the one person he believes will truly miss him. Mum and Dad will play their part, dusting off masks of grief to wear, maybe even crying on cue. Sarah will… actually he has no idea how she'll react. With a sigh of relief probably, realising she escaped before he hit rock bottom.

He toys briefly with having one for the road. No time. He stands a little too quickly, a head rush of whisky and emotion make him steady himself against the bar, then he is moving. Beyond the bar, past the bobbing balloons that proclaim a 'Happy 2019'. His step falters. He should go back; say goodbye properly. Too late. He is outside now, walking past the line of punters shuffling impatiently in the queue, their plumes of breath fogging the night air.

No going back. It's better this way. He knows he had to get out of there before midnight; before the chimes drove total strangers into a hugging, handshaking frenzy. The thought of being overwhelmed by a tsunami of goodwill and losing his nerve scares him as much as what he's about to do. Perhaps even more.

These last twelve months, his very own *annus horribilis*, has broken him. Sarah's affair has washed away the foundations beneath an already fragile ego. It only needed a whisper of wind to finish the job, but the redundancy and debt that followed has toppled him like a Jenga tower, scattering any sense of belonging or purpose.

He is calm now. The feeling settled over him this afternoon when he made his decision to shuffle off the mortal coil. If only he could feel like this all the time, maybe things would be different. He looks up, sees the graceful arc of the Tyne Bridge hovering over the river like a half-open eye. The water glistens where the moonlight slides over it.

Dark

Cold

Reptilian

People spill from doors of packed bars like stuffing from a couch. They barely spare him a glance as he passes; the booze dulls their senses as it lifts their spirits. A looping climb up Sandhill and Dean Street, a short walk to the old Swan House roundabout, and he'll be on the home stretch.

Something moves in the gloom as he approaches the foot of the bridge. He slows, sees the shadow take form as his eyes adjust. Clumps of darkness morph into legs, arms, and a head bowed under the weight of a tangled bush of hair. A man is slumped against the wall, one hand wrapped around what looks like Asda Smart Price lager, half its contents pooled by his feet. A tumble of drunken words spill out, knitted into meaningless babble.

'Pleash… C'n you… Ahjustneed… Pleash'

A hand reaches out to him. He adjusts his course, angling away. If he had any change, he would give it. It's not as if he'll have much use for it after tonight. He's almost past when he realises his mistake. Passing headlights drive back the shadows for an instant. As they do, he sees it. Spilled lager glints, laced with something darker. Something crimson. Blood. He closes the gap with quick steps, bending down on one knee like a suitor.

The man senses him, tries to lift his head. Words spill out again, a mumbled mantra, but this time he hears them for what they are. Not a plea for money, but one for help. He's asking for the police.

'It's an ambulance you want, mate,' Christopher says as their eyes meet. He sees the source of the blood, a ragged gash over the eyebrow. It has cascaded down, coating half his face like a bloodied Phantom of the Opera. His nose is squashed like silly putty. Someone has well and truly done a number on him.

'Poleesh. Swines schtole my lager. Get the poleesh. Ahm pressin' charges.'

The man manages a grin, or a grimace. Either way he's one tooth short, and those that are present and correct glint pale yellow, like old ivory with every passing set of headlights. They stare at one another, then the unthinkable happens. Christopher laughs. It comes out like a bark, fast and loud. He laughs in spite of the absurdity of this situation; of his situation, or perhaps because of it.

Something about the fierce glare in the man's eyes, his prioritising the safe return of his booze over much needed medical attention, shakes a second laugh loose. The man joins in, but his disappears into a coughing fit that sounds like someone put gravel in a blender.

Christopher looks around, but selective blindness seems to be the order of the day as the world floats past without a glance. He digs in his pocket for his phone and makes a call. Twenty minutes is what the lady tells him in a voice that reminds him of his gran. She asks if he can wait with him until they get there. Does he have a choice? Of course, he does but he can hardly say no. He settles on the ground with his back against the wall. Keep him talking, they say. Ask him questions. So, he does. He asks if he can call anyone for him. The man starts talking and just doesn't stop.

Not all of it makes sense, the air turning blue whenever he remembers the great lager heist. Mostly though he talks about missing his daughter, and the grandson he's never met. Christopher checks his watch, the minute hand tiptoeing towards twelve. He can't stay. He won't stay. He needs to get up now, or risk losing his nerve. He tries to stand.

The man stops talking and starts to cry. Whether it's the thought of his grandson, or just general drunken melancholia, Christopher can't say, but the pitiful sound sends him sliding back down the wall.

He sits. Listens. Listens to a rambling sermon of how life kicks you in the balls every chance it gets. Of how it never used to be like this. Of a daughter forever young in her father's eyes because that's when his happiest memories of her were made, memories that even years of self-destruction cannot erase.

Twenty minutes turns into thirty, thirty into an hour. When the blue lights of the cavalry finally splash across the road, it's ninety minutes since the call. All the while Christopher asks one question over and over. Why the hell has this man not thrown in the towel years ago? The answer doesn't come until he watches them load him into the ambulance. Family. Through all the shitty times, he clung on to the hope that someday he'd find his way back to his.

'Can y'call mah daughter?' he hears him ask the paramedic.

'Let's get you patched up first, mate.'

Christopher watches the blue lights dancing fainter and fainter and resolves to call the hospital tomorrow and see how the man is.

Tomorrow… He's just made plans for a day that until that very second, did not exist for him.

He jumps as his phone vibrates. Alice's face fills the screen. Family. She's the only one he cares about, and he knows in that instant that he cannot leave her alone in the world, not tonight. Not ever.

He answers, voice thick with emotion. He tells her he's not far. Just had to get some air. On his way back now. He hasn't forgotten owing her a dance. He ends the call and starts walking. There's always a way back to family.

# Family Time by Graham Smith

As a cop, I spend half my life hunting people. Whether it's murderers, rapists, or the kind of scum who mug little old ladies, there's always someone to be found. Naturally, some are easier to find than others.

As a rule of thumb, the more serious the crime, the harder it is for us to find the person we're looking for. This of course only applies to those who know we're on their trail. Most criminals are stupid and therefore they're of the opinion that cops are stupid as well. This idiocy often means they're so arrogant and cocksure, they don't make any effort to hide themselves away. They think a sibling or cousin's house is a good place to hide. It's not.

My latest quarry isn't stupid, he's a thug, a rapist, and a full-blown alcoholic, but he isn't stupid. My life would be easier if he was.

The last known address I have for him is a bedsit on the edge of town. I knock on the door and look around at my frost-covered surroundings. Four doors along, one of the homeowners has gone postal with the Christmas lights and has sheathed, not just the house, but every available space in the garden with flashing decorations.

Each time I exhale, the cold air makes me look like I'm vaping. I want to stamp my feet to drum some heat, or even feeling into them. I don't though, the stamping may be taken as an act of aggression and, while the person I'm hunting is handy with his fists, he's a coward at heart and won't answer the door if he thinks there'll be any kind of confrontation.

I rap my knuckles against the chipped paintwork of the door and long for home. Home has a woman I love, two kids I adore, and warmth, blessed centrally heated warmth. From inside the house I hear someone yelling over the blaring of Slade. The volume is turned down half a fraction and I hear the sliding of bolts. The door opens enough to let a face fill the gap created by the security chain.

The face is curious, and haggard. There's drink imbued redness in the cheeks and a defeatist attitude in the hanging jaw and unkempt hair. The man who owns the face hasn't so much been kicked by life as used as its doormat.

Rheumy eyes assess me. They take in that my jacket isn't closed enough to hide my suit, or the tie with reindeers on it.

'Who are you? What do you want? Ain't got no money. Ain't got no debts, so if'n you're one of those bailiff fellers you can piss off. I don't own nobody nuthin.'

I'm surprised he hasn't recognised I'm a cop. Maybe he's a victim not a perpetrator. I explain who I am and who I'm looking for.

'That prick? He's long gone. From all account he got kicked out when he fell three months behind on his rent.'

I ask if there's a forwarding address for the man I'm after.

'Nope. Trouble that dickEven-head's caused me I'd be happy to give you it, but he's scarpered. There's many a bailiff asked for it too. You won't find him here, but when you do find him, I'll bet that he's either in debt or is sponging off some poor cow. That Sandi at number sixty-two, he was always tapping her up for a few quid. Would give her some sob story and she'd go running for her purse.'

I try a couple more questions but get the same whole-load-of-nothing answers.

I hadn't expected this to be easy, but I'll be delighted to be wrong. With option one exhausted I'm left with no choice. I have to try the second address on my list. This could be more than a little tricky. Mothers are protective creatures by nature and my quarry's mother was a notable handful. She'd been in regular contact with my colleagues over the years for crimes ranging from solicitation to petty theft, and back via handling stolen goods and a dozen other misdemeanours. She was one of those us cops joke would have their own parking space at the probation office as she's there so often.

Like her son, she's done time for aggravated assault and there is no telling what shape I'll find her in at 7.00 p.m. on Christmas Eve. Pissed and argumentative is my best guess. Although there is no love lost between her and her son, there is little chance she'll tell me where I could find him. Not only am I a cop. I'm the one who's stopped her from seeing her grandkids. She hates my guts on principle and despises me because of the personal.

Like I said, this was never going to be easy.

****

Deirdre's house, if you can call it that, is a mid-terrace ex-council property that was bought by a developer who gave it a basic tarting up and then rented it back to the council so they could home those who couldn't look after themselves.

Rose Avenue is full of houses that have the same story as Deirdre's. There's abandoned cars in front gardens, children's toys lie where they've been dropped, and there's not a garden path that isn't overgrown with weeds. The journey here hadn't been far enough that my car's heater had a chance to make a proper assault on the blocks of ice masquerading as my feet.

When I make my way up the path, there's an argument going on between the neighbours that would do Shane MacGowan and Kirsty McColl proud. I have to turn my head so they don't see my smile.

Deirdre's door opens and she stands there, arms folded, with her face harder than the prow of an Arctic icebreaker.

'The fuck do you want, dick-head?' A sneered scowl. 'You got fuck all on me or mine, 'cause we ain't done nowt. Haven't you and your lot done enough damage? It's months since I seen my grandchildren and that's all your fault, you pig bastard.'

As expected, Deirdre is full of Christmas spirit. Having said that, she hasn't slammed the door in my face, nor has she thrown anything except words at me, so this has gone a lot better than the last time I saw her.

I make sure I'm out of immediate reach as Deirdre is an equal opportunities fighter and hold my hands up in what's intended to be a placatory gesture.

'I'm not here to cause trouble. Not for you, not for you know who. It's him I'm looking for.'

'Are you after money? Good luck with that.' Her face took on an expression that on someone else would have been concern. 'The twins. They're OK, aren't they?'

As much as Deirdre is a troublemaking harridan, she loves her grandkids. Naturally this is in her own twisted way, she'd been caught using the twins to distract a store security guard while she'd helped herself to a range of goods; hence the high court injunction preventing her from seeing them.

'They're fine, this isn't that kind of visit.'

'Thank fuck.' Her face went back to gargoyle setting. 'So, what do you want him for?'

I tell her why I'm hunting her waste of space offspring. Her face softens as I talk, and for a moment or two, Deirdre shows me a human side I've never seen before.

After much thought, she looks at me with suspicion. 'Are you on the level, or is this a cop trick?'

'I'm on the level.'

I am too.

My hunt for Deirdre's son has nothing to do with my job. It is personal. Had I been hunting for him for professional reasons, I would have been able to use the police databases to help me with my search. I could have run his name through any number of programs and used my colleagues to help me find him.

As my reason for finding him is deeply personal, I can't do any of that. All police computers require a unique logon that identifies the user and searches are randomly checked. When I find my quarry, there's a fair chance things might get a little tasty, so I don't want my name associated with his as there'll only be one winner should a fight situation arise. I have a temper that I can keep buttoned down in the normal course of things. He, on the other hand, he has a way of pushing my buttons and bringing out the worst of me. I know that if he gets me riled and punches start getting thrown, I won't be able to stop until I've gone too far.

Deirdre gives me the kind of look which could terrify a rampaging elephant. 'If I tell you and it's a trick, I'll be right down to the station to make a formal complaint against you and then I'll be straight onto the press.'

I give her what I hope is a reassuring nod. 'That sounds fair to me. As I explained, Deirdre, I'm not doing this for me. I'd be quite happy to never see him again.'

Once again, she gives me a long assessing look. I'm shivering on the doorstep, but there's not even a hint of gooseflesh on the bare arms she has folded against her chest.

'He's staying in a place out Westside way. Don't know the address and don't care none about him. You'll like as not find him in one of the pubs in that area. If not, I can't help you any more than that.' Her eyes sharpen. 'Like you, I ain't doing nothing to help him.'

'Thank you.'

I mean it. Knocking on Deirdre's door was a gamble I never expected to pay off. I'd learned more than I ever expected to. Now it's time for me to uphold my end of the deal I'd struck with her.

Deirdre recites her mobile number when I ask for it, and I send her half a dozen pictures of the twins.

Tears sparkle her eyes when she looks at them.

She doesn't thank me, that would be far too great a step across the line that's drawn between cops and criminals, but the way her top lip wobbles before she slams the door in my face says everything. Those pictures will be treasured. If she can find the money to pay for it, she'll have them printed at a supermarket and mount them around her house.

**\*\*\*\***

Westside isn't what you'd call a salubrious estate. A charitable soul might use a term like *run-down*, an honest one would describe it as the seventh circle of hell. This is a place where few people who aren't housed on the estate dare to walk its streets alone. At the station, there's a strict warning about the estate and how we must never come here alone, and even when we do enter the estate, we need to have an Inspector level of authorisation so backup can be in place.

This is a part of town where the dispossessed and the never-hads congregate. There's tribal boundaries and no sense of community, yet the inhabitants of Westside will always band together against outsiders. And cops.

It's possible Deirdre has thrown me to the wolves by sending me here, yet Westside is also the kind of place where he'd fit right in, so it's equally probable that she was telling me the truth.

I park my car several streets from the edge of Westside and walk the rest. Whatever goes down here, I don't want my car being collateral damage if things go south for me.

The carrier bag thumps against my leg as I stride along the streets. I'm walking fast for multiple reasons. One: it's cold and the exercise is warming. Two: the less time I spend in Westside, the happier everyone will be. Three: There are low whistles emanating from unseen places. I know these are warnings. I'm a cop and the kids hanging out in hidden cubbyholes will all have made me as such. Two things can happen when the locals learn of a cop's intrusion into their territory; either everyone will go to ground, or an unwelcoming committee will be formed. Neither of these options will help my cause.

The first pub on my list is a dive called Borderlands. Like any border, it's the home of many a territorial dispute.

Every pub on the Westside estate is pretty much the same. Rough places with bars on the windows and barflies on the seats. As I approach Borderlands, a shape emerges from the shadows. Maybe seventeen at most. Not sober. Or clean from drugs. Thin legs are encased in fishnet tights and topped by a miniskirt. She pulls her jacket open to reveal her upper body. I keep my eyes on hers.

'You looking for some company?'

She's either so far out of it, or so new to her profession she hasn't made me as a cop. Neither of these traits will help her going forward. I shake my head and keep walking. I have no interest in the girl or her journey to this point in her life. That's for another day. If she had three square meals a day for a month and some happiness in her life, she'd be pretty. As she is now, she's on the top of a slippery slope looking for anything that'll stop her downward trajectory.

I push the door to Borderlands open and step inside. The air is thick with cigarette smoke and there's nary a sign of where it's coming from customer wise. A barman has a cigar stump poking from his mouth, but it's not lit. In one corner an old man is holding a whisky glass like it's the last life ring on the *Titanic*, in another a woman sleeps, her body upright, mouth hanging open and dripping drool onto a faded Christmas jumper.

There're no other patrons in sight and that doesn't surprise me. Even for a place like Westside, Borderlands is the bottom of the proverbial barrel.

I leave and make my way on to the Tavern.

Even fifty yards away I hear the Christmas music bellowing out from the Tavern. Noddy Holder is proclaiming the time of year and he's got company from several lusty, if not tuneful, voices.

I make my way inside and see a crowded bar filled with merriment. Even those who live at the fringes of civilised society like to kick back and have a good time at Christmas. I don't grudge them it. If anything, I think it's great they can have a good time and forget about their worries for a short time.

Like Borderlands, the Tavern doubles as an exchange market for anything someone has to sell or wants to buy. In the space of a week it will see as many stolen goods as the station's evidence room. Patrons can sell a fresh salmon and buy a TV, DVD player, or anything that has been recently acquired from a house outside the estate.

I cast my eyes around the room. There's something of a throng on an area of carpet where people are gyrating, arms aloft with mouths belting out the latest Christmas tune to be blasted out by the DJ in the corner.

Halfway along the far wall I see the man I'm hunting. He's got a flabby arm around a peroxide blonde whose clothes are festooned with Christmas motifs. Who he's with is none of my concern. In fact, I'm glad he's got someone new as it means he'll leave his ex alone.

He's a scumbag in every sense of the word, but I'm not here for trouble, I have another purpose.

His eye catches mine and I see instant aggression. Whatever plans he has for the peroxide blonde are forgotten as he rises to his feet. His back straightens and he grabs the attention of two of his mates. All three men top six feet and seventeen stone.

I gesture to the door and leave.

Jimmy, the lying, cheating wife-beater of a rapist comes out first. His buddies at his elbows. One has a strand of tinsel round his neck and the other has a hooked nose. Tinsel and Hooked Nose make intimidating faces and gestures while Jimmy lights a cigarette and pretends he's not worried about me and whatever I may want from him. To further enhance his pretence at nonchalance, Jimmy moves forward until he's on the point of invading my personal space.

'Listen, pig. It's Christmas Eve and I'm having a good time and bothering no one. Fuck off back to your bitch and leave me the fuck alone.'

I drop the bag in my left hand to the ground – nothing in there will break – and snap a punch off. Jimmy goes down hard. A backhand elbow to the chin floors Tinsel and Hooked Nose is felled with a right cross.

Jimmy is gasping for breath, yet he can still moan. This means I judged the liver punch perfectly. A liver punch hurts like hell as it jolts the nervous system and that can lead to debilitating pain and even the brain putting the recipient of the punch on the ground so it can focus on getting the blood it needs. The blow I landed on Jimmy wasn't full power.

Considering his lifestyle, he's already kicked lumps out of his liver, so there's no way I was going to risk doing any real and permanent damage.

I wait a minute until Jimmy rises to one knee. I'm far enough back to prevent him throwing a punch at my groin.

With my eyes on Jimmy I pick up the bag and put it in front of him. His eyes are full of scorn when I tell him what's in the bag and what he has to do with it. The scorn changes to fear when I tell him what I'll do if he doesn't do as I've instructed him.

**** 

Christmas morning is everything I could have possibly hoped it will be. Two little faces light up with delight and excitement as wrapping paper gets shredded and squeals of excitement grow louder.

The presents I receive are of the usual socks and aftershave variety, but that doesn't bother me in the slightest. I like to make other people happy and seeing the children I love opening presents on Christmas morning is a window into a world of ecstasy. My fiancée, Jane, sits beside me, our fingers entwined as the kids play with their new toys.

There's a knock at the door, Jane looks at me with apprehension as we're not expecting any visitors yet. I smile and rise to my feet. 'I'll get it.'

I open the door to find Jimmy standing in front of me. His chin is shaven and he's wearing a clean jacket and a shirt that's felt the effects of an iron. In his hand is the carrier bag I'd left with him last night.

Behind me there are shrieks as two kids get the surprise they'd most hoped for.

'Daddy!'

'I told you he'd come.'

I step aside and let my fiancée's children hug their father.

'Come on in, Jimmy. I'll put the kettle on.'

The kids clamber all over their father and tell him of everything that's happened in their lives in the nine months since he bothered his arse to see them.

Jimmy plays nice and uses his natural charm on his kids.

He doesn't deserve their adoration. He's unaware of how often they've mentioned him. Or cried themselves to sleep, missing him. Jane and I have dealt with all that. When I heard Peter insisting to his sister that their dad would show up at Christmas, I knew I had to make sure Jimmy didn't let them down. The bag of presents I'd given him was mostly cheap tat, but the kids would love them because of who the giver was. Also, I didn't want to give Jimmy anything that was of resale value.

When I look across the room, I see Jane watching her kids with her ex. Jimmy made her life hell, but she never once bad-mouthed him in front of the kids.

Jane looks up at me with understanding – she'd questioned where I'd gone last night, and I hadn't given a convincing answer as I'd tried not to tell her an outright lie – at my part in Jimmy's presence and mouths 'thank you' to me.

I didn't hunt Jimmy down for her thanks. The kids will never know it was me who got him here. All they'll remember is he came and that's more than good enough for me, after all, Christmas is a time for families, and I've just made mine happy.

# About the Authors

# ALEX KANE

Alex Kane is a psychological thriller writer who lives in Glasgow. She is a huge fan of the genre, with her favourite authors in the genre being Lisa Hall, BA Paris, and Sarah Stovell.

If she is not writing, she can be found playing with her cat, reading, or drinking tea and/or gin (sometimes all of the above).

**A note from the author…**

I'd like to thank Emma Mitchell for organising this anthology for Help for Heroes. I've loved writing this short story and am extremely excited to read the others.

# ANNA FRANKLIN OSBORNE

I have always worked in healthcare, and more recently in education, and like so many other parents, hit a tiny crisis a few years ago when I felt that my purpose in life had narrowed to not an awful lot more than dashing between my two jobs and being a mummy taxi.

I managed to find time to begin singing with a choir, and that helped me feel that I might have a more creative side to myself. One evening, my husband was out and, quite suddenly, I decided to start writing. I immediately hit the first obstacles of terrible handwriting and a broken laptop, so my writing career began that night in bed, typing into the note section of my smartphone, with no clear idea of what I wanted to say but resulting in a severe case of RSI and several short stories over the next few nights.

My husband was delighted that I had suddenly found this passion and kept encouraging me to write a novel, which I really felt I did NOT have in me. Later that summer, however, we were walking along a D-Day beach for no other grander reason than our ferry home from France being late, and I began telling our kids about my three great-uncles who were part of that day, and my grandmother who sewed parachutes for the paratroopers jumping over Normandy. Neil looked at me and smiled and said, 'you do actually have a story there, you know...'

*Walking Wounded* was written over a period of a year, on a tiny tablet which I bought specifically because it fitted into my handbag – as I said, 'if it's not with me at all times, this just won't happen.' I wrote every day in 10 minute bursts while I sat in the school car park waiting for my daughter to emerge from school, I wrote parked outside ballet lessons and maths lessons, I wrote early in the mornings while everyone was asleep.

*Walking Wounded* is a war story and family saga, focussing on those left behind while their menfolk went to war, how they survived and how their relationships evolved through periods of violence, loss and reunion. The main story is about May, a young woman struggling to find her own identity as the youngest in a large family, forced into a stormy marriage through a mistake she is too proud to admit, and explores the web of loyalty, guilt and duty that shaped the decisions of the women awaiting the return of their menfolk as WW2 draws to a close. Spanning the period from the armistice of the Great War to the exodus of the ten-pound Poms to Australia in the 1950s, its internal violence is mirrored by the world stage upon which it is set.

# BILLY MCLAUGHLIN

Billy McLaughlin is a Scottish born writer with eight books currently under his belt. Four of the books, including 2019's serial killer thriller, *Four*, are part of the DI Phil Morris Mysteries. His first full-length novel, *Lost Girl*, arrived in May 2016 and has gone on to achieve more than 15,000 downloads. The follow up, *In the Wake of Death*, has received rave reviews for its dark tone and psychological elements.

His most downloaded book came in the form of 2017's, *The Dead of Winter*, a novella that focuses as much on the broken relationships of a small community as it does the crime itself. One reader described it as being like 'a full series of Broadchurch.' Once again, praise was levelled at the atmospheric tone with another reader suggesting that the material would work well as a movie.

Billy is passionate about reading but recognises the need for bite-sized thrillers for people who enjoy reading but simply don't have the time. As he begins works on his ninth book, he finds himself even more excited about the writing process. A plot, title and cover are already mid-production for book nine and he cannot wait to share them with you.

# CARMEN RADTKE

Carmen has spent most of her life with ink on her fingers and a dangerously high pile of books and newspapers by her side.

She has worked as a newspaper reporter on two continents and always dreamt of becoming a novelist and screenwriter.

When she found herself crouched under her dining table, typing away on a novel between two earthquakes in Christchurch, New Zealand, she realised she was hooked for life. The shaken but stirring novel made it to the longlist of the Mslexia competition, and her next book and first mystery, *The Case Of The Missing Bride*, was a finalist in the Malice Domestic competition in a year without a winner.

Carmen was born in Hamburg, Germany, but had planned on emigrating since she was five years old. She first moved to New Zealand and now lives in York, UK, with her daughter, cat, and sometimes her seafaring husband comes home.

# GORDON BICKERSTAFF

I was born and raised in Glasgow but spent my student years in Edinburgh. On summer vacations, I learned plumbing, garden maintenance, and I cut the grass in the Meadows. If I ran the lawnmower over your toes – sorry.

I learned some biochemistry and taught it for a while before I retired to write fiction. I like DIY and I do some aspects of DIY moderately well and other aspects not so well. I live with my wife in Scotland where corrupt academics, mystery, murder and intrigue exists mostly in my mind.

I write the Lambeth Group series of standalone crime/conspiracy thrillers: *Deadly Secrets, Everything To Lose, The Black Fox, Toxic Minds, Tabula Rasa,* and *Tears of Fire.*

They feature special investigators Zoe and Gavin. More will come in due course.

I enjoy walking in the hills, 60s & 70s music, reading and travel.

*A note from the author…*

Many thanks to Emily for story inspiration and Emma Mitchell for all the work in pulling this anthology together.

# GRAHAM SMITH

Graham Smith is a time-served joiner who has built bridges, houses, dug drains, and slated roofs to make ends meet. Since Christmas 2000, he has been manager of a busy hotel and wedding venue near Gretna Green, Scotland.

He is an internationally best-selling Kindle author and has six books featuring DI Harry Evans and the Cumbrian Major Crimes Team, and four novels, featuring Utah doorman, Jake Boulder. His 'Lakes' series which has three novels featuring DC Beth Young has received much critical acclaim.

An avid fan of crime fiction since being given one of Enid Blyton's Famous Five books at the age of eight, he has also been a regular reviewer and interviewer for the well-respected website Crimesquad.com since 2009

Graham is the founder of Crime and Publishment, a weekend of crime-writing classes which includes the chance for attendees to pitch their novels to agents and publishers. Since the first weekend in 2013, ten attendees have gone on to sign publishing contracts.

# H.R. KEMP

Hi, I'm H.R. Kemp and I'm thrilled to have a short story included in this anthology. I've had several short stories published; the most recent appeared in *The Writers' Magazine* in October 2019. My writing journey began in earnest after completing Graduate Certificate in Creative Writing at Adelaide University in 2011 and with the support and critiques of my writers' group, The Novelist Circle. I'm preparing to publish my first conspiracy mystery/thriller novel *Deadly Secrets* in 2020. I'm currently rewriting a second novel (another conspiracy mystery/thriller) and the beginnings of a third novel are sitting in the bottom drawer awaiting my attention.

I live in Adelaide, Australia, although I grew up in country areas near Melbourne. My long career in the public service spanned roles as diverse as Management Trainer, Team Facilitator, Statistician and Laboratory Assistant although my first degree was a Bachelor of Science (Chemistry) and I have a Graduate Diploma in Education.

Besides time with my family, travelling and discovering new places is a passion for me and I have wandered through many fabulous countries and cities around the world. These are often incorporated into my writing as locations for scenes in my novels. I keep a daily travel journal and take copious photos along the way. I'm an avid theatre goer, enjoy art exhibitions and galleries, and of course, I love to read. Each year, I take full advantage of the Adelaide Writers' Festival in March to discover new authors and to hear my favourites.

My Facebook: https://www.facebook.com/hr.kemp.31

My Facebook author page:

https://www.facebook.com/hrkemp01

My website: https://hrkemp13.wixsite.com/hrkempwriter

# JANE RISDON

Jane Risdon has spent most of her life working in the International Music Business rubbing shoulders with the powerful and famous, especially in Hollywood.

Married to a musician, and later working alongside him managing singers, musicians, songwriters, and record producers, she's also facilitated the placement of music on successful television series and movie soundtracks.

Her experiences have provided her with a unique insight into the business and her writing often has a music related theme. She is published traditionally by Headline Accent.

With long-term friend, award-winning, best-selling author, Christina Jones – one time fan-club secretary for Jane's husband's band – Jane has co-authored *Only One Woman* (Headline Accent) which is set in the UK music scene of 1968/69. Available in Waterstones and on digital platforms.

Recently Jane completed a collection of her first short crime stories – *Undercover: Crime Shorts* – published by Plaisted Publishing House, available from Waterstones and the paperback and eBook is available on most digital platforms.

Jane has contributed to fifteen anthologies, online newsletters, and magazines as well as print magazines and she is a regular contributor to many of these. She also has regular radio appearances in the UK and USA chatting about her writing and books. She is a regular blogger and also hosts guest authors too.

Jane is working on the sequel to *Only One Woman* as well as a series of crime novels – Ms Birdsong Investigates – featuring former MI5 Officer Lavinia Birdsong. Her experience of working at the Foreign and Commonwealth Office in her pre-music days has given her plenty of material for her crime/thrillers.

### A note from the author…

I'd like to thank Headline Accent (my publishers) for enabling me to contribute a story to this worthy anthology, thanks to Katie especially.

My thanks to Emma Mitchell for including me in this wonderful book and for her hard work curating it; much appreciated, and I'm sure our readers will acknowledge her hard work too.

Last, but not least, I want to thank the special person in my life who puts up with my pre-occupation with writing and who reads everything I write with such gusto and enthusiasm, and without whom I'd have given up years ago.

# JOHN CARSON

John Carson is the author of the DI Frank Miller and DCI Harry McNeil detective series set in Edinburgh. He is Scottish, but now lives in New York State with his wife and two daughters. He shares his house with two dogs and four cats.

# KA RICHARDSON

My name is KA Richardson, and I'm a crime writer based in the north-east of England. I write around my other work commitments so am constantly on the go.

I love reading many genres, love speaking to people and spend a lot of time people watching in coffee shops, though if I'm honest this is more for the purposes of character building and plotting.

I enjoy watching cop shows from both the UK and the USA and am a fan of sci-fi.

I began thinking about writing as a career in 2010 and completed my MA Creative Writing in 2011. I love to be inspired, and enjoy spending time with friends and family, as well as like-minded folk.

# KRIS EGLETON

Kris grew up in a world of two halves. Born and raised in the East Riding of Yorkshire she spent some of her summer holidays in her mother's homeland, Norway.

Her writing is eclectic, as she writes in several genres. Her forte is short and flash fiction. She gained a BA in Arts and Humanities, followed by an MA in Historical Research in 2015, graduating in her sixties. She feels she has always been a writer but has done more since being widowed thanks to her local writing group and her son who lives with her.

# LEXI REES

Lexi Rees was born in Scotland but now lives down south. She writes action-packed adventures brim full of witch doctors, fortune-tellers, warriors, and smugglers, combining elemental magic with hints of dystopia. She also writes fun activity books for children.

Her fantasy adventure, *Eternal Seas*, was awarded a "loved by" badge from LoveReading4Kids and is currently short-listed for a Chanticleer award. The sequel, *Wild Sky*, is available now.

She's passionate about developing a love of reading and writing in children and, as well as her Creative Writing Skills workbook, she has an active programme of school visits and other events, is a Book PenPal for three primary schools, and runs a free online #kidsclub and newsletter which includes book recommendations and creative writing activities.

In her spare time, she's a keen crafter and spends a considerable amount of time trying not to fall off horses or boats.

# LOUISE JENSEN

Louise Jensen has sold over a million English language copies of her International No. 1 psychological thrillers *The Sister*, *The Gift*, *The Surrogate,* and *The Date*. Her novels have also been translated into twenty-five languages, as well as featuring on the USA Today and Wall Street Journal Bestseller's List. Louise's fifth thriller, *The Family*, was published in autumn 2019 by Harper Collins.

    *The Sister* was nominated for the Goodreads Debut Author of 2016 Award. *The Date* was nominated for The Guardian's 'Not the Booker' Prize 2018. *The Surrogate* has been nominated for the best Polish thriller of 2018. *The Gift* has been optioned for a TV film.

    Louise lives with her husband, children, madcap dog, and a rather naughty cat in Northamptonshire. She loves to hear from readers and writers.

# LUCY CAMERON

Born in London and having lived in South Wales, Liverpool, York, and Nottingham, Lucy currently lives in a shed in her dad's garden in Scotland where she wears thermals for warmth and writes by candlelight.

Lucy studied Fine Art at university which allowed her to get a glittering career in… food retail. Working sixty hours a week in retail management hampered Lucy's writing until a career-break took her to Scotland and the rest, as they say in history… Or should that be (crime) fiction? Having taken a walk on the dark side, Lucy now splits her writing time between crime fiction and comedy fiction writing.

Lucy's debut novel *Night Is Watching* was published in April 2017.

# MALCOLM HOLLINGDRAKE

You could say that the writing was clearly on the wall for someone born in a library that they might aspire to be an author, but to get to that point Malcolm Hollingdrake has travelled a circuitous route.

Malcolm worked in education for many years, even teaching for a period in Cairo before he started writing, a challenge he had longed to tackle for more years than he cares to remember.

He has written a number of successful short stories, has nine books now available and is presently writing the eighth crime novel set in Harrogate, North Yorkshire.

Born in Bradford and spending three years at Ripon College, Malcolm has never lost his love for his home county, a passion that is reflected in the settings for all the DCI Bennett novels. As well as the Bennett series he is writing a new series set in Merseyside.

Malcolm has enjoyed many hobbies including collecting works by Northern artists; the art auctions offer a degree of excitement when both buying and certainly when selling. It is a hobby he has bestowed upon DCI Cyril Bennett, the main character in his successful Bennett series.

# MARK BROWNLESS

Mark Brownless lives and works in Carmarthen, West Wales. He has been putting ideas on paper for some years now but only when the idea for *The Hand of An Angel* came to him in the autumn of 2015, did he know he might be able to write a book. Mark likes to write about ordinary people being placed in extraordinary circumstances, is fascinated by unexplained phenomena, and enjoys merging thriller, science fiction, and horror.

Mark's new novel, *The Shadow Man* is a terrifying horror thriller imagining what would happen if you found out the memories of your childhood were untrue, and that something sinister was lurking behind the facade of your life. Could you face what had happened back then? Could you face *The Shadow Man*?

Mark is also fascinated by myths and legends such as those of Robin Hood and King Arthur. This has culminated in the release of his short story series, *Locksley: A Robin Hood Story*.

# MEGAN STEER

Megan started writing at the age of nine. She loves English and enjoys competitive All-Star Cheerleading.

Megan's Poem, as featured at the start of *When Stars Will Shine*, was written at school when she was just eleven years old.

*Keep an eye out for her in future, I'm certain there will much more to come from this talented young lady: Emma Mitchell, Editor*

# OWEN MULLEN

Best-selling author Owen Mullen is a McIlvanney Crime Book of The Year long-listed novelist.

Owen graduated from Strathclyde University, moved to London and worked as a rock musician, session singer, and songwriter. He had a hit record in Japan with a band he refuses to name; He still loves to perform on occasion.

His passion for travel has taken him on many adventures from the Amazon and Africa to the colourful continent of India and Nepal. A gregarious recluse, he and his wife, Christine, split their time between Glasgow, and their home in the Greek Islands where Owen writes.

# PAUL MOORE

I was never one for learning at school and couldn't wait to leave and get out into the big wide world. It wasn't until I was twenty-seven that I read a book since leaving school and I was hooked! Due to health reasons I stopped doing manual work and for the first time in my working life I've had to properly use my brain. I started writing children's stories at first but I just couldn't get what I wanted from it and then I decided on crime. After all, it's the genre I read. I was in a photo taken on a mobile phone and at the time I remember feeling very cold and emotional; when I saw the photo, I saw a spirit is beside me. This of course got my interest and the paranormal sometimes creeps into my work. I'm a proud Londoner and it's where I base a lot of my stories.

***A note from the author…***

Thank you to every soldier that has served or who is currently serving in the armed forces.

# PAUL T CAMPBELL

I have been published in three Poetry Anthologies. I love writing and am currently in the final stages of editing the first novel in what I hope will be a thriller trilogy, set to be released in the New Year.

# ROB ASHMAN

Rob is married to Karen with two grown up daughters. He is originally from South Wales and after moving around with work settled in North Lincolnshire where he's spent the last twenty-two years.

Like all good Welsh Valley boys Rob worked for the National Coal Board after leaving school at sixteen and went to university at the tender age of twenty-three when the pit closures began to bite. Since then he's worked in a variety of manufacturing and consulting roles both in the UK and abroad.

It took Rob twenty-four years to write his first book. He only became serious about writing it when his dad got cancer. It was an aggressive illness and Rob gave up work for three months to look after him and his mum. Writing *Those That Remain* became his coping mechanism. After he wrote the book his family encouraged him to continue, so not being one for half measures, Rob got himself made redundant, went self-employed so he could devote more time to writing and four years later the Mechanic Trilogy is the result.

Rob published *Those That Remain, In Your Name,* and *Pay the Penance* with Bloodhound Books and has since written the DI Rosalind Kray series. These are *Faceless, This Little Piggy, Suspended Retribution,* and *Jaded* which are also published by Bloodhound.

When he is not writing, Rob is a frustrated chef with a liking for beer and prosecco and is known for occasional outbreaks of dancing.

# ROBERT SCRAGG

Robert Scragg had a random mix of jobs before taking the dive into crime writing; he's been a bookseller, pizza deliverer, karate instructor, and football coach.

He lives in Tyne & Wear, is a founding member of the North East Noir crime writers' group and is currently writing the second Porter and Styles novel.

# STEWART GILES

After reading English & Drama at three different English universities and graduating from none of them, I set off travelling and finally ended up in South Africa, where I still live. I enjoy the serene life running a boat shop on the banks of the Vaal Dam.

I came up with the DS Jason Smith idea after my wife dropped a rather large speaker on my head. Whether it was intentional still remains a mystery.

*Smith*, the first in the series was finished in September 2013 and was closely followed by *Boomerang* and *Ladybird*. *Occam's Razor, Harlequin*, and *Phobia* (a series of short stories detailing Smith's early life) were all completed in one hazy 365 days and *Selene* was done and dusted a few months later.

*Horsemen*, the seventh in the DS Smith thriller series is out now.

*The Beekeeper*, a departure from the DS Smith series was released through Joffe Books on 22 May 2019.

# VAL PORTELLI

The author's pen name Voinks began many years ago. It started as a joke when a friend bought a holiday home abroad, then gradually spread through the family, so it was an obvious choice when her first book was published.

Despite receiving her first rejection letter aged nine from some lovely people at a well-known women's magazine, she continued writing intermittently until a freak accident left her housebound and going stir crazy.

To save her sanity she completed and had published her first full-length novel. This was followed by a second traditionally published book before deciding self-publishing was the way to go. In between writing her longest novel to date at over 100,000 words, she publishes weekly stories for her Facebook author page and website.

She writes in various genres, although her short stories normally include her trademark twist of 'quirky.' From having too many hours in the day, she is now actively seeking out a planet with forty-eight-hour days, to have time to fit in all the stories waiting to be told.

She is always delighted to receive reviews, as they help pay for food for the unicorns she breeds in her spare time.

*A note from the author...*

Thanks to everyone involved, in particular Emma Mitchell, for her tremendous efforts in bringing this anthology to completion.

I'm proud to have been involved, and able to contribute to such a worthwhile cause.

Printed in Great Britain
by Amazon

44960661R00197